Ain't No Grave

Ain't No Grave

MARY GLICKMAN

INTEGRATED MEDIA
NEW YORK

ISBN: 978-1-5040-9097-1

Published in 2024 by Open Road Integrated Media, Inc.
180 Maiden Lane
New York, NY 10038
www.openroadmedia.com

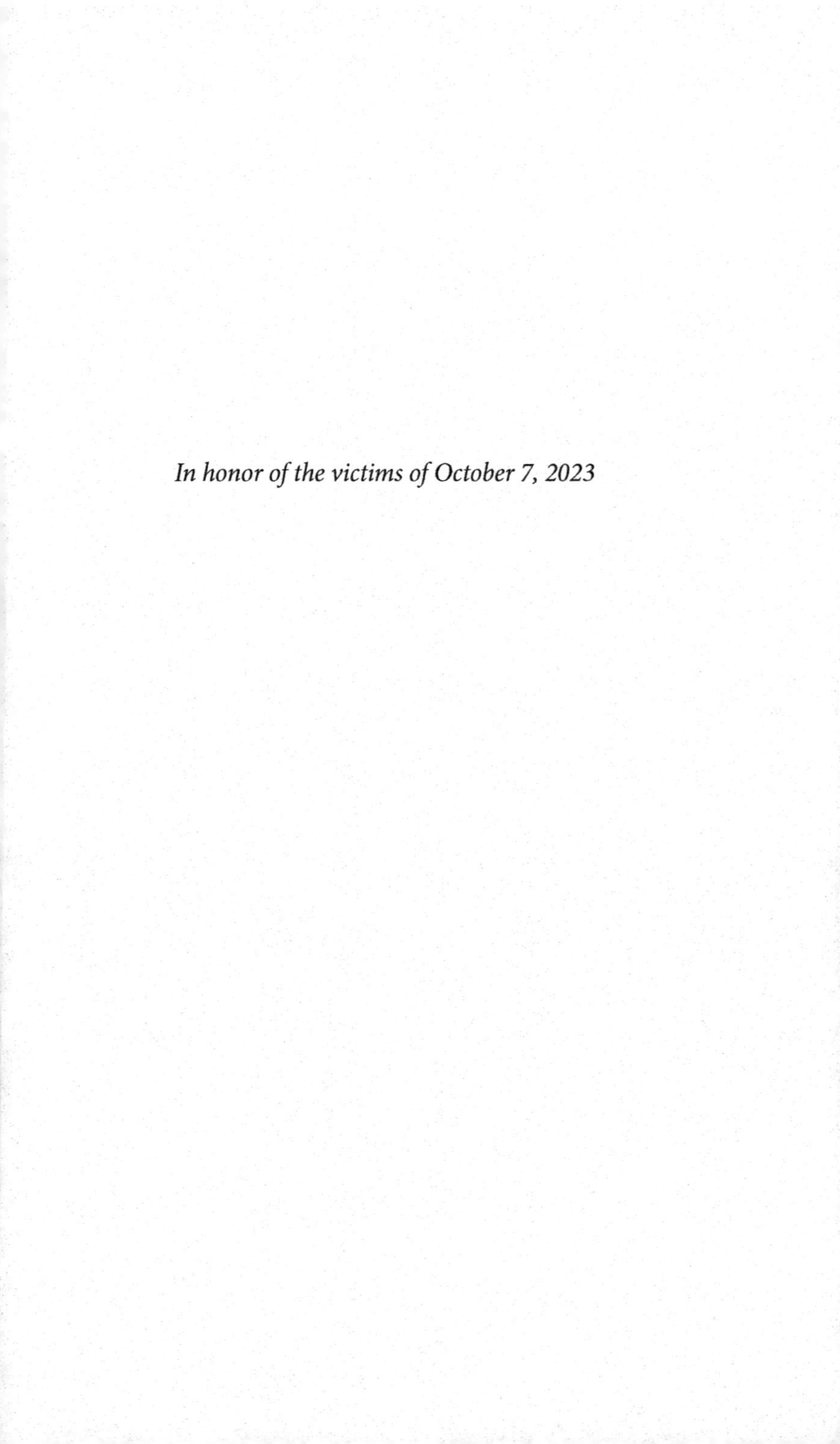

In honor of the victims of October 7, 2023

Ain't No Grave

Oh, shame is a prison as cruel as a grave
Shame is a robber and he's come to take my name
Oh, love is my redeemer
Lifting me up from the ground
Love is the power where my freedom song is found

Ain't no grave gonna hold my body down
Ain't no grave gonna hold my body down

Oh, fear is a liar with a smooth and velvet tongue
Fear is a tyrant
He's always tellin' me to run
Oh, love is a resurrection and love is a trumpet sound
Love is my weapon
I'm gonna take my giants down

"Ain't No Grave"
Lyrics by Claude Ely, Jonathan David Hesler,
Melissa Helser, and Molly Skaggs

1.

Heard County, Georgia, 1906

There were many things nine-year-old Maxwell Isadore Sassaport would never have done if it weren't for the influence of his best friend, Ruby Alfreda Johnson, among them, visiting a witch woman in the most isolated territory of the backwoods. Max was a good boy, obedient and loving. Lying and theft were normally far from his mind. But Ruby tickled the adventurous side of him. She tickled it good.

When he awoke that morning, Max did as his daddy trained him. He picked up the pitcher kept by the side of his bed and poured water over his hands and into the basin it sat in, murmuring thanksgiving for the return of his soul to his body. For a minute or two he imagined places his soul might have wandered while he slept. No matter how many times he questioned Daddy on the matter, he'd never got a satisfactory answer.

Daddy was eccentric in his choice of which Jewish traditions he kept and which not. His choices boiled down to what he felt like doing in the privacy of his own home and what he dared not do in the company of his neighbors, a mixed crew of both philo- and anti-Semites, all of them in stark ignorance of what Jews were really about.

When Max came of age a few years later, there was no *bar mitzvah.* He didn't notice. He only vaguely knew what a *bar mitzvah* was. There were no other Jews in Buckwood, Georgia, to compare with his own. As far as Max knew, the only Jews around were Mama, Daddy, Bubbe, and Zeyde. Sometimes a stray cousin or uncle passed through, but that was it. Daddy would have liked to teach the boy to keep a kosher home. Mama flat-out refused to maintain one. "There's no *shochet* out here," she said. "We s'posed to live on plants? No, we'll eat like everybody else, and that's final," Her mother and father, who'd grown up kosher but dropped it with reluctance somewhere between Kiev and Raleigh, lived with them. They protested some out of guilt. They got nowhere. It was true that without a kosher butcher, there wasn't much in Buckwood they could eat. They gave up.

Accordingly, after performing his family's crude brand of *tashlich*, Max sat at the kitchen table to enjoy a hearty breakfast of biscuits and sausage gravy.

Usually, after breakfast and before school, Max helped Daddy in the notions shop below their apartment, dusting shelves with a sawed-off broomstick topped with a crown of chicken feathers, just as Ruby helped her daddy in the fields, digging furrows, sowing seeds, and pulling weeds. Saturdays, while Daddy felt the need to do business himself, he let the boy off the rein for the Sabbath. Ruby's people were Seventh-Day Adventists, but as there was no church of that denomination closer than fifty miles away, she had the day free too. Sabbaths were their best time together all week, filled with long lovely hours of play and dreamy conversation while lying flat on their backs in the sun.

Saturday past, the two had discussed a matter of extreme importance. It was no secret to them that white and black children could enjoy intimacy only until a certain age, the age "when they should know better." Once they knew better, the friendship was over. Max and Ruby sensed that time approached and it frightened them. They loved each other. If they were separated, there would be no replacement friends. Each was a unique article within their milieu. As his classmates never tired of reminding him, Max was the singular Jew-boy in his school and town and Ruby was extraordinarily tall for her age, towering over her contemporaries, boys and girls alike. Her mother told her she'd inherited the grand stature of her Masai forebears, which meant little to Ruby Alfreda. "Masai, shamai" she'd say, waving an arm dismissively in imitation of Max's grandfather whom she knew some. If anything, she resented those tribal ancestors who'd given her a trait she did not want, one that distinguished her to the point of social exclusion and stinging cruelties from other children both black and white.

The affection between Max and Ruby was proof positive that difference can be as bonding as similarity. Max belonged to a family that while not wealthy enjoyed financial security. Sassaport's Fabrics, Fancy Goods, and Notions was the sole retail merchant in a town frustrated by the inconvenience of mail-order goods, half of which arrived late, damaged, or otherwise not as expected. Husbands looking for a piece of luxury to gift their hardworking wives could leave Sassaport's with a yard of velvet, another of lace, a cut-glass vial of scent, or even a snow globe featuring President Teddy Roosevelt on a reared-up horse. Their wives could purchase anything from silk-lined dancing shoes that their eldest daughter might attract a beau of quality at a family wedding to vibrantly painted chamber pots acquired to discourage their husbands from pissing out the bedroom window. Children came to the store for the selection of penny candy displayed in a tower of mason jars in the front window next to beard pomades and bouquets of dyed feathers meant to be pinned to a lady's hat. Max may have been the solitary Jew-boy in town and thus the subject of rude inquiry about his family's supposed horde of gold coins or the horns hidden by the hair of his head, but access to penny candy gave him a grudging cachet even among the bullies who pestered him.

Ruby was the fourth and middle child of a sharecropper. From the tenderest age, she suffered far more hours of hard labor a day than schooling, but as she was black no one beyond her family much cared. Nonetheless, unlike her brothers and sisters, she could read and write. Max taught her how under the stately weeping willows of Yellowjacket Creek. For her part, Ruby taught Max what her mother taught her about wild vegetation, edible and non, medicinal and poisonous, along with what omens were signified by the west wind, speckled fish, and the habits of hawks. It was a fair exchange.

Both children were exceedingly smart. While they knew their days as companions were numbered, what bothered them, what perturbed them utterly was not knowing on what day that end might occur. Ruby's brother Joshua told her it happened suddenly. One day you had a white friend and the next you did not. It was a grave, inescapable matter. Sometimes, Joshua swore, whole families moved in the night to achieve the goal. Ruby wasn't sure she believed that but knew she and Max had to find out when they'd be torn asunder before it was too late. If they had time to prepare, they could design a network of secret places to rendezvous or maybe run away.

"I've got it!" Ruby said suddenly that fair Saturday in September while they lay together on the grass watching the hooks of their fishing lines bob in the creek's currents. "We can go up to Mayhayley's house and ask her. She'll know."

Mayhayley Lancaster. The oracle of Heard County, Georgia.

A woman who could find a lost wallet or identify a future husband using common playing cards and the ashes of her fireplace. Her reputation was widespread. Her predictions were remarkably reliable. People were known to travel from Alabama and Florida for her services. How she did what she did was anybody's guess. She claimed she was born with a caul, which the world of the faithful believed a clear sign of the Lord's favor, one that bore the gift of prophecy. No one knew anyone alive who could corroborate the claim, so maybe it was true, maybe not. The very mention of Mayhayley's name sent shivers down Max's spine. He heard his grandmother's voice admonish him the only time he ever dared mention the seer at home. "Thou shalt not suffer a witch to live!" Bubbe said, shaking a long bony finger and looking very much a witch herself. The boy was impressed. He knew many people who were afraid of Mayhayley and stayed that way until they'd a need of her services, but Bubbe was the first person he ever knew of liked to kill her.

Bubbe knew the seer from her schoolmarm days, when Mayhayley was young and before she lost her left eye. Her friend Sadie's child was in her classroom. Back then, she wasn't so bad. She didn't tell fortunes for money yet but she dressed like something between a whore and a Rough Rider, all the while thumping a Bible every Sunday over to the Lebanon Baptist Church. Impossibly tall like Ruby, she was gaunt to boot, with the long cheeks of a horse. Her face was plain as a pancake. On church days, she wore rouge in reds and purples as if her unremarkable features were worthy of ornamentation. In the younger days, she was judged peculiar maybe, but not outright crazy. Bubbe opined it was the loss of her eye due to a fateful fall with a flinty rock in hand that tipped her into lunacy. For all that, she was shrewd. It was rumored she was quietly buying up vast acres of farmland with her sorcery money and studying the practice of law as well. She lived in a ramshackle wood and tar paper cabin miles out of town and also smelled bad.

Ruby Alfreda Johnson discounted all that. In convincing Max to approach the witch, she emphasized the accuracy of Mayhayley's predictions. She could tell you more than where that lost earring was or who you would marry. She could tell you when you would die. That astonished him.

"All for a dollar and a dime," Ruby said, getting to her feet and brushing off her skirt. "A dollar for her and a dime for her dogs. You bring the dollar next week and I'll bring the ten cent."

Max's eyes bugged. He scrambled up and faced her square.

"A dollar? Me?" he said. "Where am I gonna get a dollar?"

Ruby looked at him as she would an idiot child.

"Same place I'm gettin' my dime. From wherever your mama hides her hard money. Don't tell me you don't know where that is."

The boy felt a rush of anticipation and anxiety both. It was as if a trail of fire ants had crawled up his leg and bit him only nothing hurt.

"I don't know if I can do that, Ruby."

She punched him but not hard in the tricep.

"Course you can."

Her certainty irritated him.

"But why do you only have to get a dime and me a whole damn dollar?"

She gave him the idiot child look again, raised her palms to heaven, then rolled her eyes.

"You think there's a whole damn dollar anywhere in my mama's possession?"

He reddened, feeling guilty for having pointed out the great gulf between her station in life and his. To his credit, he never saw them as opposing ends of the same pole. He just saw them as friends. Best friends. For whom, he quietly realized, he would beg, borrow, or steal.

"Alright, then," he said.

He pursed his lips and breathed in deeply. His chest filled with quiet determination.

"I'll do it."

She threw an arm around his shoulder and, being the taller, lay her head on top of his.

"It'll justify the whuppin', Max. I promise."

He trusted her. He figured Mayhayley Lancaster would indeed be worth whatever punishment his father summoned although he never hit him so it wouldn't be the whuppin' Ruby risked.

That morning, he lollygagged at table, pushing his gravy-soaked biscuit around the plate with a fork. As soon as she'd fed her boy, it was Mama's habit to bring breakfast downstairs to Daddy and his grandparents who both worked the shop's floor. Max waited while she noisily descended the back steps to Daddy's storeroom with a coffeepot and plate of sweet rolls in hand. He waited until he heard the storeroom door open and shut, then scurried over to the pantry. Standing on a chair, he reached up to the third shelf behind the back row of spice bottles for a medium-sized tobacco box made of tin. He lifted it out. It had an air-tight seal. It was hard to open. But he pulled and pulled and got the job done.

Inside was a heap of glittering silver coins, all jumbled up. There were so many, Max decided no one would notice any were missing unless they sat down to count them. He grabbed two quarters and a half-dollar and stuffed them swiftly into his trouser pocket. He had trouble getting the top back on the box tightly. The front edge kept popping open. He pushed the box against the wall and pounded it with his fist to get the lid shut tight, cursing when he realized he'd dented the thing at one of the corners. It was a tiny dent yet there it was. He called out to heaven, "Don't let Mama find it." The trudge, trudge, trudge of her footsteps ascending the stairs came to him.

There was nothing else to do but put the box and chair back in place and rush to his seat at the table where he resumed poking around an empty plate. His face went dark as he worked to still his breath. Mama appeared. She halted mid-stride on the way to her sewing pile to place a hand on his brow.

"Hmm. You feel cool but you're lookin' flushed and you're sweatin' too. I'm not entirely sure you should be goin' out to play around with that Ruby today."

Max gave her his most irresistible good-boy look, wide of eye, pleading of brow.

"Oh, Mama, please? Please mayn't I go? I'm feelin' fine, I swear!"

She relented.

Once out of the house, Max ran as fast as his short, plump legs could carry him to a prearranged spot past the edge of town. He felt the coins through the rough cotton of his pants. They burned. He pushed down his guilt and ignored it. Mama might not even notice they were gone for a month. Plenty of time to worry.

The road was a thoroughfare of dirt and overgrown weeds tamped down by the steady hooves of horses and mules. It led more or less directly to Mayhayley's house. At the place where a peddler had piled up a heap of stones to point the way in and out of town, he turned into a field of wildflowers and ran until he achieved the stand of willows at Yellowjacket Creek. Though the wildflowers reached almost to his neck, Ruby stood near waist high in them. She held a hand up to her brow. Her head moved right to left, left to right searching for him. His heart leapt. He raised an arm above his head.

"Here I am," he shouted, waving madly.

Ruby hopped up and down. They reached each other and stood hugging and laughing. Max's guilt resolved itself. Their adventure had begun.

Adventure was the trademark of their friendship. They'd met at a critical moment for each, in the aftermath of danger. One morning, Ruby was pursued by a gang of insecure, jealous boys who wanted to "cut her down to size." A girl child their age had no business being bigger than them. Their leader, a stocky, pig-faced boy, waved a pocketknife above his head. About the same time, Max was chased by a band of shiftless young Methodists who threatened to tie him down and re-circumcise him. Although both children escaped mutilation by being fleet of foot and knowing where to hide, afterward their lives felt worthless. It was not the first time they'd been bullied and it would not be the last. In their eyes, the future looked like an endless cycle of loneliness and flight.

By afternoon, each was chin-deep in grief and headed for a crumbled deer blind near the creek, a secret refuge they thought no one else knew. They entered from opposite directions, each intending to sit there for as long as it took to come to peace. On entering, they near collided. Stunned, they stood stock-still and stared at each other. Max saw the sadness in Ruby's eyes; she saw the same in his. The tall black girl and short white boy understood each other immediately. Without speaking, they went deep inside the deer blind's wreckage together. They sat on a fallen board, side by side, moon-faced, calming their breath. When the latter was achieved, they introduced themselves.

"You that boy Max by the candy shop, ain't you?" Ruby said.

He appreciated that she didn't say Jew-boy, just boy. He nodded.

"And you're Ruby. I heard of you," he said. "Kids say a giant came down from the sky on a beanstalk and fooled with your mama and that's why you there's so much of you. I always thought that partic'larly stupid."

She appreciated his assessment.

"So what you doin' settin' in here, Max?" she asked.

"Same as you, I s'pect. Hidin' from a cruel world . . ."

She broke into a smile then, a big one. He wasn't sure what was funny but he found her beautiful.

"It's hard bein' the onliest one, ain't it?" she said softly.

He agreed. They talked for hours then, finding much in common. By the time they brushed themselves off and left for home, they'd vowed friendship everlasting. Two years later, nothing had changed. They kept constant company. They supported and protected each other. The idea that anyone had the power to separate them was a nightmare to them, a tragedy.

"It's gonna be a trial of a walk to the oracle's house," Ruby said.

She wore a muslin shirt stitched by her mother, a long flour-sack skirt, and tattered high-button shoes, the best she had for long distance walking. Around her waist she'd tied a piece of rope from which dangled a draw string burlap bag and a small jug sealed with a cork. She patted them.

"I figured we'd need water and some'at to eat."

Max appreciated the way Ruby always thought ahead. He counted on her to prepare for every eventuality. He thought of himself as more the battering-ram type, a boy who shouldered his way forward without a plan, playing it by instinct, no matter what the obstacles. It was a fantasy and he knew it. His shoulders could barely knock aside the thicket of wildflowers around them. But he had ambitions.

He grinned.

"That's absolutely right. Thank you for thinkin' on it."

Ruby grinned back. His praise always warmed her. They set out.

They walked the morning away. At first, they chatted and joked around but after a while grew thoughtful and taciturn. The landscape encouraged quietude. No wagons or riders passed them on the road. The air was dead, still, hot. Thick stands of trees by the side of the road offered no breeze to cool them. Oak and pine stood silent, motionless, cast in shadow, bearing grave witness to Max and Ruby's larceny, their eager pursuit of sinful acts.

As the noon approached, Max stopped, sat in the road, and voiced his opinion that maybe, just maybe, Ruby didn't know where she was going.

Ruby stuck her chin loftily in the air. She reached into her deep skirt pocket and withdrew a hand-drawn map on a scrap of cardboard.

"My brother Franklin made us a map," she said. "I'm fair curious how he came by the route—he wouldn't tell me—but he swears this is it."

Max took the map. Nothing was labeled as Franklin didn't know his letters, but the boy recognized his pictographs, both the major twists of the road, the hills, and the place where river and creek met.

"Where are we now?" he asked.

Ruby pointed to a spot dotted with Franklin's symbol for pine trees. They looked relatively close to a big X, presumably Mayhayley's house.

"Right to there. Less than an hour to the place where we turn in."

Max was satisfied. He apologized for doubting her. He got to his feet. They continued.

By the time Mayhayley's house rose in the distance, their water was gone. Ruby's hard tack and boiled egg were gone too. The dust of the road mingled with their sweat to make dark, dirty trails from their hairlines to their chins.

"Too bad we can't wash up," Max said.

"I doubt Miss Mayhayley minds . . ."

Ruby took his hand. They squeezed their palms together for courage and walked on down the semi-cleared path that led from the road to their destination.

When they were a few yards from the front door, they halted next to a brick well, their eyes large as saucers as they took in what was before them. The cabin was made up of more kinds of wood than either of them knew, scraps of tin, and newspaper balled up tight as a stone. It had a long stick and mud chimney from which smoke spewed despite the warmth of the day. By the front porch, a possum and two squirrels dangled dead, hung by their tails from ropes nailed into the ceiling. An outhouse stood close by. Next to the cinder block stairs leading up to the front door, a small, square herb and vegetable garden was encased in a wire mesh against those who would prey upon it. Chickens pecked the dirt outside the wire.

Mayhayley's mule and a pack of rangy dogs lounged behind a wood fence that reached from the front all the way around the back. On seeing them, the latter bounded up as close as they could get, barking. The children leaned into each other. Ruby pointed out in as brave a voice as she could summon that the dogs did not growl, at least there was that. Max heard her and felt a little calmer, but on the whole he was close to terrified. The door creaked open.

Miss Mayhayley Lancaster emerged from the shadows to stand at the top of the stairs, wiping her long white hands on an apron. She wore several skirts of different patterns and lengths, a yellow gentleman's shirt, which was likely white when it was new, and, surprisingly, the very latest hat, a gray felt cloche to which she'd attached the dried cockscomb of a rooster. Around her waist was the same rope Ruby tied around her's. Mayhayley's had burlap sacks and vessels hanging from her rope as well, but larger ones and there were more of them. The sun faced her. She wore a glass marble in her empty eye socket. The blue pupil and network of veins she painted over it did not obscure the light that bounced off that strange, immobile eye, light that came at the children in piercing rays. It near blinded them. They squinted and held up their hands against it. She's like the burning bush, thought Max. Like the Holy Spirit, thought Ruby.

"What you two ragamuffins lookin' for 'round here?" the seer said. Her voice was surprising. It had a soft tone and round notes. It was younger than expected, but maybe Mayhayley was too. Legends, myths, and seers live old in the mind of their observers. The children thought her voice was part of her sorcery, that she altered it to seduce them like the Hansel and Gretel witch Uncle Washington told them about but it was quite natural.

Ruby was six months older than Max. She was already ten. As oldest, she took it upon herself to speak.

"We are here to have our fortune told," she said. "We have the dollar and the dime." She pulled out—pennies from her shirt and nudged Max with an elbow. He produced his two quarters and fifty-cent piece.

Mayhayley regarded the money, stood aside her door, and gestured.

"Come on in, then."

The children ascended the cement block stairs not hesitantly exactly, but slowly. Each handed over payment on entering the cabin. The first thing Max noticed as he passed the witch and dropped his coins into her palm was that she didn't smell bad. She smelled like everybody else.

The interior of Mayhayley's house brushed all other thoughts aside. It felt small, cramped. There was a fireplace with a caldron on a spit. Flames licked the pot's bottom. Whatever brewed within it smelled spicy and sweet and earthy too. A narrow mattress framed by pieces of ironwork lashed together lay close by, parallel to the fire. Stacks of books leaned against it. Playing cards were spread over a homemade bed quilt in groups of three and five. Against the far wall was a table, two chairs, and a sink on a stand with a mounted butcher's board beside it. There were more oil lamps than Max had ever seen in one room though none were lit. On the walls were pinned whole pages of newspapers and magazines, mixing up portraits of ladies' garments and hairstyles with politicians and statewide news.

The children settled into the two chairs. Mayhayley put their coins in a blue jar on the mantel and stood before them, hands on hips.

"What is it you two want to know before your mamas come lookin' for their dollar and a dime?" she said.

Fear spiked in their hearts. How did she know they stole the money and from whom? Maybe she'd read their minds. Mayhayley laughed. It was a man's laugh, completely out of sync with her speaking voice. They watched, slack-jawed, as she dropped her hands to her sides, sat on the bed, gathered the cards, and shuffled them while regarding her guests intently.

Swallowing a ball of fluid lodged in his throat, Max nodded at Ruby. She spoke for them both.

"Miss Mayhayley, m'am," she said, standing up. "I am Ruby Johnson and this boy is Max Sassaport, my dear and only friend. We are afeared our parents will separate us soon and we would like you to tell when this will happen. Also what can we do about it."

She sat. Max lifted his chin. He was proud of his friend. For a girl without much experience in a classroom, she knew just how to behave in front of a former schoolteacher. It made the place they were in a little more normal around the edges, so he was afraid less and relaxed as much as could be expected.

Mayhayley reached into one of the sacks around her waist and put something from it into her mouth. It looked like animal hair, though whether dog, possum, or squirrel one could not tell. She chewed a bit then turned to the fireplace behind her and spat whatever it was into the flames where it sputtered then flared. She laid out the cards. She didn't study them long.

"Y'all gonna get ripped apart like an old shirt eighteen months from now," she said, "and there ain't nothin' you can do to stop it."

She regarded them, one after the other, to see if her words sunk in. Continued.

"You will not frustrate the plans of your parents. You will not meet in secret. You will not speak on the street. Still, I see that you are united in spirit in which case time will pass and you will find each other again in another place. A city, I believe. Look for me. Lord knows why, but I'll be there too."

Her words rang inside their heads. They were difficult to comprehend. In eighteen months, they would no longer be allowed to keep company. They expected that. But how could it be that they would never speak to each other again, even casually, on the street? Where they came from, everyone talked to everyone else. Black or white didn't matter.

Max and Ruby understood the good people of Heard County feared too much familiarity between them. Both races thought the separation of near-grown children served the purpose of

God and man, sparing everybody a kind of trouble nobody needed. But no one kept Ruby's daddy from stopping by Max's daddy's store on Thursday nights, when blacks were welcome inside Sassaport's Fabrics, Fancy Goods, and Notions. He'd look over the display of seconds and discounted items no white man would buy. The men would talk to each other and trade pleasantries. One needn't pretend the other was dead, a ghost. If that could be true of their daddies, why couldn't Ruby and Max also talk easy in public? Why couldn't they at least have that?

What Mayhayley said made no sense. Then again if everything Mayhayley said were true, at least they'd get back together when they were grown, a time so many years ahead that it glistened over the horizon in a golden fog. But the oracle would be there too?

She shuffled more cards, laid them out.

"After that, I don't know. Maybe I'll know then." She laughed her manly laugh. "I don't see every damn thing straightaway."

She turned over a few more cards.

"I see you, Miss Tall Drink of Water, will grow into a beauty and a man will want to marry you who loves you more than life. Appreciate him."

Ruby blinked twice and shook her head. Ideas of romance had never entered her head before, but now they lodged there. In short time, they became a major concern.

"And you, young master Max, you'll have to work harder to get a wife than you will to make money. You'll always have enough money. People will court you. You won't never mind that."

Max straightened his back against the chair. It was all too much for his young self. He was stuck on the first thing she said, that in another year and a half, he and Ruby would no longer speak to each other and wouldn't for years and years. A future beyond that he couldn't absorb.

Mayhayley rose.

"Time to get goin' now, children. It be near dark afore you get home."

They got up and went to the door. Mayhayley gave them permission to draw water from the well. They filled Ruby's jug, said goodbye to the witch, and set off. Instead of talking, they prodded each other and made faces, producing queer, expressive sounds as they could find no words straightaway. When they were at the end of the path to the main road, the witch called out to them.

"Remember this: y'all goin' t'have to stop your thievin' ways." she said. "Or nothin' good will come to you. Walk with the Lord."

Max gulped. They turned onto the road. Ruby consoled him in a quiet voice the witch could not hear.

"She's feelin' bad because she's the one received stolen goods."

Max shrugged. His mind was young, fickle, elastic. It traveled elsewhere, deep into his relief that their separation was not imminent. He looked forward to the next eighteen months. Their end sounded far away. Maybe during all that time, they'd think up a way to stay together, a way Mayhayley hadn't seen. She wasn't divine. She could be right and wrong simultaneously. When he got around to it, he'd ask Ruby if she thought that was true. But as days passed and punishment for their thefts took hold, he forgot, so he never did.

2.

Ruby's theft was discovered before she'd a chance to get home that day. Two hours before, Mama noticed her glass jar of coins hidden at the bottom of a gunny-sack underneath a collection of cloth scraps and salvaged paper had been interfered with. Like most women for whom pin money comes hard, Mama counted her stash every day. She added to it by taking in laundry, although she gave more than half her earnings to her husband. What was left she spent where she had to but still managed to put away a penny or two every week. The clink-clink they made hitting the jar was like music to her. It made her smile. It gave her peace. To find the jar light broke her heart.

Francine Johnson was a wily mother. She knew her children and deduced which one was the thief after the briefest deliberation. When Ruby sauntered through the front door humming a prayer song, hoping her parents would buy her innocent act, they grabbed her. Her daddy pulled her by the elbow into the center of the room for interrogation.

"What did you do with that ten cent?" Bull Johnson demanded.

Ruby's siblings gathered in the shadows near the light of the cook fire. They held fast to one another, casting a giant lumpen shadow on the wall. The shadow looked like a beast or a demon. No matter how hard Ruby tried to lie when Mama and Daddy asked over and over if she knew anything about missing money, her face was turned to the demon on the wall. Frightened more of the devil than her parents, she failed miserably in all her fabrications. She confessed but she didn't tell the truth.

"I took the pennies, yes, I did. But I lost 'em, playin' with 'em. They dropped from my hands into the creek and then I couldn't find 'em. I looked and I looked and I looked. I looked as hard at that creek bed as an angel of God looking for an honest man. But no siree."

Daddy wasted no time. He sent her to the patch of wild grown weeds big as trees behind the house to select a switch he could beat her with. She thought that was it. A lecture and a beating. But afterward, as she stood in the middle of the room, facing the demon, weeping with her hands on her sore bottom, her mama decreed that Ruby was going to work out in the world until she paid back the dime. She'd learn the value of a penny let alone ten cent.

Max's theft was not discovered until much later. It might have been sooner were it not for Uncle Morris. All the way home from Mayhayley's, Max prepared excuses for why he was late and practiced saying "I don't know where them bits went" with a straight face and calm voice. He thought he had it down pretty good. When he got to the store, he found his uncle Morris, who visited town four times a year at the change of seasons, in conference with his father. The brothers were intensely involved. They ignored his arrival. Feeling relieved, Max sidled up next to them out of curiosity.

At forty-three, Uncle Morris looked older than he was, as ancient as Zeyde. The yellow fever got him down in Santiago during the war of '98. Its ravages aged him. His skin went permanently sallow. He was scrawny. He stooped. The bindle and valise he carried everywhere through the countryside, trading this and that, had, over time, bent his back and tilted one shoulder toward the ground. Another man might have found stay-at-home work or better yet, sitting-down work. But life on the road was a romance for Morris Sassaport. He enjoyed wandering, ever wandering, making friends in the cities, farms, and backwoods. It gave him a connection to the ancestors, made him feel like one of them, a pioneer. Morris disparaged modern life. He never sat a horse if he could walk. He'd never sat a Roundabout, Model C, or Studebaker at all and swore he never hoped to. He'd been stubborn that way since he returned from the gunfire in Puerto Rico.

"Life and death, m'boy," he told Max. "Look 'em square in the eye and you'll find yourself wantin' only to do what God Almighty made you to do by your own lights alone and none of that gov'mint honor and remember the *Maine* and glory-chasin' bullcrap will ever cuddle up to your mind agin."

All of it went over Max's head. He thought Uncle Morris was crazy, teched, *meshugah* but he liked him anyway. He told good stories and always had surprising items in his valise, things he bartered Daddy's conventional stock for, things Daddy often thought were worthless. Sometimes, a Morris purchase made him raise his voice and tear at his hair, which confounded the boy. He thought his uncle's finds were mesmerizing, even magical on occasion. He stood on his toes to see what it was the man presented to his brother this time around. From their conversation, he realized it was something rare.

Like all good salesmen, Uncle Morris created a sense of wonder about his prize. He reached into his valise with exaggerated care and withdrew a red checked handkerchief he placed in the palm of his right hand. It bulged in the center. He held it out toward his brother and slowly unwrapped it with his left hand, corner by corner.

"And there you have it, Yacov," he said, addressing Daddy by his Hebrew name. Everyone else called him Jake. "What will you give me for this marvel?"

Max leaned in to see what Morris had unveiled. He didn't see much. Some metal and glass. In acknowledgment of his presence, his father placed a warm hand against the back of his neck. Max knew the two men were engaged in a contest by the way each stared the other hard in the eye. He hoped his father would win. He wasn't sure why or how he could tell who won since both the stakes and object of the contest were unknown to him, but he rooted for Daddy anyway.

Uncle Morris played his trump card. He broke the stare off to glance down at his nephew. He smiled. Suddenly, the hand with the handkerchief made a graceful sweep that ended six inches below the boy's nose. With a wink toward Daddy to indicate Max was a prime example of the typical consumer, Uncle Morris asked,

"What do you think, kid?"

Max regarded his uncle's treasure. His brow wrinkled up.

"It's just a doorknob," he said.

"Yes!" Morris said. "But what a door it once opened! Max, this knob, this ordinary, just a cut-glass knob is the one that opened the door of the room in which Fenton Smalls waited for the mob to hang him."

Max was impressed. He knew who Fenton Smalls was. The man had passed shortly before Max was born but he knew. He looked up at his uncle round of eye, jaw-dropped.

"Look here," Morris continued, "you can see what he scratched in the metal piece where the knob fits the door. 'Let me out' it says in Smalls's own hand."

Max took the knob and held it close to his face. Fenton Smalls was a black man charged with the rape-murder of a white woman over to Macon. He was confined for several days in the back room of the local courthouse awaiting trial. Directly after opening argument by the prosecution, Judge Calloway saw no purpose in continuing and called a recess to give opportunity for what followed. Soon as the courtroom cleared, half a dozen men snatched Smalls from the holding room and took him to an oak tree bordering a nearby field where he was hanged, and then burnt, some said while he was still alive.

Fenton Smalls was not some ignorant field hand rounded up by police who could find no other suspect of an unsolved crime. He was a literate man, a journalist for the black newspaper out of Macon, *Wings of Freedom*. Some said his pen not his manly parts brought his fate down upon him. It might have been true. Fenton Smalls made a lot of enemies during his short life, fighting for justice in an unjust world, but barely a white man alive in Georgia thought Smalls might be innocent anyway. They read about the case in the *Atlanta Constitution,* and the *Atlanta Constitution* was the next thing to gospel. A trial was too good for him.

It took time for Max to find and read Smalls's desperate inscription.

"It's writ tiny," he said.

Morris had an answer for everything.

"That's why I want to sell it with a magnifying glass, the size of a loupe, the kind women use for the sewin'. I know you got 'em in stock, Yacov. I'll only need the one. Plus I will throw in a short stack of postcards I acquired over to Marietta featuring Smalls's charred up corpse laid out underneath the hangin' tree. Some of 'em are from days after the fact. There's picnics goin' on in the background. They sell like hotcakes."

Max's father held up a hand cutting his *shpiel* short. He knew he could sell a knob with provenance—people loved something with a story behind it—but the idea of selling postcards of a black man's corpse along with ones of white people celebrating over it was something he could not stomach.

"Morris, you've been too long on the road if you think I'm going to sell those cards," he said.

Morris tilted his head right and then left while he thought up a compromise.

"Fair enough. I got ones of the room he was drug from, too, with the furniture overturned in the draggin'. He put up quite a fight, evidently. How's about those?"

Morris offered to mock up a wooden box to showcase the knob nestled atop the red checked handkerchief next to the loupe. He'd affix Jake-approved postcards to its sides, make a fancy little sign to hang on the wall above it.

His brother lifted his shoulders in a shrug of acquiescence. He could do that. He'd have to sell from the back room, though. No women allowed or the shop would get a reputation. It was the postcards clinched the deal. They enhanced the value of the object. Made it appear legitimate. He wouldn't have the doorknob long. He stuck out his hand. The brothers shook on it.

"I'll do the best I can," Jake said. "But don't expect too much."

It was time for supper. Bubbe called them upstairs. Everyone was hungry and eager to hear Uncle Morris's bulletins from Marietta, Macon, and Atlanta along with a market report on what farmers around wanted for the coming season. It was nearly time to harvest the cotton, weeks of hard work performed in the hope of cash money at the end of October when the crops were sold. Schools were closed for the month that families might have all hands on the cotton. If the price per bale went low, November was still the richest month their customers had all year. Those who didn't buy in November, didn't buy from December on either. It was vital to have November goods folk'd ride into town for. They always bought more than they came looking for. The talk at dinner was loud and boisterous. Everyone wanted their opinions of what to stock on the table, even the women and Max. They all forgot he'd got home late.

The next day, while Max slept in of a Sunday morning, lying flat on his full belly, Ruby's mama rented her out as a laborer at a farm down the road. It was a white man's farm. A rich one, a friend of their landlord. She worked in the night and on Sundays after her family chores were done. She cleaned stock stalls, sorted leaves in the tobacco barn, rolled cotton in the gin until her hair was full of lint. Soon enough, Ruby proudly paid back the dime but her mama took all her pay above it. It wasn't fair. If she was old enough to work outside the home, Ruby reasoned, she was old enough to keep her money.

Between making restitution and bringing in the cotton with the family, Ruby didn't see much of Max in October. Most Saturdays since the theft, her mother made her stay in and study the Bible with the family to improve her character. Max was mostly free. Without Ruby, he was bored, lonely, and depressed. Sometimes, he visited the deer blind and sat down and wept because he could not see her.

The time they did find together was more precious than ever to both of them. When Ruby managed to evade her mother's watch, she got word to him by enlisting her sister Paulette as messenger. Then they'd meet by the creek as before. Each time they reunited, they hugged hard and talked for hours. After a few minutes, it felt as if nothing had changed although there were things Ruby laughed at Max didn't understand. He told her life without her companionship was dull and dreary. He felt dead already most of the time. He wanted to make enough money for the two of them to run away. She laughed her queer laugh and paid no mind to him but that was alright. He didn't tell her he already had a grubstake, having found the perfect money making venture. He wanted to surprise her.

He got the idea the day his father decided to delay selling the Morris box until November when farmers could afford to compete in a bidding war. Max thought that very smart. "Even kids my age have a few coins after harvest," he told Daddy at dinner and a spark went off in his mind. A venture came to him that was brilliant, fool-proof.

First, he drew up a handbill that he distributed to all the boys at school the first week of November. "Come see what's left of Fenton Smalls," it read simply. "Group rates available." Their reaction was as he hoped. All of them knew about the doorknob and postcards through eavesdropping on their daddies and mamas' gossip. By lunchtime, he had a roster full of appointments.

At the end of the day, he gobbled his evening meal and told Daddy he had a chore to finish in the store, one his father had assigned to him at breakfast that he'd purposefully left undone. He made up an excuse for why he hadn't got to it, something to do with schoolwork. He went downstairs to the shop's back door, opened it, and allowed his queued-up schoolmates to file in for a look at the Morris box. He charged a penny for groups of three and two cents for groups of five. Word spread. Some of the boys even wanted to see the box twice. He made money every night before his father sold off the knob for a sawbuck. Max didn't care. He had a windfall on his hands. He was rich. The next time they met, he tried to give Ruby a tied-up cloth holding the proceeds from the doorknob inscribed "let me out" by a lynched and burnt black man. He didn't tell her where it came from. Money was money, he figured. She didn't ask. She already knew. Franklin told her all about Max's enterprise when he was informed of it by the boys at the cotton gin where he worked when they needed day labor.

"Do you know what that l'il cracker a yours is doin'?" Franklin asked her.

She shook her head. Her brother spit out the gruesome facts with drops of venom flying from his tongue.

"How can you entertain kind thoughts about a white boy who'd do somethin' like that?" he demanded.

Ruby's eyes filled up. She wasn't so much shocked as heart-broke. She never knew Max to have a callous, hateful moment in the past. She thought a while, torn between loyalty to her one and only friend and loyalty to her very blood.

"Oh, Franklin," she said at last, her voice cracking just a little. "He ain't mean. He's just simple. He don't think things all the way through. I won't hear no more about it."

Her brother tried to say more, but Ruby covered her ears with her hands and loudly hummed, drowning him out. He wanted to shake her until she listened. But he knew his sister and realized she'd only dig her heels in deeper if he tried. He threw up his hands and dropped the subject. Ruby pondered on it more than once afterward.

When Max presented her his mound of coins in a tied-up cloth, all she did was test the heft of his coins in her palm, give him a long hard stare he wondered the meaning of, and hand it back.

"Money ain't gonna buy me out," she told him. "Mama said the other day it's time I started livin' a woman's life. That farmer I worked for wants me back permanent."

Max persisted.

"You don't have to do that. We can leave with this."

He shook the tied-up cloth, rattling pennies and nickels together.

She gave him one of those incomprehensible laughs and waved her hand in a gesture he didn't understand.

"In the first place, we're too young yet to run away," she said. "In the second, if I kept that money, what makes you think I can hold on to it? It wouldn't take Daddy two days to find it. And what you think my daddy's gonna do if he finds I got a pile of money I shouldn't? I don't need him raisin' cane."

Max tried to puzzle out why her daddy would raise cane if she were found with extra money. He still hadn't turned ten yet, though the date drew close. Ruby was now nearly ten and a half. She knew many things he didn't. He wondered why she thought they were too young to run. Ten-year-old runaways weren't unknown in Heard County.

Her eyes got big the way they did when she was bursting to tell him something and then it came out.

"I do got a secret, though. The boss over to the gin gave me somethin' extra for helpin' him out when everyone else gone home. Mama's never found out about that. I dug a hole in the backyard and buried it. That money's mine."

Max would have asked her why she couldn't just bury his money with hers but his mind had moved beyond economics. They only had a couple hours together. He didn't want to waste them. He suggested a turtle hunt.

It was low tide. They poked with sticks around the mudflats and along the high grass that bordered them. Ruby squealed when they discovered their only turtle of the afternoon. Its shell was about three inches in diameter. She held it up against the blue sky with two fingers. The turtle's head was tucked inside its shell. Its legs pawed the air. Max took a turn holding it. They named it. They talked to it. They sang to it and returned it to the mudflat that was just beginning to refill with water. Tiny hummocks of wet mud pierced by the airholes of burrowed crab glistened in rainbow colors under the sun. It was a beautiful warm day, not too hot. They lay out next to each other on the creek bank and closed their eyes. Within seconds, Ruby was asleep.

Max knew she was awful tired. She had to be with harvest just over. Her eyes looked pouchy. She'd lost weight. What was left of her looked tight, wiry. Long ropes of muscle had replaced baby fat. He put his thigh next to hers while she slept. His resembled a plump turkey drumstick, hers the foreleg of a crane. He hadn't noticed them being so different before. The change touched something deep inside him.

My darlin' friend, he thought, with his heart full of emotion, my darlin' friend. He knew of no other words to express himself, mostly because he couldn't identify the powerful feeling her ropy limbs provoked. The words were copied from his daddy who gave him the only phrase of endearment he knew. When he was moved to do so, Jake Sassaport called Mama "my darlin' wife." The way he said it made Mama flush with pride. It gave her a surge of strength. Her shoulders squared, her chest filled with air. Max wanted to give Ruby the same gift. He told her so the best way he knew how.

"My darlin' friend," he said, aloud this time but softly. "My darlin' friend."

Ruby snored some. She didn't hear him. He laid back on the grass and shut his eyes too. Though he didn't have half the reason Ruby had to sleep, it wasn't long before he slept beside her.

A big heavy boot kicked his side. He woke up. Ruby wasn't next to him anymore. The big boot belonged to her father.

That afternoon, Bull Johnson and his mule had delivered hay bales to farms around. He was on his way home when, due to a trick of the light, he spied two child-sized figures lying together near the blind. They looked odd. He wasn't sure they were alive. He parked the mule and went to investigate. The last thing he expected to find was his baby girl sleeping next to that Sassaport boy. Wild thoughts of Ruby hurt by him, damaged by him, assailed the man. He raised his daughter up to stand by him and booted her companion.

Max scrambled to his feet. He tried to speak but couldn't at first. He coughed. Tried again.

"Good day, Bull," he near whispered to Ruby's daddy, a man named for the years he pulled his own plow before he bought a mule. It didn't occur to the boy that he addressed by his given name a man three and a half times older and at least four times bigger. Such familiarity came natural. He'd never heard a white boy call a colored man mister or sir, even one nicknamed for his strength.

Bull struggled to contain himself. His breath came loud. His fists clenched and unclenched. His voice broke when he asked the big question in as even a tone as he could manage.

"What 'xactly, young man, you doin' here layin' about with my Ruby?"

Max swallowed. He could hardly tell Bull Johnson they'd fallen asleep while plotting to run away. He turned twelve shades of red. His answer was short but came out of him in one breath. It was a speeding train of words that left him panting.

"Jest playin'," he said. "We been huntin' turtles."

The great hulk towering over him grunted. He didn't speak. He got sadder and sadder and still didn't speak. Ruby emerged from behind the man's legs. She stepped around until she was face-to-face with him.

"Daddy, Daddy, leave Max alone, please. Mama don't need that kind of trouble. Nuthin' happened. Nuthin' at all."

Bull studied her with a world of sorrow in his eyes. His chest, however, expanded until it looked like it would bust his shirt buttons. She reached up to put a hand on his cheek.

"Daddy," she said, quietly, "we're only ten."

She went to Max's side and took his hand. Her gesture made him feel proud, ready to join her wherever fate and their friendship led. He was still scared though. Ruby gave Bull a bright, shiny look, her feet firmly planted, her head erect, while Max worked up a frightened version of the same thing. Only the most heartless of men would fail to be moved by them.

Ruby's daddy was not a heartless man. Before their very eyes, he deflated like a worn-out balloon the day after the Fourth of July. His shoulders caved. His mouth softened. For a few moments, the children beamed solidarity at him while he thought the situation over then Bull heaved a manly sigh and said, "C'mon, chillun. I'll get y'all home."

Max and Ruby climbed into the back of the wagon. The bed was strewn with hay scraps they gathered together to make pillows and cushions for themselves. Whether it was an accident, a mere happenstance, or an act of God that gave Bull Johnson notice of the uncommon bond between them, it got him to worrying. He was not a man to leave matters to chance. It was true they were only ten, but they would not stay ten forever.

He dropped off Ruby to home first. No need to put pictures of the two together in Max's parents' heads. The one in his own was rough enough. They were going to have to do something about those children sooner rather than later. First, he and Francine would need to talk and then somehow approach the Sassaports on the matter. He didn't like to tell anybody but tall, willful Ruby was his favorite child. He hated to imagine how distressed she was going to be.

The Johnson family lived in a dog-trot house, four rooms

separated by corridors open to the air, which helped cool them during the hot months. It required a lot of plugging up during the cold. The boy children had one room, the girl children another. There was a family room for eating and cooking while Bull and Francine had the luxury of their own room, which they shared with three hound dogs and a scrappy cat. The house had a long front porch with two chairs and a heap of barrels for sitting, flowerpots for spring and summer, stacks of wood for everyday cooking and heat in winter. It looked rickety to Max's eyes. To Ruby, it was just home. In her mind, the house, the barn, the ten acres of fields behind it where they all worked together belonged to her as much as to the landlord.

Franklin, Paulette, Jackson, and Marla sat on the floor of the porch, dangling their bare feet over the edge. They played a game with sticks and stones. It appeared Paulette was winning. Ruby scrambled off the wagon to join them, giving a back-hand wave goodbye to Max, which hurt his feelings a little. It comforted Bull.

The ride into town took a while, but it beat walking. When Bull turned into Main Street, Max moved to jump off the wagon bed and go the rest of the way on his own, but Bull took hold of his shirt collar to pull him back. "I'm takin' you to your door, son. The back door."

Folk on the street saw them coming and someone went in the store to tell Jake Sassaport his son was being transported home by Bull Johnson from God knows where. Bull drove around the back and the family rushed forth, lining up to give Max what-for. As it happened, their agitation had none to do with Ruby or Bull, but their expressions told no lies. Max was in the soup.

Buying time, he thanked Bull profusely for the ride and slowly dismounted from the wagon bed. Soon as his feet touched the ground, his daddy had him by the arm while his mama, standing square before him with her hands on her hips, scowled at him. His grandma stood behind her, shaking a tin tobacco box. The granddaddy stood back radiating shame that such a child was his.

Bull lifted his hat and gave the family a big smile.

"I'll just leave the li'l prince to y'all," he said and rode off without waiting for a reply. He didn't know what was going on but surely didn't want to be part of it. Nonetheless, he heard Rose Sassaport's demand.

"Where'd my dollar go?"

Then the boy's reply, "I only borrowed it."

Curious, Bull turned his head to catch Max holding up his cloth of coin.

"Here, I give it back this instant, as I was plannin' to do," the boy finished, a gesture he hoped would defuse his troubles. He couldn't help adding with a touch of pride, "There's more there than a dollar. Took me two months, but I got me a fortune."

Alas, he'd only opened up a fresh can of worms. Jake Sassaport took the sack and tested its heft. He blinked. His mouth opened a hair. He passed the cloth to Zeyde who was similarly impressed. "*Gott in Himmel*," the old Jew muttered, wide-eyed, handing it over to Bubbe.

"Where in heck did you get that money?" Daddy asked with full-bodied consternation.

Bull laughed so hard inside his shoulders shook. He'd heard the stories. He suspected he knew how the boy got rich. It delighted him the little squirt would get what he deserved. He grinned as he made his way back down Main Street on the way to home. He shook his head and clucked his tongue, marveling over white folk so careless with money it took months before they noticed it was missing. Then he cracked his whip over the ears of the mule as he wanted to get home before dark.

Bull's wagon exited the alleyway in a blast of dust that might have been smoke. It sparked the curiosity of those lounging on rockers beneath the awnings of Main Street. They rose en masse and went to the alleyway between Jim Buck's Smithey and Sassaport's Fabrics, Fancy Goods, and Notions where they could see what was going on. They clustered in a knot and gawked. Mama paled beneath their scrutiny. She put a hand inside the crook of her husband's elbow.

"No need to do this in the street," she said.

Her husband looked around and agreed. He ordered Max upstairs with an outstretched arm and pointed finger. The boy trudged to his fate, head down. During his inquisition, there were no demons cast upon the wall, only parents and grandparents bearing down upon him. Bubbe asked what did he need his mama's dollar for in the first place. With an ease he did not know he possessed, he lied.

"I wanted to buy off them bullies what chase me," he said, looking pitiful while he did so, "and then when I reached in my pocket to get it, it was gone. 'Member that hole you stitched up in my school pants, Mama? It was afore you done that."

Rose Sassaport winced. She grew up in Savannah and completed a high school education there, which set her apart from the country women around her. Had she not fallen for a handsome merchant, she might have been a teacher. Poor grammar hurt her ears worse than mendacity from the mouth of a thieving child.

"*Those* bullies *who*, son," she said, "and *before* I *did* that."

Max then told most of the truth about his side show of Uncle Morris's box. Bubbe pinched him on the arm, enough to raise a bruise next day on his pale, baby flesh. She would have done it twice but Mama blocked her hand. Daddy was stunned then angered that business had occurred behind his back in his own establishment but by nightfall, as he lay abed with his wife, he confessed he admired the kid's ingenuity.

"To tell the truth, Rose," he said, "I didn't think the boy was that smart. You know how he's always starin' out a window, all dreamy? From now on, I'm goin' to take more interest in what he's dreamin' about."

A family conference ruled on his punishment. He was to work in the backroom an extra hour every day for a couple weeks, sweeping, cleaning, counting. It wasn't hard work, but harder work than he was used to. The point was not that he would learn the value of a dollar but that he would learn more of the blood and guts of commerce.

"It was a good idea you had there, son," Jake said to him on the q.t. "But you are not the boss here. Next time, come to me."

Max promised he would, but he never came up with another worthwhile retail plan. Losing his profits was a discouragement and his parents worked him so much he barely saw Ruby, which gave him pain. In punishing him, they killed any enthusiasm he might have had for buying and selling. He began entertaining ideas of other pursuits, ones he might devote himself to when he was finished with schooling. He liked the idea of piloting a boat, but he couldn't swim. Railroad engineer also appealed. He thought of being a bar owner because everyone seemed to like bar owners, or maybe, an auctioneer because talking fast was something he figured he could learn to do without much effort. He imagined his friend Ruby at his side, sharing his path, though in what capacity remained mysterious. If Mayhayley was right, their real life would begin years hence and in a city. Now, that was something to look forward to.

3.

After their sufferings over a dollar and a dime, the two friends met in secret. Max couldn't put his finger on why, it just felt like a good idea when Ruby brought it up. Not even Paulette knew when they saw each other. They left notes arranging where and when in a rusty coffee can hidden underneath a pile of rubble in the deer blind.

They never met in the old place. In the backwoods of Georgia, there were many discreet places to hide, as many as there were copses of trees and cairns as old as the Creek tribes that built them. It was fun deciding where to go, pinning locations down. Clearly, secrecy spiced their games and daydreams. They pretended they were spies or highwaymen. Whenever one snuck up undetected on the other's position, they erupted in giggles. It may be that clandestine activity gave them a taste of rebellion, a sense of freedom neither possessed. It made them feel they could be anything, they could go anywhere. Max imagined they rehearsed for running away.

Lots of things happened the year they turned eleven. Max had a growth spurt. Ruby did not. He was now able to look over her shoulder when they stood close, facing each other. When they hugged, he felt twinges of pleasure that spread through his chest and down to his root. He didn't understand them, but he liked them. He found himself engineering excuses to hold her close without clear comprehension of what might follow. For her part, by the time she was eleven Ruby began to grow breasts. Francine made her wear two undershirts even when it was hot. Ruby didn't see her point. They were so small at first, who would care about them? But sometimes, when Bull regarded her with fresh, sharp sadness, she dropped her head and crossed her arms over her chest. Unlike Max, Ruby knew exactly what her changes meant.

Soon she attracted new friends. Her contemporaries were nearly caught up to her in height. She was less of a monster in their eyes. The boys were fascinated by her ever developing body and hovered around her when they could; the girls hovered, too, that Ruby's boys might notice them as well. It was exhilarating to be courted suddenly by both genders, each for their own designs, but she didn't forget Max. He was family. He was so dumb about so many things, she figured he needed her. She couldn't abandon him for the sake of more recent attachments. While she mistrusted his parents and grandparents the same way she'd learned to mistrust every other white person she knew, keeping her thoughts, her judgments, her emotions hidden from them, playing the role every black girl knew how to play almost from birth, she trusted Max, mostly because they'd loved and trusted each other from the git-go when nobody else did.

There came a soft spring night during that year when everything around smelled moist and new. Ellen Frances, one of Ruby's new friends, a pretty brown child as poor as Ruby but with airs copied from the family her mama cleaned for, passed by the house. Ellen Frances and Ruby talked sometimes when their mothers sent them for milk at the four-cow dairy farm the black folk patronized. They liked each other well enough.

"Hey, Ellen Frances," she called out.

Ruby sat on the edge of the porch, swinging her long legs. Ellen Frances asked if she'd care to join her for a moonlight walk.

"Come taste the night air with me," she said. She waved the corner of a hand-me-down yellow shawl draped around her shoulders in a welcoming gesture.

Ruby found her movements elegant. She scrambled off the porch without using the stairs in her rush to fall in beside her.

"Where we goin'?" she asked.

Ellen Frances shrugged.

"It don't matter," she said. "We just on a ramble."

She inhaled deeply, exhaled, and sighed.

"It smells simply divine out here."

Ruby inhaled deeply too. She caught a noseful of Daddy's manure pile mixed with the scent of pine needles he'd chopped up to sweeten the outhouse. Ellen Frances must be playing a pretend game, she decided, then sighed also to be companionable. They walked to the end of the property and into the public road, a narrow channel created by the passage of wagons and four-in-hands, grown over with grass in the middle and lined by trees on either side. While they walked, Ellen Frances hummed a song she'd acquired working in the big house kitchen while her mama's lady played piano and the mister sang in the room next door. The mister was the round, haughty boss of a tobacco farm. He never seemed to do much but ride his horse and count his money. He employed most people of the town who did not tend their own farm and some who did. From time to time, Ruby saw him here and there astride his big buckskin draft. She could scarcely believe that the man she knew sang frivolous songs in a parlor.

The one Ellen Frances hummed intrigued her. Max was not musical. He had a singing voice like barbed wire. Everything he sang sounded exactly the same. In her home, only religious songs were sung. She had to ask.

"What you singin'?"

"It's the latest tune from New York City," the girl said. "Mama's lady been learnin' it this week. I been helpin' Cook these days so I'm hearin' it all the day long. I can't help but get it stuck in my head."

"Do you know the words?"

"Some."

"Let's hear 'em."

While she sang, Ellen Frances swung her arms like a mother rocking a baby or a sailor keeping time to a shanty.

Cuddle up a little closer, lovey mine,
Cuddle up and be my little clinging vine,
I like to feel your cheek all rosy
Make you feel all comfy-cozy . . .

"That's so stupid!" Ruby said.

Ellen Frances rolled her eyes and continued to sing.

'Cause I love you head to toesies, lovey mine . . .

When she got to the end, the girls held their sides and rocked on their heels with laughter, as if romance were the dumbest, silliest thing in the world. For Ruby it was. She'd watched enough besotted grown-ups make idiots of themselves to have formed an opinion. She might entertain herself with notions of who the great love Mayhayley Lancaster predicted might be but she wasn't in any hurry to bind herself to a man. She figured he'd come along soon enough without her bothering to look. It was a fact of life young girls couldn't stay single too long or there'd be trouble.

Her big sister Celia married at fifteen to prevent trouble. Her husband was the son of a cropper down the road. The two were so crazy about each other the families married them off quick. Celia went to live with her in-laws but in the first two months ran home to Mama three times, crying about her treatment over there. Francine gave her Bible verses to follow, ones encouraging a wife's submission to her husband. Bull had a man-to-man with both his son-in-law and his daddy, which probably did more good. While not an endorsement of romantic bliss, as time went by the marriage became just what was. Celia looked tired all the time. She looked older than her twenty years. Without saying a word, she gave Ruby plenty of reasons to put off searching for a man.

Two young black men three or four years older than Ruby and Ellen Frances leaned on the great trunks of slippery elm by the side of the road. They took off their hats as they passed. "Evening, ladies," they said then quit the trees to follow them. Both walked so close behind, Ruby imagined she felt their breath on her back. She sped up to get a few feet away. They matched her pace.

"Ellen Frances, honey," one said, "introduce us to your friend."

Ellen Frances halted and reached out to seize Ruby by the wrist. She turned toward the boys, twisting Ruby about in the same direction. Ruby wrenched free of her. She stepped backed. By then, Ellen Frances was up in the face of the boy who spoke.

"Miss Ruby Alfreda Johnson, may I present Misters Randolph Roth and Lewis Taylor," she said. "These boys work at the tobacco farm Mama's mister owns."

Ruby didn't know which surprised her more. That Ellen Frances knew the pair or that she then put an arm around the waist of Randolph Roth, then drew away from the others. Ruby was alone on the road with Lewis Taylor. He got beside her.

"Look. I don't expect much from you," he said. "We just met. But if we're walking together, maybe you could hold my hand. That's all. Jist hold my hand."

Lewis Taylor wasn't bad-looking. His hair was neat. It was combed back and glistened with store-bought pomade by the light of the moon. He had no spots that she could see. His mouth looked soft. It wasn't cruel. She didn't give him her hand but she did walk forward instead of turning toward home. They walked a while at a pace the others set until Ellen Frances and Randolph Roth cut into the woods beyond the tree line and disappeared. Lewis Taylor raised a hand to wave them goodbye as if their departure was as normal as eating an apple or wearing shoes on Sunday.

A knot of anxiety settled at the pit of Ruby's stomach. Ellen Frances had cast her off. She walked alone in the night at the age of eleven with a strong boy her father would consider a man. She took deep breaths. She tried to marshal her courage and still the beat of her heart. Part of her looked for a way to run.

She turned about face.

"It's got dark," she said. "I have to go home."

"I'll go with you."

There was no getting rid of him. She shrugged.

"Suit yourself."

They walked along silently, briskly. Every time she turned her head to glance at him, he was staring at her and a wave of heat rushed up her neck to her cheeks. They went on. He didn't seem to ever look away from her. He didn't watch where he went. She expected him to step in a burrow or get swiped in the head by a low hanging branch. Max would have. Neither happened.

When she got home, she felt the obligation to be gracious to him. He'd taken it on himself to see her home. In the end, he'd been a gent. She faced him.

"Good night," she said, which was all she could think of to say.

He raised his hat and smiled. He had good teeth. He left. She felt a fool for her fears.

Ruby thought of Lewis Taylor a lot after that. She thought of him when she got up in the day and when she lay down in the night and numerous times in between. She wondered if he'd come by or if she'd run into him again on the road. After a few days, neither occurred, which made him a puzzle she must solve. She reflected on the looks he gave her, speculating on their meaning and whether her refusal to hold his hand was what kept him away. Exactly seven days later, she started her bloodtimes. In later years, she considered it was the thinking of Lewis Taylor so intensely brought them on.

She told Mama how things were with her. Mama gave her a bundle of folded rags and a talk about watching herself. It was pretty much the same talk she gave her every time she had a birthday or learned a new skill. It was very much like the talk she gave her the first day she worked at the farm down the road last year, the one that started, "You're gettin' all grown up. It's time you got more careful . . ." only this one ended on a different note. That one ended: "Just do your work and come straight back." This one ended: ". . . soon you'll have a husband and a home of your own to worry about. You won't have time for playing around then."

Max, Ruby thought. Mama means playing around with Max. There'll be no time for Max in what's to come.

For a while, she fretted about it. But when she lay down her head to sleep that night, it was thoughts of Lewis Taylor came to her first in a trickle and then in a flood. She tried to talk to Max about him. There was no one else she could confide in.

The next time the two friends met, they met in the woods near a stretch of creek north of the place on Yellowjacket where they met in the years before the dollar and a dime. It felt familiar, comfortable. Ruby sat with her back against a turkey oak. Max lay at her feet, propped on an elbow, a hand by his ear, beaming affection. He melted her heart. She hardened it.

"Do you know how old I am today?" she asked him.

"Eleven somethin'."

"I am eleven and eight months exactly," she said.

Max knew where she was going before she figured out how to take him there.

"If Mayhayley's right we have two months left," he said. Sadness weighted each syllable. "That's not much.

His tone made her eyes sting. She coughed to keep her voice calm, low.

"No, it's not."

He looked up at her with piercing sincerity.

"We have to run."

There it was. The thing she expected, the thing she feared. Here is where the truth will hurt, she thought, and said it anyway.

"I don't want to."

Max's features contorted themselves into a portrait of unhappiness and confusion.

"Why?"

She took a deep breath. She knew she had to follow through, to make a decision here, a grown-up one, and by the time she exhaled, she'd made it. She told him more of the hurtful truth as well as she understood it.

"Lewis Taylor. Lewis Taylor is why."

Max's lower lip pushed out. He squinted as if holding back tears. Ruby wiped a palm over each of her eyes to block her own then lifted her chin to show determination.

"I don't understand. Who is Lewis Taylor?"

She took another deep breath and said what had preyed on her mind for two weeks. It was the first time she said it out loud and to another human being.

"A boy I like," she said.

Her words had an echo. "A boy I like, a boy I like, a boy I like" sounded inside Max's head at least five or six times and still he did not comprehend them.

"How do you mean 'like'?" he asked the one girl, the one person he'd ever loved outside his blood relations. She looked away from him. Her voice went soft.

"Oh, Max," she said. "You know."

Her words penetrated like a thousand needles pushed into his brow.

"Oh," he said. "OK."

She stood up and brushed her hands against her skirt. She looked for the straw hat Francine made to keep the sun off her while she worked. She picked it up from the grass, shook it, and tied its burlap straps under her chin.

They didn't speak. Anger and hurt bubbled around the edges of Max's mind. He got to his feet, thinking to tell her how stupid she looked, standing there liking Lewis Taylor, when he felt the earth beneath him shift. It made a loud, impossible sound. All of it came from inside his head, but a panic hit him nonetheless. He walked briskly away from the sound, away from her; he would have run but that seemed unmanly, so he walked and he walked until he could hear the earth no more.

He saw Ruby three more times after that. The first time, he tracked her down. They hadn't seen each other for weeks. He'd checked the coffee can by the old deer blind daily and there was nothing from her, not even an "I'm sorry" or "I miss you," which might have soothed him. So he hid out near the entry of the neighbor's farm where she worked the late afternoon and evening shift. The man's farm had thick cement pillars with cement finials in the shape of pineapples flanking the entryway through which both visitors and workers were required to pass. Max plastered himself against the backside of a pillar so no one could see him although he could peer around the edge to look on the street and see who approached. In time, he saw Ruby arrive for her shift, walking toward him with four other black girls, all barefoot in flour-sack dresses. He hissed at her as she passed through the pillars.

"Psst. Ruby. Psst."

She heard him and fell back from the others. She looked surprised.

"Why you doin' this to me?" he said before she'd a chance to speak.

Ruby knew what he meant. Days before, she'd tired of waiting for Lewis Taylor to saunter by her porch. She got together with Ellen Frances at the dairy. The two arranged another rendezvous with the boys. That night, Ruby let Lewis hold her hand. When they said good night, it was she who kissed him in the dark. Since then, she thought of Lewis constantly in ways that had never occurred to her to think of a boy before. She certainly never thought of Max that way, and when he appeared like that, out of the blue, talking nonsense, trying to make her feel bad while she was on her way to work, it irritated her.

"Max, why don't you ever see things as they are?" she said with a sharp edge to her voice. "Lewis Taylor is a black man. You're white, in case you haven't noticed. Why do you think there is anywhere in this whole wide country we could, you know, run to? Max, you have been my dear friend, but I need to think of the future."

She turned on her heel and marched off to work, catching up with the other girls. They put their arms around each other and put their heads together. One of them broke away to look back at Max. Her expression was pinched, mean.

A few weeks later, he caught Ruby leaving the farm in the evening when her work was done. She was alone. He called out to her from behind the pillar.

"Ruby," he said sweetly. "Ruby."

Few stars were out that night. The moon was obscured by clouds. She peered through darkness looking for him.

"Max?"

Along the gravel path that led to the big house was a stretch of gas lamps. They were on wrought iron poles and well spaced. The closest cast thin columns of light near the entrance. Max stepped into one.

"Yes."

He'd spent a lot of time thinking about what he would do once he had her attention, but at the sight of her, all plans abandoned him. He had to say something. It might be his last chance. He got close to her.

"I miss you," he whispered.

Ruby's blood ran hot and quick. She felt confused about Max. Part of her missed him terribly while the other part wanted him out of sight and mind. Her confusion descended over her in full. It had weight. It crushed her. She said the only thing she could think of to get out from under it.

"Go away, Max. Next time you pop out from anywhere, I'm gonna yell for help."

Without waiting for a response, she ran down the road toward home, leaving Max drop-jawed in the lamp light.

Max had not anticipated Ruby would ever speak to him that way. It nearly destroyed him. The first day, he cried every chance he got. He couldn't weep in front of Mama or Daddy or the grandparents. He couldn't weep at school. But every moment he had alone became a festival of sobs. He lay in his room or hid in the back of the shop or sat in the privy with a sock in his mouth to stifle the pitiful sounds he made, mourning Ruby Alfreda Johnson. The next day, he decided crying was unmanly so he suppressed it by grinding his teeth whenever he felt the teardrops gather. His jaw was perpetually sore. He remained flat out miserable. He had no room for any other emotion. It drowned his anger with her.

Eventually, his mother noticed his eyes were always red. She took him to the doctor expecting a diagnosis of pink eye. The doctor found no infection. He attributed the boy's affliction to allergies although it was the start of winter and pollens were few.

It took about a month, but in time, with effort, he achieved a kind of lonely resignation to his fate. He no longer clenched his teeth five hundred times a day. On occasion he was able to smile at some memory of Ruby without tearing up. In the meantime, he kept busy. He spent extra time at school, reading whatever Mr. Austin suggested, which was a good thing as it stimulated his intellect. At night, after dinner, he straightened stock and filed invoices in the store's back room.

One night while he worked, there was a frantic knock on the door, rapid and insistent. He opened it. Pressed hard against the outside of the door was Ruby, clutching the torn neck of her shirt with two hands. Her breath was short, her skirt was streaked with blood. Her legs wobbled. She pitched forward into the room, wild-eyed.

"Ruby, what happened to you?"

She felt her way to a stool and sat. He wasn't sure if he was supposed to touch her but he put a hand on her shoulder. She swatted him away then spread her legs and put a hand on each knee. She bent over her lap with her elbows crooked.

"What happened to me, Max? You want to know what happened to me?" She gave out something between a moan and a cry. "Lewis Taylor happened to me," she said.

She reached out and grasped him by the sleeve.

"I have to get out of here, Max. If I stay, my daddy will kill him. Daddy can never know. Promise me, Max. My daddy will never know."

His mind was reluctant at first to acknowledge what his bruised, bloodied only-friend-ever was talking about. Lewis Taylor had hurt her, that much he was sure, but the how and why were unthinkable. He could imagine her daddy killing him though. He'd like to himself.

His parents were asleep in their bed in the living quarters above the store. The strong, intrepid Ruby he knew looked frail, helpless, terrified. He'd never seen her like that. It didn't take him but a second to know what to do.

"Let me get money," he said. "Stay here."

He tiptoed up the stairs worried that she'd leave before he got back. He entered the kitchen by the back door, went to the pantry, took up Mama's tobacco box, emptied its contents into his pockets, and put it back. He crept downstairs even more quietly than he'd gone up, his heart pounding less from fear of waking the household than fear that Ruby would be gone when he opened the door. Please let her still be there, he prayed.

She was. A great bolt of gratitude pierced his heart. He flushed with it. He dug into his pockets and emptied a stream of silver onto her lap. Her hands went to her cheeks. She was shocked at the amount of it—there must have been more than ten dollars in coin—and water welled in her eyes.

"Max. There's so much."

"We'll need every cent," he said.

She smacked her tongue against the back of her teeth, shook her head.

"No, Max. You can't go."

His head reared as if she'd punched him in the jaw.

"Why not?"

"You know why."

Ruby glanced down at the pool of money in her lap. Then she looked Max square in the eye.

"If you want this back . . ."

She bit her lip, hoping he'd say no.

His jaw tightened. He looked older.

"No. No. It's yours."

Ruby stood up and they hugged. Max felt the shape of her breasts against him, but they did not give him the pleasure they once had. Holding her filled him with raw grief. Every last frayed nerve she had trembled through her torn dress. Time was of the essence. She needed to get going before Bull Johnson discovered there was something amiss.

"I have to go," she said. "Now."

He nodded agreement. He opened the back door for her and was hit by a blast of cold night air.

"Wait," he said.

He fetched a wool blanket from the front of the store and wrapped her in it. She thanked him and worked up a wan smile.

"Remember to look for me in the city," she said.

"What city?" Max asked.

"I don't know. But it'll happen. Mayhayley said so."

"I'm counting on it," Max said.

He watched her walk down the alleyway and into the street as long as the dark would let him.

4.

Ruby was gone. The first night, Bull Johnson thought she would walk through the door any minute. He was ready to give her heck for staying out so late and worrying her mama. But she did not walk through the door all the night long. He imagined she was injured then, maybe even dead, or kidnapped, and needed him. His imaginings tormented him.

When daylight came, he searched for her everywhere he could think up and failed to find her. He talked to all the neighbors. No one had seen her. There was no note, no errand she'd been on, no message passed to the family through a friend. Francine talked to that Ellen Frances she'd been spending time with, but the girl was wide-eyed and ignorant on particulars. She couldn't say for certain when she'd last seen Ruby or what they'd done together lately.

For three days, he searched for her. He combed the town. He walked the woods. He prayed by the river. He looked down wells and quarries. When he tried to catch some sleep in the still, gray hours before the dawn, he couldn't shut his eyes for more than thirty seconds before the whimpers of his quietly, endlessly sobbing wife came to him loud as sirens. He could not help her. His burden of loss could only turn inward to the great black hole that was his soul's collapse. For a man who fails to protect, who can not comfort, there is no rest.

On the fourth day, he acknowledged the unthinkable. Ruby, his spirited, strong, beautiful daughter had disappeared. Without a trace. Just like that. She might never be seen again.

Didn't mean he gave up. When he was done searching all the places black folk lived, played, and worked, he turned to the white. He went with hat in hand to back doors all over and those who answered him regarded him with pity wondering how it was that proud Bull Johnson had turned to beggary. Others were irritated he'd come to bother them likely about some black man's business they wanted nothing to do with. But when he told the tale of his daughter gone missing without a trace, even the hardest heart felt a rush of human feeling and that night held their own girls close. About Ruby, no one knew a thing.

Time came for last resorts. Early on, Bull considered Maxwell Sassaport. Franklin and Paulette told him their sister hadn't bothered with him for months. As far as they knew, their friendship had withered on the vine so he put off talking to him. But Bull was not a man to leave a stone unturned. After striking out everywhere else, he resurrected the idea. He remembered how that young white boy and his Ruby stood together to challenge him when he'd caught them sleeping next to each other by the creek. He remembered their bright eyes and backs ramrod straight. He knew enough of life to know such deep affection can be crushed but never dies.

When evening fell the Thursday after Ruby went missing, he walked through the front door of Sassaport Fabrics, Fancy Goods, and Notions. It was colored night. He nodded to the handful of blacks looking through the shelves for what they could afford. They gave him sad-eyed looks in return though no one spoke. He might as well have walked into a funeral or brought one with him on his shoulders like a nightmare hobo carrying trouble to the unaware. He went right up to Jake Sassaport who stood behind a cash register set atop a broad counter fitted with a yardstick and a long hinged blade used to measure and cut what needed it.

"Mister Jake, sir," he began in an obsequious tone that made the other black folk cringe inside, "you are my last hope."

Jake Sassaport's back straightened. He braced himself. Clearly, Bull Johnson was about to ask for a handout. Times were pretty good. Business was brisk. But there was Rose's empty money box to replenish and he could hardly give Bull anything in front of other customers who'd then expect a break on the price of whatever they were in the store to fondle and look at and most likely never buy.

"I sholy don't know how I can help you," Jake said, as if a charitable appeal was already on the table. He narrowed his eyes to look determined.

"You can let me talk to your boy." He tilted his head to one side.

"What about?"

"My Ruby's gone missin' four days now. I thought maybe he'd know a place for me to look. I been everywhere I can think."

Jake blushed crimson. He felt he'd been unfeeling. Everyone took note of it. In later times, they'd say how Mister Jake turned as red as a Yankee apple because you know he's got the soft heart. 'Member how that time, they'd say, the late frost killed half of everybody's crop and Mister Jake gave credit behind the missus's back? The blacksmith didn't do that. The seed store didn't.

"I'm sorry, Bull, I had no idea," Sassaport said. "He's in the back. I'll fetch him."

Max came through the back with his head down, studying the floor. A stillness settled over the store at the sight of him. It was obvious his jaw was swollen, his cheeks black and blue.

He had a bandage wrapped several times about his left wrist. He blinked a lot as if his eyes recently got back to normal after sustaining injury. Jake scoped the room with raised eyebrows daring anyone to ask him what had happened to the kid. It was nobody's business how his son's face got like that. No one dared ask. Bull hoped he'd fallen off a horse or something.

"Mister Maxwell," he said. "I been lookin' for my gal, Ruby Alfreda. I wondered if you knew where she was."

Max spoke just above a whisper.

"No, I don't."

Bull stared at him a few seconds hoping the boy would think harder and come up with something. Max didn't so much as look up. Bull turned to leave, defeated, despair oozing from him like a bad smell.

"Thank you, Mister Jake," he said.

Halfway out the door, Bull gave the store a backhanded wave so much like Ruby's that Max couldn't help himself. Soon as he could evade his father's notice, he went out through the back and ran after him. He caught up with him just outside of town.

"Bull! Bull Johnson!" he yelled out.

Bull turned around.

"Bull, I didn't want to say in front of Daddy, but I think I know who can help you find Ruby."

"Who, Mister Maxwell? Please tell me who."

Max lost his nerve. He looked aside.

"Well, I might not be right."

Bull leaned over and put a hand on each of the boy's shoulders. He wanted to shake him. He could see his intensity frightened him. He restrained himself.

"I don't care, boy. If there's only half a chance, I'll take it. I want my girl back."

Max wasn't sure if he should say what he wanted to say. He

couldn't tell Bull what happened to Ruby at the hands of Lewis Taylor. He couldn't betray her like that. But he wanted to know where Ruby was almost as badly as her daddy, that big man who stared down at him and gripped his shoulders a little harder. Max blurted it out.

"Mayhayley Lancaster. Ruby is acquainted with her."

Bull straightened. He knew what Mayhayley Lancaster was. Everyone did.

"Mayhayley Lancaster," he said. Then he said it again. "Mayhayley Lancaster."

Max walked alongside Ruby's daddy toward the road that led to her home. They were silent. Then Bull said, "Mayhayley Lancaster is acquainted with my daughter." He said it in a faint voice. Maybe he was talking to himself.

"How exactly are they acquainted, Mister Maxwell?"

Max spilled every bean he had, lying only when necessary to keep his vow to his friend. He told Bull they had an adventure together and went to Mayhayley Lancaster on a lark. He told him about the dollar and the dime.

"So she lied to us about where them pennies went," he said in his faint voice.

"I lied too," Max said, as if that would make Ruby's mendacity less sinful. "But you and me could go up there to Mayhayley's house. I'll introduce you to each other."

Bull was cautious about going into the backwoods to visit a white woman's home, especially one he did not know. There was never a guarantee under such circumstances that he'd be welcome. He might just as well be shot at. Having a child with him was like carrying a passport in a foreign country. Made him look harmless. He agreed, gratefully.

They made a plan for the following morning. Max skipped school. He waited behind a blackberry bush at the edge of the woods until Bull's wagon pulled up. He darted out and scrambled up to sit beside him.

"Sure you know how to get there?" Bull asked.

"I could hardly forget the way," Max said. "That was the most exciting day of my life."

Bull couldn't help but smile at the boy's zeal. It made him comfortable enough to ask.

"If you don't mind, Mister Maxwell. What happened to your face?"

The boy twisted his lips then spat it out.

"My bubbe beat me," he said.

"Your who?"

"My granny. I stole some money. She'd a killed me if Mama hadn't come in and stopped her."

"Musta been a lot of money."

"It was. More'n ten dollars."

Bull Johnson whistled. It confounded him that a white boy, one who had enough of everything, who had wishes not needs, would steal a fortune. The two of them were all by themselves in the green woods. Being alone with whites was different that being in their company with a crowd. One to one, relations were most often friendly. He asked another question.

"What'd you do with it? The money."

Max told Ruby's daddy the same lie he told his own. He'd repeated the lie often enough that by this time, it came out smooth, unfettered by guilt or embarrassment.

"I gambled it away."

Bull knew of card and dice games that took place behind the schoolhouse some nights. He'd threatened his own boys with bodily harm if he ever caught them sneaking around there.

"Huh. I hope you learned your lesson."

Max hadn't learned any lesson at all. He would steal that

money ten times over to help Ruby at her darkest hour. He'd take the beating ten times over too. But he said, "Oh, I did. I very much did."

Each fell into a pensive quiet. Bull considered whether or not he was a fool to put so much hope in Mayhayley Lancaster. He'd heard plenty of stories over the years about the Oracle of Heard County but he never truly believed them. It wasn't his nature to fall in with the dubious enthusiasms of others. He was more God-fearing than that. Adventists preached against soothsayers. To follow them evidenced a lack of faith in the Almighty, whom one should trust with one's fate absolutely, without question. I guess I'm just that desperate now, he told himself.

They rode past landmarks Max remembered from his previous trek. He mentioned them to Bull, pointing out a tall gray rock shaped like a sword and twin oaks whose trunks wound about each other in steadfast embrace. They arrived at the entry to Mayhayley's property. Bull parked the wagon and tethered the mule.

"Don't want to ever ride up to a stranger's house. Always better to walk," he told the boy. "Makes you look fair harmless."

They drew close to the cabin. The dogs rushed around a corner from the back like before, barking wildly. Max was struck once more by the structure itself, its haphazard placement of mismatched boards, the gaps between them stuffed up with newspaper. Everything looked crooked this time. He didn't remember that from his first visit. Maybe there'd been a little quake or something. It happened thereabouts from time to time. In a handful of spots, green weeds grew out of the cabin walls. He knew for sure they hadn't been there earlier. It struck him as more than odd. It wasn't the season for green things to sprout. Smoke rose from the chimney as before although the weather perhaps warranted it now.

"Look a that, Bull," Max said. "Ain't it just about the most ramshackley cabin you could ever see?"

"I seen worse."

Bull removed his hat. To Max's eyes, he looked scared. Why a big man like Ruby's daddy should be frightened of a scrawny, one-eyed woman, witch or no, puzzled him. He took the man's hand.

"It's alright, Bull. I swear she's not half so bad as she looks. She might even be kind."

The door opened. A woman stood on the narrow stoop above the cinder block stairs. She was not the witch but a pretty young woman in a gingham dress and a gardener's bonnet. She held a pail with a spade and claw sticking out the top.

"Y'all here to see my sister?" she asked in a dull, incurious manner.

"Yes'm," said Bull, "if your sister be Miss Mayhayley Lancaster."

"You got your fare?"

"Yes'm."

Bull reached in his pocket, fished around, and withdrew a dollar, a nickel, and five pennies. He held them out in his broad palm. The pretty woman put her hands on her hips and frowned.

"Well, come t'here and give it me. I sholy ain't goin' down to you."

He did so. Max walked up the cement stairs behind him. Mayhayley's sister stood aside holding the door open to allow them in. The witch was in the front room just inside the door reading a thick book by the fireplace. She finished a page before looking up.

Max found Mayhayley different and the same at once. Rather than a marble in her eye socket, she wore an eyepatch over it, which was a relief. Instead of several skirts and a gray felt cloche, she wore wide-legged men's pants and big outsized boots. She had a military cap on the back of her head but from what service or what era or even what country was indeterminate. Yet she had the same long face, the same gangly limbs. She studied her two visitors a while, then gestured for them to sit in the chairs Ruby and Max had occupied a year and a half before. She remembered him.

"Y'all banged up, boy," she said. "Didn't I tell you to quit that stealin'?"

He hung his head.

"Yes'm."

She got up and put a knobby thumb and two crooked fingers on his chin, turning his head this way and that to study his wounds.

"The good book says spare the rod and spoil the child. Your granny did the right thing."

"Yes'm."

Bull stared at Max and then the witch. Was it possible they got together somehow before this moment and concocted a dialogue that would convince him of her powers? It wouldn't be the first time two whites conspired to take advantage of a black man. But no, there hadn't been time for that. And he'd already handed over his money. There wasn't any more for them to get.

Mayhayley addressed Bull next.

"You here about that gal of yours?"

How she knew what he was there for was a mystery but this was it, the moment he would find out if his beloved daughter was alive or dead, safe or in peril. His eyes filled.

"Yes'm."

Unexpectedly, she put a hand on his shoulder and squeezed. Her voice softened.

"She was just fine though some the worse for wear when I saw her."

Relief washed over him. He couldn't help himself. His brow knit, little cries issued like bubbles from the back of his throat. He wasn't sure he believed her though.

"When was that?"

"Two days ago."

Bull gaped at her, mouth open, then decided to believe. She was alive. His girl was alive. He didn't think about what worse for wear meant. He was occupied thanking his Lord over and over in a low murmur. Max leaned toward him and patted his back, shedding a few grateful tears of his own.

The witch smiled down at her handiwork.

"Sallie, honey. Bring the boys here some tea. I feel like doin' the leaves on a crisp day like today."

Sallie, the pretty young sister, poured hot water from a pot that hung over the fireplace spit into a plain porcelain teapot. She took a handful of dried leaves the color of blood she got from a tin on the mantel and tossed them in the water. Bull and Max kept their silence while the tea steeped. Once it was poured into cups, they drank in a hurry so Mayhayley could have something to work with. She read Bull's leaves first, pushing the leaves around the edges of his cup with a spoon. Part of what she said came from things Ruby mentioned when she'd passed through and the rest came out of the sphere where her mind went when she was called upon to use her gifts. Even she didn't know where that was.

"Your gal had enemies in the town. She didn't want you to know as she feared your actions against them. So she left. Simple as that. She has some coin, enough to get her where she's goin' and in safety, but I made a promise and cannot tell a livin' soul where that came from . . ."

Max sighed with relief inside. He hoped it didn't show.

"Now, where she's goin'. She wasn't sure but I am. Time goes by, she'll get to Atlanta where there's plenty of work for young people in the factories if they don't mind long hours 'n jist a li'l bit of pay. God knows, the life in Atlanta ain't too kind to the child workers. Some of 'em get hard sick with the diphtheria and malaria from the harsh times and the poor water. But she's a strong girl used to work—she might get sick but it won't kill her. And as time goes by, she'll send money to help with the others. She's a good girl. She'll make you proud."

Bull looked much relieved. He felt more at peace than he had since the night he realized Ruby was gone. He wanted to know who Ruby's enemies were.

"Who in Buckwood would want to hurt my baby?" he asked Mayhayley.

She shrugged, put a finger to her lips, and winked her good eye. She might know, she might not, but either way Bull wasn't going to get it out of her.

Max shifted from side to side, waiting for the witch to turn to him. He hadn't paid her anything. The dollar and a dime was Bull's alone. But it felt like she was going to tell him something, and he wanted more than anything to hear it. Mayhayley looked him over.

"Boy, you ever lie with snakes?" she asked.

It sounded like a real question. A sincere one. But lie with snakes? What was she even talking about? He shook his head.

"You should try it. It's a life-changin' experience. What you do is you find a place where they lie all by themselves, nestled and entwined. The day my life changed, I found 'em in the house I was born in, the one what's over yonder down the hillside. It was lyin' in ruins then and it still is. For safety's sake, you take pages of the Bible with you and when the snakes come near, you read 'em out loud then stuff 'em in your mouth like this . . ."

Mayhayley mimed the balling of paper. She put the imaginary balls between her teeth then shot her neck back while she swallowed them. Her cheeks blew out in circles, the balls passed down her gullet in lumps so vividly Max had to wonder if maybe they were real after all. The witch continued.

". . . and then you lie down with them snakes. No reason to be afeard. 'For the Lord gives wisdom; from His mouth come knowledge and understanding' and you have eaten of His Word. Them snakes'll love you then. Let 'em wind all over you as they desire, over your arms and twixt your legs. They'll hiss to you the secrets they know and one thing is certain, you'll never be the same agin. You'll have the Lord in your belly and the snakes as your friends."

All the talk of snakes agitated Max. He didn't care where he was or who she was, he wanted the words she spoke, words suffocating him with fear and confusion, to burst into flame and die so he said, "Why you tellin' me this, Miss Mayhayley? What I got to do with snakes and the Bible?"

She smiled so wide he could see the places where her back teeth were missin, upper and lower.

"I see you, boy. I see the day ahead when you gonna need to know what's comin'. For there's a great darkness comin' at you over the horizon. So dark and so deep, you won't know what it is until it is upon you. But you need to know and you need to be prepared or you'll get sucked into the devil's pit and never get out. Now I can't see what you gonna do. I just know it's there. So I'm tellin' you how to get the second sight, same way I did. Lyin' with snakes and eatin' the Lord's words. Then you'll know what to do when the time comes. Maybe. I'm not one hundred percent sure it'll work as you didn't get born with the caul like me."

She turned her back on him then, went back to her chair by the fire, sat, and opened her book.

"The caul may be essential. I do not know 'bout that."

She said no more. Sallie emerged out of nowhere like a ghost or a fog and told Bull and Max it was time for them to go. They complied.

They rode most of the way home in silence until Bull asked Max, "What she mean about you and some great dark thing?" Max answered him, "Heck if I know."

He started to whistle a song, pretending he didn't care. He cared, but he didn't want to think about it. By the time years later, the great dark thing indeed presented itself before him, the rough loud cries of the damned drowned out the memory of Mayhayley's words. So he stopped thinking about them for the moment and turned his mind to his daydreams of meeting Ruby in Atlanta when he would be a man and able to care for her. He hoped she'd have him.

5.

On the road to Atlanta, 1908

Mayhayley Lancaster liked to give honest service for honest money. When there was a reason not to—it wasn't a regular occurrence but it happened sometimes—it troubled her. There was no good reason to tell Bull Johnson his daughter had been violated. Only a coldhearted fool would do that when he had no recourse short of murder to right the wrong done her. But maybe she should have told what route the girl was on, or that she'd have help along the way, or that she'd given Ruby a pair of Sallie's old boots, a patched cotton jacket, and a money pouch to wear around her neck beneath her shirt so's she might keep her coin safe from thieves. Lost in rumination, hoping she'd done the right thing, she stared into the fire long after Bull and the boy left pondering Ruby's immediate fate until it appeared to her in a vision.

The vision served up images of Ruby following Mayhayley's caution that if she wanted to get to Atlanta, she should stick close by the shores of the Chattahoochee, which was the surest way not to get lost. That she'd listened was a blessing. Along the Chattahoochee, there were hills and hollows but none too high and none too low. The girl already knew how to fish, how to start a fire with what lay at hand, what the wild greens to eat that wouldn't kill you were. Down the road, there were towns here and there where she might find a little work, shelter, maybe make a friend. That'd be enough for a while. A girl like Ruby needed to go slow, find her footing, before she tackled the big things. In times to come, her worst problem would be healing her insides and her heart, but not even the Oracle of Heard County could help her there. Nothing could save her from the hard business of working all that out by herself. Mayhayley prayed on it and slept well, considering she felt right on every count. But there was much she missed.

She missed that Ruby found wearing the Sassaport money around her neck burdensome. It was heavy and the leather cord creased her skin. The pouch rubbed against the space between her breasts until she was chafed raw. If the sun was out, the coin caught a fiery heat. It burned. She transferred the kit to her skirt pocket. Much of it spilled out the day she climbed a particularly difficult slope just above the Chattahoochee water line at a place where the road diverged and there was only rock and mud to follow until it looped back. She slipped twice, landing on her backside. The coin escaped, rolling down the riverbank and into the water like so many glittering breadcrumbs. By the time Ruby discovered their loss, they were impossible to find. What remained was a pittance. At first, she sat in the dirt and wept. Once she started in to weep, other troubles plagued her, the hideous touch of Lewis Taylor and regret that she'd abandoned Max among them. She wept herself out and started on the road again. There was nothing to be done about the lost coin. Such was the fate of ill-gotten gains. She prayed to Jesus for forgiveness that she'd accepted it in the first place and begged pardon for the one who'd stolen it for her out of love.

Perhaps because she was a barren woman fond of children, neither had the seer taken into account that Ruby appeared older than her years. She looked to be thirteen or even fourteen, which made her practically adult in most eyes, especially those of men. But she didn't need Mayhayley to tell her where the assumptions of men could lead. She'd learned that on her own.

The walk to Atlanta was a long one, 250 miles or more. The roads, where there were roads, stopped and started. In between were grass-trammeled paths interrupted by boulders and trees the roadmen never plowed through. Even after losing her money to the river, Ruby often chose to climb up and over rock rather than be out in the open. There were men on the road, black men and white men, men in wagons, men on horseback, ones on foot like her. She avoided them as best she could and hid in bushes, in caves. Some passed close enough to her hidey-holes to set her trembling. She only came out if the men had women with them or families. She saw no one like herself, a female traveling alone.

She passed the time thinking of home, of her family and Max. Sometimes, she missed Max so much she had to drive him from her mind to stop the hurt. For the most part, she was successful but whenever she was at her most desperate, his voice would come to her. It comforted, counseled, or admonished her, whatever fit the occasion. It was something of a miracle so she tried to follow whatever his voice told her even though he was younger than she and an innocent. Her mama always said a person should never argue with the miraculous.

In the night, the air turned bitter. Animal calls she did not know rang out through the cold stillness. They screeched, growled, and chattered as if to raise the dead. Ones she did know—fox, owls, raccoons, and wolves—scared her just as much as those she did not. She looked for caves to sleep in or trees she might climb where she tied the blanket Max gave her between sturdy branches and nestled inside, inhaling the scent of home and friendship. When she found such a place, she was still not secure. Too often, the piercing cries of creatures being eaten by their enemies rang out. One night, she heard the slurp of predators licking their prey clean of meat and blood, and it was very close. She prayed.

"Sweet Jesus, let me find a family I can travel with, for safety's sake," she said into the dark. It was a good prayer, although somewhere in her head she heard Max say, *Don't go after the first one that comes by.*

She was on the road a week, her progress slowed by the need to hide from all manner of danger, when she spied a white family in a wagon watering their mule by the riverbank.

The wife, scrawny, wan, her lips tight, her eyes like two beads of polished stone, sat up front the wagon next to the pater familias, a broad, lantern-jawed man who looked like he could handle whatever trouble came his way without help from anybody. Their children sprawled over the open wagon bed amid a poor variety of pots and pans, two sacks stuffed with Lord knew what, and a few iron tools. They were three boys and a girl. The boys were around Ruby's age. She thought they looked stunted. Their chins jutted forward. Their noses were sharp, thin as the beaks of birds. The girl was just a li'l bit, maybe seven or eight. Compared to the boys, she was pretty in her way but looked fragile like she might shatter if you knocked into her too hard. She made Ruby think of the china dolls in Sassaport's window at Christmas time.

The lot of them looked safe enough. There were beaver and raccoon pelts hanging from poles attached to the buckboard, which made them appear substantial as well. Ruby stepped out from a thicket of hawthorn just inside the tree line and descended to the road ahead of them. She walked along the bend slowly to hasten an encounter with those behind. If they gave her a chance, she'd talk them into letting her ride with them. She'd offer to be a help to them in return.

While she walked, hopeful, waiting for their wagon to draw near, the Max voice chided her. *Didn't I tell you not to get with the first one?* She hit the side of her head with her fist to make him go away. He did. Luckily, her fellow travelers didn't seem to notice. They caught up and approached her in the cordial manner of country folk. Ruby was relieved. It could have gone another way.

"Hello, gal," the daddy said. "Where you headin'?"

"Atlanta," Ruby said. "To find work."

"That so?" the mama said, giving her a broad smile. "I wouldn't think a girl like you would have to look so far. They's plenty farms hereabouts. You from pickin' stock, ain't that right?"

In all Ruby's life, no one ever called her "pickin' stock," but there didn't seem to be anything nasty in the way the woman said it. She sounded friendly. Ruby nodded.

"Your mama know you're on the road?" the daddy asked. "There people lookin' for you?"

Ruby lied.

"No, sir. I'm the eldest and they hope to see me bring home a fortune. Sent me off with coin and all, but I lost it along the way."

She tried to make herself look pitiful, drawing in her shoulders and widening her eyes. The man and woman put their heads together for a moment and then the man said,

"Well, gal, you're in luck. We're headin' to Atlanta too. My wife could use some help, if it's work you're lookin' for. We'll get you to Atlanta in exchange."

It was an unexpected offer. For Ruby, it felt like a blessing from the Lord.

The man's wife spoke up, laying out her terms.

"This is what you need to do for us in return," she said. "First thing is help me with fetchin' firewood and cookin'. Maybe do the washin' if we stop long enough."

"I don't mind, m'am."

"I don't know how much a chore it is and how much a penance, but you can watch our babies while we look for work along the way and should we find it, praise Jesus, until the day we got enough to move on. If we all like each other, you can work for us in Atlanta too. For that, we'll feed you and give you a place to sleep."

Ruby thought it over and gave a truthful answer.

"M'am, I can watch over them babies for you while you're lookin' for work and once you find it, but when we reach Atlanta, I need to look for hard money work myself. I can't be stayin' with y'all for longer."

"Mebbe we'll convince you," the man said.

He put out a hand to her, which she grasped with two of hers. He hauled her up then set her in the wagon's bed. The oldest boy stuck out his foot so that she landed hard on her knees. She sat up quick.

"Ow," she said.

The boys snickered. The l'il bit got wide-eyed and stuck a thumb in her mouth. Their mama turned around and whomped the closest boy on the head.

"Now you be kind to this gal," she said. "Or you gonna be in the workhouse yourself afore you know it."

The boys knew she didn't mean it. They did what they wanted. Over the next days, Ruby was poked, pinched, and otherwise tortured by the Bickell boys, a situation their mama either didn't see or chose to ignore. Likely, she was grateful they were occupied. To have them off her hands was a grand and holy blessing.

Mr. Bickell halted the mule for suppertime and the family ate together. Ruby fetched firewood for the cooking at eventide then washed out the pots and pans in the Chattahoochee after. She ate apart from the family by choice. Like their mama, she found any break from the young demons something to thank the Lord for. When inside the wagon bed, she kept to a far corner with her legs bent, the better to kick them away should they sidle up. She took the l'il bit in her arms as a shield when she had to. Whenever they were off the wagon, the eldest boy specialized in tripping her. The youngest preferred to follow her around until he had a chance to stomp on her toes. When the family lay down to sleep in the back of the wagon by night, close as ticks on a blade of grass, Ruby stretched lengthwise along a row of their collective feet. Once, the youngest turned himself upside down to bite whatever part of her lay close by while his parents snored. But the middle boy was the worst. He liked best to pinch her breast or feel her bottom as near between her legs as he could get. Mostly, she was successful in deflecting him but it riled her blood. She almost wished he'd get his wish so she could beat him down while his daddy and mama watched.

If it hadn't been such a long walk to Atlanta, she would have quit them. As it was, she apologized to the Max inside her head a hundred times for ignoring his advice. But the soles of Sallie's boots had worn out, a testament to the thousand piercing stones they'd met on the road. She tied soles to uppers with scraps of cloth torn from the lining of Mayhayley's cotton jacket. She wasn't sure they'd make it to Atlanta. So far, it seemed better to ride with the Bickells than walk barefoot. Once they got to the city, she'd leave them without delay and never look back.

She didn't last that long. Opportunity presented itself and she snatched it. The family stopped at Clotis, a mill town three days from Atlanta by foot. She was tasked with clearing debris caught up in the wagon wheels while Daddy and Mama Bickell went off to barter a few pelts for supplies. The children begged to go with and did, tethered to their mother by lengths of rope, even the eldest. Their humiliation warmed Ruby's heart.

Once she had the wheels cleared, she wandered through Main Street and by chance overheard that the lumber mill was looking for someone to sweep up as the usual child was lung sick, coughing up more sawdust than she could gather. Straightaway, Ruby found the company office, offered herself for hire, and was accepted. She bid the Bickell family goodbye.

For ten hours a day, Ruby swept up the mill floor. It was child's work. Only a child's frame could fit under the mamouth saws and get at the shavings gathered there. One as near grown up and tall as Ruby had to crouch low for hours at a stretch, but she had the stamina to do it. Mindful of her lung sick predecessor, she took care to cover her nose and mouth with a bandanna while she worked. Debris from the saws flew through the air all the way to the warehouse corners. She created towers of excess shavings that was then bagged by others. In return, she was given a noon meal, generally turnips swimming in a thin broth, a place to sleep on the floor in the colored folk dormitory, and three cents a day. On Saturdays, the daily stew had a few specks of meat. One of the boys who bagged the shavings, a green-eyed black boy a couple years younger than she, a boy called Willie Gordon, was a talker.

"This is good work," he said, "but you can make lots more money in Atlanta. They got factories up and down every street and houses for the workers too. None a that sleepin' in the back on the cold ground as we do here. I'm goin' to Atlanta myself, soon's my baby brother's old enough to come with."

He told her when Sunday came 'round in the city, a boy could enjoy amusements like the flickers or the bands that played in the parks or he could watch the goings on at the beer gardens, which was almost as entertaining.

"You kin fill a bucket with beer and take it home for a nickel, long as you tell 'em you're gettin' it for your paps," he said. "Ain't that a scream?"

Willie told her such stories every day. Some Ruby knew were fanciful, like the ones about beautiful black women and handsome black men dressed in silks and velvet who strode through the streets of Atlanta wherever they wanted. According to Willie, they wore feathered hats and carried pearl-encrusted walking sticks. They mixed freely with whites who tipped their hats to them as they sauntered by. Willie laughed when he told her that, but even without his exaggerations, the city sounded like a paradise.

She remembered the dream she once had. It felt bittersweet now. It was a dream of a place she'd share someday with Max, a place where laughter and affection reigned. That dream had been crushed. But the young cannot live long without dreams so Atlanta took the old dream's place in her heart. She dreamt of a home of her own, meat every day, time off every week to do whatever she liked, and enough money to send some back home to Mama. She didn't need a boy to share it with, not even Max, although she might have liked to share it with him for the joy of it. In the meantime, there was Willie telling her stories, making her laugh. He reminded her of Max some. He had the same look in his eyes when he spoke to her. She grew fond of him.

She saved her pay. It wasn't long before she bought used boots from another worker and then she started saving again. The time came when she had money enough to quit Clotis and finish the trip to Atlanta. Her only regret was that she'd miss Willie. She'd learned friendship was precious in life and wanted to keep in touch, but Willie didn't read or write. If she wrote him a letter, he'd have to find someone to read her words to him.

She'd written to Max twice since she'd been gone. Both times she lost courage when it came time to post them. Doubtless, the postman back home would deliver a letter addressed to a minor directly into the hands of his parents as it was pretty much an unheard of occasion. Her letter would be the cause of much curiosity. Everyone on Main Street that day would crowd around when it was opened. She imagined Rose Sassaport's reaction when neighbors peering over her shoulder learned her son was in communication with a black runaway. The shame would cripple her. Max might hear about the letter but he'd never see it.

The day she said goodbye to Willie Gordon, they stood together by the side door of the mill while Willie told her about his baby brother's bad night. He had fever and yellow eyes. Ruby didn't hear him. Her thoughts were occupied with saying goodbye. She interrupted him.

"It's time for me to leave Clotis," she said.

His face changed. His nose flared, his lips drew together until they were surrounded by fine lines like the spokes of a wheel.

"No," he said. His voice rasped. "You can't go."

She saw something go dark in his wide green eyes. She put a hand on his arm.

"I have to," she said. "I'll let you know where I am. When your brother is bigger and you're ready, you come to me."

She promised she'd write. Mill workers got their mail no matter how young they were. He could take the letter wherever he needed and have it read to him. If she was able, she'd put a penny in the envelope for him to take to the reader.

Willie's shoulders went back. His chin went up.

"Maybe I'll find a way to learn to read my own self," he said. "It'll save you the freight."

Ruby wasn't sure how that might happen in Clotis, but she wished him luck and hugged him tight. "Farewell, Willie," she said with a tenderness she'd thought was dead inside her. She got hold of herself enough to let Willie go and walk to the colored dormitory without a backward glance.

Her possessions were stacked against a far wall. She gave the old man who watched out for everybody's things a nickel. All her worldly goods were wrapped up in Max's blanket, which she'd bound with ropes she could put her arms through and so carry it on her back. Lifting it up and on, arming herself with courage, she set out. As she reached the end of town, she thought she saw Willie in an alleyway watching her go. *Look at him, Max*, she said to her interior companion, *he breaks my heart he's so pitiful.* Although his voice had gone quiet in the months she'd been in Clotis, the Max-in-her-head responded. *He'll be alright*, he said. *You need to be on your own just now.* She agreed.

Ruby arrived in Atlanta on a Sunday. It was a sparkling spring day. The sun was high, the air clear. It dazzled her. She'd never seen so many huge buildings all crammed together. She'd never seen a paved street. Atlanta had them in abundance. Everything around her looked bright and new. There were stores everywhere, ones that sold only one or two types of things; tobacconists, tailors, cobblers, butchers, pastry shops, concerns selling sewing supplies, hardware. People in good shoes and Sunday finery thronged the sidewalks. They were both black and white. The whites entered cafés and restaurants. The blacks window shopped. None had pearl-encrusted walking sticks, and it was they who doffed their hats to whites while giving way on the sidewalks.

There were as many automobiles as horses on the thoroughfares. They spewed smoke into the air like dragons. One driven by a black man in uniform stopped at a lamppost in front of a church full of song. He hopped out the car and opened the cab door then pulled down a set of steps and stood aside. An elegant white couple emerged, the gent in a fine wool coat with a boutonniere, the woman holding a prayerbook. They ascended the stairs to the church. The driver leaned against the lamppost and lit a cigarette. *Ask him*, Max urged her inside her head. *Ask him.* Ruby approached the driver.

"Sir," she said, keeping her distance as she always did with grown men, "do you know of a factory where a girl like me might work?"

The driver looked her up and down. He grinned.

"You can work in my factory anytime," he said. "How old are you, girl?"

Ruby didn't get city humor yet. She answered him as if his words meant what they said.

"I'm near thirteen," she said. "What kind of factory do you have?"

He coughed out a puff of tobacco and laughed. He looked her over a second time. His face softened.

"Here's what you do, child. Head down that way and don't even think of making a turn and after a while you'll get to Cabbagetown. Ask someone there."

She thanked him and did so, passing over the next hour from grand thoroughfares with stately homes with lush gardens to treeless streets of tenements built so close together there was barely room for the clotheslines strung between them. She found her way to Cabbagetown, where workers for the Exhibition Cotton Mill lived. Opposite that was Happy Hollow, built as a worker village cheek by jowl to Atlantic Steel. Between them was the colored part of town, constructed of scraps scavenged from Happy Hollow and Cabbagetown in the same ramshackle design as Mayhayley's house. Facing the length of it was a foul trench used by all three neighborhoods when the honey trains were late and the outhouses backed up.

After knocking on a half-dozen doors, she was advised to try a plain but suitable rooming house for coloreds. She paid four days in advance to the landlady who took her to a second floor room and left her there sitting on a thin mattress clutching her bundle of possessions in her lap. The room's dimensions were narrow. There wasn't a window. It might once have been a closet. Besides the mattress, there was a small table with a chamber pot beneath it and a bowl for water on top. The bowl was dry. Ruby studied the ceiling, the walls, the floor. She counted cracks. Cooking smells came to her along with all kinds of cries: angry, laughing, adult, childlike, loving, miserable, hungry. They came to her through the paper-stuffed wall and from under the door. There were more voices in that windowless room than on Main Street at New Year's Eve back home. All that was missing was the sound of gunshot at midnight. It made her glad she couldn't see out.

Monday morning before anyone was awake, she washed up as best she could in the landlady's kitchen and went to the National Pencil Factory to ask for a job. She'd been told it was a good place to work. It was run by a Jew from New York. Ruby knew everything she knew about Jews from Max. By her lights, it would be a lucky thing to work for a Yankee Jew. Far as she knew, Yankees were good at business and people said Jews were too. Max's daddy certainly did alright. She knew enough not to favor Yankees in public but in her heart she felt happy for a chance to work for Leo Frank. She imagined him fair, generous, smart, a friend to the worker.

By the time she returned to the rooming house, she had a job. Mr. Frank's floor manager told her he would make her a rotating worker at first, one who filled in where she was most needed on any given day. After that, they'd figure out where she best belonged. The tasks would be simple, rote. She'd have no trouble learning them. There'd been a fever going through the eraser room. They were shorthanded and having trouble meeting their quota. That's where she'd start, screwing the brass bit between lead and eraser onto the wooden shaft. She'd work a ten-hour shift for fifty cents a day. While it was less than the white workers made, it was a princely sum compared to wages at the lumber mill.

On her way home, she stopped for groceries at a cart run by an old man who spent the day sitting in a chair by his wares. At eventide, his granddaughter drove a mule into town to take him and whatever he didn't sell back home for the night. Ruby told him her name and he told her his—It was pronounced Le-ROY, he said, not LEE-roy. She purchased some cheese and bread with a bottle of milk, saying "Thank you, LeROY," and he smiled, making her feel that she was at home with a kindly neighbor. Sitting on her bed in her closet room, she celebrated her new job, eating cheese and bread with gusto, guzzling milk like it was wine. How she longed for Max! More than anything, she wanted him to come find her. Life in paradise had arrived.

6.

Without Ruby to relieve him of his loneliness, Max floundered. His mind often drifted to dark fantasies. He imagined beating Lewis Taylor lifeless, but as he didn't know who he was or what he looked like, he regarded any unknown young black man he encountered with suspicion and resentment. He still wanted to run away. Unfortunately, he could not secure the money to do so. His mother wised up and relocated her tobacco tin to a more secure spot. He had yet to discover where that was although he looked, he looked in every nook and cranny of the house. Maybe, he thought with a shock, she put it in the bank.

His people didn't trust banks. After Zeyde's father left the old country, London bankers stole the deposits from his bank account. No Sassaport in his line ever banked again. Zeyde slept with his greenbacks strapped to his middle by a four-inch wide band of cloth secured by hooks and eyes. Bubbe claimed his money girdle was the reason he snored so badly. His lungs couldn't fill properly under the burden of all that cash. It closed his throat.

Daddy didn't wear his money like Zeyde, but he was cautious. The shop money was kept in a large safe in the attic, a safe to which only Rose had the combination. Max might as well try to pull silver dollars out of the walls as get his hands on that money.

He woke up every morning hating his life. He hated Buckwood for being bland and Rubyless. He hated school where bullies reigned. He was tempted to bust out with just a couple sandwiches and a bottle of water. He'd figure out the rest on the road. But something always deflected him. For one, his grandmother died suddenly of a stroke, the week before Max turned thirteen. Her loss was a shock that ripped through them all. The whole family mourned, some more than others, Zeyde and Rose in particular.

Rose went quiet. She barely spoke to anyone and only remembered his birthday because Daddy reminded her. Zeyde was worse. All the day long, he either wailed an indistinct *kaddish* while keening back and forth, side to side on the balls of his feet, or sat immobile staring into space. Daddy needed help with Mama and help in the store. Out of duty, out of compassion, as a way out of his own sadness, Max stepped up. He quit school and worked at his father's side every day. When Daddy had to go upstairs to look after Mama, Max was left in charge of the store, sometimes for hours. He loathed every minute.

For him, retail was a prison. He longed for another life, any other life. He hadn't chosen a different path yet, there were too many choices, but he investigated those that attracted him most. He took books out of the new library to study ships and navigation and railroads. When he was alone, he practiced the kind of banter he imagined barkeeps employed. He read newspapers from New York City and pondered a career as a journalist. The job of stringer sounded particularly free, adventurous. It was, he thought, the perfect city boy's job, providing the boy was wily and sophisticated. Max fancied himself both.

He grew more between thirteen and fourteen than he had the year before. His shoulders became sturdy, his voice got low. He grew a fringe of black beard, sparse and downy. Daddy considered he was old enough to learn how to handle his own money so he gave him a salary and watched him manage it. What he learned amused him. His son was a saver. Other boys his age rushed to waste their money on things like dime novels, tobacco pouches, and baseballs. But not Max. Every cent got tucked away. He'd make a good steward of the family business one day. Retail, his daddy told Mama, was in his blood.

His thirteenth and fourteenth years brought some good fortune. The gang from school no longer tormented him. After all, he'd left. When they came into the store, he was in charge. They wheedled him about the price of whatever they sought to buy as if they were pals. He delighted in refusing them or seducing them into paying far more than an item was worth. It was the only time his work pleased him.

Whenever he wasn't working at the store or reading at the library, he took long, thoughtful walks. He wrote letters to Ruby about every last thing on his mind then burned them out in the woods, next to the old deer blind. Their smoke curled into the sky in a stream of black ash and gray plumes that thinned out and spread to the four corners of the earth where, he was hopeful, it would find her and whisper to her his heart. Sometimes, he put out his hand and felt hers wrap around it.

Years passed. His shoulders got broader still, his beard thicker. When he was sixteen, he found many young women receptive to his advances, but none of them were Ruby so none could reach his heart. Eventually, he took neither pride nor pleasure from their favors and realized since they were not Ruby, he preferred to be on his own.

The day he left home was nothing special. He hadn't argued with his parents. No one came in the store to abuse him. He was neither bored nor overworked. It was a mild day at the end of winter, a good day for walking, but the weather was not part of his decision. Uncle Morris was in town, staying with the family. It was a tale from his life on the road that put the idea into Max's head that he belonged on the road too.

". . . and that redheaded widow lady high up near Tookan, Persephone, 'member her?" Uncle Morris said at table.

The family nodded. Who could forget her? Whenever he spoke of her, Morris got dreamy-eyed. She was a siren, he said, able to ensnare a man with her voice alone. The first time he met her, he was on his usual trek in the foothills, selling the wares in his pack, bringing folk what they'd ordered the previous season, taking orders for whatever he might bring them next. He walked winding trails that ascended and descended until he got to the place where the mountains began and there was only rocky ascent. Then he walked back.

One bright afternoon, he heard an unearthly sound, a musical sound the likes of which he'd never heard before. Its melody was more than sweet, dipping and soaring like the hills around them. It had a languid rhythm, a soothing one. Its tones were round as a bell. They echoed. He imagined it was the song of a band of angels giving praise before the Holy Throne and he followed it off the main trail, up a narrow path to see if he was right. There, in the center of a treeless clearing, was a small cabin, barely big enough for two. A redheaded woman sat on a porch rocker in a sack dress singing, just sat there warbling away with her mouth fixed in a perfect "O." Her chest moved in and out. Her throat quivered. Other than that, she was motionless. Moved, Morris put down his pack and sat cross-legged and drop-jawed in the grassy dirt and listened.

After a time, the woman stopped singing and lifted her arms to run her hands through her long red hair. He noticed then she had the look of a pretty little thing gone old. Her round blue eyes were sad. The skin around them was weighted down and flecked with lines. Her lips were well shaped and full, but her neck was a mess. Meanwhile, her limbs, legs as well as uplifted arms, were taut with long, willowy muscles, which were nonetheless bruised at the biceps and thighs. He wondered how they got that way. He wondered if the earth had tried to drag her beneath itself to let her song charm the underworld but failed, leaving its marks. She noticed him then, stared at him awhile, then beckoned. He got to his feet and approached her.

He spent that night at her cabin, he told them, but gave no more details. They made their own conclusions. Later, he learned everything he could from the people in the next town about the redheaded widow Adela, although as a man with some self-taught classical learning, Morris renamed her Persephone in his heart. He paid a sales call to her every year since but never saw the inside of the cabin again. She met him outside her front door rain or shine. He let the family draw their own conclusions about that too.

The week before Max left home, Morris caught them up on the latest stories about Persephone. People all over loved to talk about Adela, the widow of upper Tookan. He liked talking about her too. It made her feel close by.

"She got two husbands now," he said. "I brought her the French corset she ordered last time I was through, one I took great pains to acquire for her down in Franklin. She wanted silk and whalebone next to her skin and lace over that. Had to be ecru, too, which is a color I found out, close to the color of flesh.

"A young man answered her door. He was in overalls. His hair was mussed. He had a cowlick and his feet were bare. He had as much beard as old Maxwell here, which is to say, not much at all. He said somethin' about my wakin' him up. I told him I sure was sorry about that and handed him her package, boxed and wrapped in paper, which he took to rippin' apart like it was his own. When he saw what was inside, he grinned wide and called out 'Adela, Adela!'"

The widow had come to the door in a patched nightdress, her hair as mussed up as his. She grabbed the package from him and gave Uncle Morris an angry look. She spoke in a dark, scratchy voice as ugly as her other voice was beautiful.

"What made you give that lad my under things?" she said. "Now they's ruined."

Morris had been dumbstruck a minute and when he spoke he stuttered.

"W-wh-why? He jist eyeballed 'em. Didn't touch 'em or nothin'."

Persephone stepped out onto the porch and closed the door behind her, practically in the boy's face.

"They were not meant for his eyes," she'd said. "They were meant for the other one."

He could not figure what she meant and told her so.

"T'other! T'other!" she said as if he were deaf and needed everything repeated.

She went back in the cabin and bolted the door.

Uncle Morris knew the sound from their night together years before. She'd pulled the beam down then too. "You never know who might come up when you want only to be alone," she'd said, which struck him as either stupid or crazy. Who was going to show up in that clearing with no one living thereabouts for at least a mile or three, especially in the middle of the night?

Max piped up.

"Who was the other one?"

Morris slurped some tea then put down his cup.

"I didn't have a clue. When I went along to my usuals, I asked them if the redheaded widow still lived alone. They said, 'Oh, no, she married young Thom Baker.' Then, to a man, they'd grin and put their mouths next to my ear. 'Only there's another one what comes every Thursday when Thom goes to market.' Their wives would cluck their tongues or laugh, according to their nature. I had some time before I was expected east. I decided to see what this t'other one was like."

He slurped more tea.

"That Thursday, I took of the darkness to hide myself behind the widow's tool shed near the tree line. Sho enough, long about two hours after dark, she sat on the porch and sang her song. I couldn't see her from my hidey hole, but once again her song thrilled me down to the root. She went back inside when she was done and not a quarter hour later, what she had summoned arrived. I swear there were heavy footsteps going up the cabin door. I heard 'em clear as church bells. So I took a chance and peeped around the shed to see the widow Persephone Adela open the door dressed in that corset and not much else. She stood on her tippy toes. She raised her arms and kissed. Who did she kiss, you ask? Who?"

Mama, Daddy, Max, and even the perpetually grieving Zeyde leaned forward, nodding heads, eager for Uncle Morris to answer his own question. He clucked his tongue and nodded back.

"Air. She kissed air. There was no one there I could see. Yet, she smiled, looked down, and took an airy hand in hers, pressed it to her lips, and led a ghost into the cabin. Yes, I'm absolutely sure that's what it was. The ghost of her first husband. Thing was, she was as happy as I'd ever seen her."

The family gasped. Uncle Morris finished up.

"I hear she divorced that young Thom Baker shortly thereafter too."

"No!" everyone said and discussed other ghosts they'd heard of for the rest of the night.

Max was taken mightily by the story of Persephone Adela. He thought about it constantly. If such summoning from the very depths were possible, he decided, then he could make Ruby come to him, through distance and time and beyond life itself, if required. Later that night, he laid down before sleep with his eyes scrunched up tight, attempting to summon her. She did not come. He failed again and again, night after night. But his failure only inspired him to try harder. When he walked alone in the woods, he thought of her so hard, he called to her not in a whisper but in a shout. Once, lost in conjuring, he shouted out her name from bed in the middle of the night.

It roused his family, Zeyde included. He told them he had nightmares. They advised exercise and a shot of schnapps before sleep.

It occurred to Max that maybe he couldn't summon Ruby as long as he was in Buckwood, a place she'd fled in fear. The thought preyed upon him, robbing him of peace. He walked to Yellowjacket Creek and tried to conjure her from beneath the willows. It didn't work. Maybe he wasn't far away enough. At last, he gave up, afraid failure meant that either he didn't love Ruby enough or that she didn't love him at all. More sleepless nights followed until there was nothing to do but leave home and find her.

Early in the morning before anyone was up, he wrote a note for his parents telling them he was going to Atlanta to seek his fortune and not to worry he would keep in touch. He packed up his savings and a change of clothes, took bread and jerky from the buttery, and walked off into the unknown. He stopped first at Ruby's house. Bull and most of the others would be in the fields, but he hoped to catch one of her sisters tending the chickens and goat.

He found Marla gathering eggs in the hen house. She told him no one had heard from Ruby except for bank drafts sent now and again. She didn't write because no one at home could read, but they knew she was well from the drafts and the glyphs she drew of smiles and kisses. Max felt a stab of jealousy. She thought of home but not of him. Marla wasn't sure where the drafts came from. No one in the family was. They just cashed them and praised Jesus.

It didn't matter. According to Mayhayley, Ruby would be in Atlanta sooner or later. It only made sense that he go there. If she was in Atlanta, he'd find her. If she wasn't, he'd wait for her.

Compared to Ruby's trek, his trip to the capital was trouble free. He set out to walk to Franklin, the county seat, and from there secure a ticket on the train to Atlanta. Unlike Ruby, he had no need to hide from men. He met farmers, surveyors, and haulers on the road. Many sought distraction or companionship and picked him up gladly. Once he arrived in Franklin, he ate hot food in a modest restaurant where he was given directions to a respectable rooming house for transients. He'd been on salary by Daddy for more than two years. His savings were generous. He was able to splurge on a private room where he took a bath and washed his shirt in a basin. In the morning, a fresh, rested Max got on a half-filled train to Atlanta, taking a window seat in an empty row.

It was a slow train that stopped in every town along the way. More people boarded. Two men in suits took seats across the aisle from Max. They raised their hats to him briefly and he raised his to them. He closed his eyes and pretended to sleep while they talked about their business. His ears pricked when they mentioned paying a sales call to "the Jew on Washington Street" He learned that Washington Street was a home to Atlantan Jews and their businesses for three blocks around.

Max's parents and short life had taught him that caution was required in a big city. When he arrived at the station, he bought a map and studied the route to Washington Street thinking he would be most comfortable with his own people even if he didn't really know what they were like. Directly, he headed to midtown, to Peachtree. When he was close to his destination, he came upon a neighborhood of rich homes and grand lawns, the like of which he'd never seen. They reminded him of things of fancy, like fairy castles or gingerbread houses. They were landscaped, pillared, and gabled. They had porches that wrapped around to the back and stately drives pebbled with riverstone. He stood on the sidewalk, staring at them in disbelief, amazed that so much wealth existed in one place. He forgot that he approached the quarter of the city that was home to Jews until he passed by a magnificent building and stopped on a dime to stare at it, dumbfounded.

It was a marvel of red brick, limestone, and stucco, topped by a colonnade drum dome. The tablets of Moses were carved above a peaked and columned entry inscribed with the words "The Temple." He'd never seen a synagogue before, never stepped into one. It looked a place of wonder. Max decided to ascend its steps and try the door. It opened.

He entered a vast sanctuary bathed in shafts of light that poured in from massive windows. Rows of pews faced the three steps up to a marble floor where an Ark of the Covenant was centered, with lecterns and high-backed padded chairs to the left and right of it. It was very quiet. Max sat in a pew in the far back and let the quiet suffuse him. It felt a good time to ask God to reunite him with Ruby sooner rather than later. He didn't know many prayers and only a handful of blessings, so he spoke from his heart.

"I heard you come in, son," a man said behind him.

Max was startled. His shoulders hunched. He turned swiftly to see who addressed him. It was a mature man in a high-buttoned dark suit and celluloid collar. He had a brush mustache neatly trimmed and wore a skull cap beneath which he appeared to be going bald. He had eyeglasses and a book in one hand. The other held a pen.

"I've never been in a synagogue before, sir," Max said.

The man put on his eyeglasses. He looked Max over.

"Are you a Jew?"

"Yes, sir."

"Where are you from?"

"Buckwood. Heard County."

The man nodded with his lips pursed, as if to indicate that yes, he knew the place and realized it had no Jewish house of worship. He smiled.

"I'm Rabbi David Marx," he said. "Welcome. Enjoy. Absorb."

"Thank you, sir," Max managed, forgetting to introduce himself.

The rabbi waited a few seconds to see if he'd remember to do so. He gave up.

"Alright. Alright," he muttered and left the sanctuary, exiting by a side door which led, as far as Max could see, to a portico bordered by flowering bushes, and at its end, another door.

Max did as he was told. He looked around at the white paneled walls, at the complex web of windowpanes and moldings, at the alcoves where, removed from the Ark, the scrolls were placed during services before they were read. He wished he could see them. He'd only ever seen Zeyde's picture postcards of scrolls dressed in their velvet coverings, their silver crowns, and breastplates. He wanted to hear the sound the little bells that adorned them made.

While he sat there, half in awe, half in disbelief, he

strengthened his conviction that he was exactly where he was meant to be. From Sassaport's Fabrics, Fancy Goods, and Notions, Buckwood to South Pryor Street, Atlanta had not been an arduous or lengthy trip, but Max felt he'd walked into the other side of the world. It was fate that led him to The Temple as if granting blessing on his endeavors. His heart filled with hope.

By nightfall, he'd taken a room in a neighborhood close to the synagogue, a place thick with lodging houses, but respectable ones. He determined he'd go to services on Shabbat if he found a job that let him off on Saturdays.

It didn't happen. He wasn't in town a week before he landed his first job with the *Atlanta Georgian*, owned by William Randolph Hearst himself. They'd hire anyone as a stringer. What did they care, they only paid a commission if the stringer came in with a story they could use. The way things worked, the good stringers were separated from the bad soon enough and from the pool of survivors the best were singled out and handed jobs as cub reporters on salary. It didn't take long for Max to realize that in a factory city, the news people wanted to read generally happened on Saturdays and especially in the evening. If he wanted to advance, he'd have to work on the Sabbath. What the heck, he thought. Daddy always did.

7.

Atlanta, 1913

Early every morning, stringers representing the *Atlanta Georgian, Atlanta Constitution,* and *Atlanta Journal* along with half a dozen less illustrious rags gathered across the street from the construction site of the Lewis B. Slaton Courthouse to trade leads on what was happening where. The stringers who followed salacious scandals looked for gossip about drunk lawyers and loose barmaids, those who fancied themselves soldiers of the working class sniffed out the deceit of banks and factory exploitation, the romantics among them went after tips on street crime, while the newest, young men like Max, scrambled to find items of human interest. The *Georgian* ate up human interest stories, especially ones about runaway horses, lost or rabid dogs, what lady wore what dress at charitable fundraisers, and gentlemen's wagers on sporting events.

Some mornings, senior reporters mingled with the stringers, scavenging stories, making friends, scouting for cubs. One of them, Harold Ross, fierce, hard-smoking, hard-talking, and twenty years of age, took a shine to Max for no reason the young man could figure. By Max's lights, the four years between them made Ross an old hand. He looked up to him. It was Ross who told Max that human interest items were best discovered by going to the bars where working folk relaxed of a Saturday night.

"Don't loiter in firehouses and bank lobbies like these stiffs," Harold advised. "Barely a man or woman alive can keep their mouths shut about their employers, landlords, and neighbors after a pop or two. If a man's lucky, he'll pick up a good item about a wayward socialite or a magnate's thieving cousin. Even better, a fight might break out."

Harold swore that publishers, his own over at the *Journal* but especially the *Georgian*'s William Randolph Hearst, loved a good fight story because the public did, and the more so if it recorded the injuries sustained in gruesome detail. The best fight stories were over a woman. Fights over money also sold well, if the contested amounts were large or small enough.

The previous night had been a quiet one. Max didn't hear a single complaint about a boss or a spouse. Confederate Day was coming up. The whole city worked double-time getting ready for the celebration. At the end of the day, there wasn't much moxie left in anyone for fighting or gossip. Even on Decatur Street, the bars were tame, full of sippers and sighs. The best story Max got was about an old hound dog that lived wild by the west side railroad tracks. It dragged a toddler off the rails just as the Memphis train came roaring in. Some of the neighbors who knew the dog thought it meant to eat the child not save him. Max went with that. His headline read: *Killer or Savior?* which was, he thought, a fine hook. His stringer pals encouraged him. It's a great story, they said. It had everything: animals, babies, life and near death; couldn't fail.

He ran the story over to the *Georgian* before one of the others could steal it. The *Georgian* was committed to a five-part series on the horrors of child labor, Mrs. Hearst's pet cause. There was no space. He begged, he wheedled. Still, there was no space. Harold Ross came to mind. "A good stringer sells what he's got to whoever wants it," he'd said. Max went over to the *Journal* and, summoning courage, barged into the reporter pool to pitch the story directly to him.

As always, Ross stood out from the others. To a man, the other reporters had smudged shirts and rumpled pants but Ross was elegant. His suit, a simple daytime worsted, was beautifully cut. His scarlet tie was silk. He lounged in a wooden chair with his legs crossed at the ankle and resting over a corner of desktop. His long, classical face suited his wardrobe. Only his thatch of hair, longer than most men's and untamed, marked him as a member of a rough-and-tumble trade. Pursing his lips thoughtfully, Harold listened then reached forward with languid grace to take Max's notes in hand. When he opened his mouth, all illusions of sophistication collapsed under a broad Western accent. It was loud enough to hurt Southern ears. At times, he twanged.

"Stupid fuckers can't find the child labor hook in here?" he sneered. "Amateurs! Listen, kid, you've got a piece of a decent story here but it's whole stories that sell. We need to know more. There's a big gap in your headline. Make it carry some weight. It may be the only words most of 'em read." He scribbled at his desk. "Here. We'll make it *Killer Dog or Baby's Savior?* and I'll get someone to draw a rendering too. Just a cartoon, maybe, but it'll get the point across. Go back to where you found this and try to find the mother and child for an interview, although I'm warning you it's unlikely anyone'll materialize. In that case, we'll fill in the gaps the way Hearst's lackeys do. We'll gently postulate that the mother is sixteen and was sweating on her factory bench when the canine event occurred. Fuck those fucking fuckers. We'll show 'em how it's done."

Max heard all the "we"s Ross used as his story slid into the older man's hands. He felt a stab of envious pride then let it go. He knew a stringer's leads were never his own but became the property of whomever bought them. Often, the stringer was asked to flesh out the details for the reporter who'd write them up. Ross gave Max a fiver and he did as he was told. He tried to find the flesh-and-blood rescued baby and mother he'd heard of on a Saturday night past midnight in a working man's bar. Ross was right. It was impossible. He reported back his poor intelligence and waited for the *Journal*'s afternoon edition.

Ross's article hit the front page, above the fold. It was brilliant. It had a new headline, *Killer Dog Saves Baby Elizabeth,* and a sketch, not a cartoon, of a dog with a linen-swathed two-year-old in its teeth. The article read as richly as the finest short fiction. What a stroke of genius, Max thought. No one can ignore a baby with a name.

And they didn't. Everybody in Atlanta read it. The name Baby Elizabeth was on the lips of people in the shops, on the street, at the factories, and most especially, at the rail yards. Ross modestly called it a parody of every bloated report Hearst's rag published. Even his chief, a serious man, got a kick out of it. The only thing the piece lacked was Max's name anywhere.

Another boy might resent Harold Ross for that, but not Max. He admired the man. He envied his boldness, his finesse. He'd demonstrated an uncommon flair for drawing drama out of a human interest story, although all the boys said he was a different man entirely when pursuing hard news. On those occasions, he was ruthless in his pursuit of facts, a wolf, an eagle. It's what made him the *Journal*'s star reporter. That was the Harold Ross Max was eager to know. After Baby Elizabeth, he quit the *Georgian* and brought all his leads first to him, hoping to learn everything the man had to offer. In time, Ross noticed he had a good nose and took him on officially as a cub reporting exclusively to him. In Ross's eyes, that made Max his worker bee. To Max, it made them partners.

A cub's salary was mean; it required supplement. In between running down facts and chasing new leads, Max walked the city, searching the streets for abandoned objects he might sell. Come Saturdays, he spread a blanket on the grass of open air markets, laid out his scavenged wares, and hawked them using every Uncle Morris sales technique he knew. Sometimes, when he sold at a better-than-expected price, he thought how proud his parents would be. He'd get a bit homesick but managed to push sadness away without much difficulty. He was young. The glories of city life constantly distracted him. He would not go home until he'd something to brag about. In the meantime, he sent home postcards. His last was of the Opera House. He knew his mother would be impressed to hear Caruso was in town.

Max never stopped searching for Ruby. Whenever he approached a black neighborhood, he was on alert. He searched for her in crowds. He searched for her in shadows rounding the corner up ahead. His ears were pricked for any sound of her voice. He asked for her everywhere and stared people in the face while asking. He didn't notice the kind of looks he received in return or when the streets got quiet around him. He was lucky he didn't find her. Passersby offended by his stare might've taken action against a lone white man appearing to interfere with a black girl on their streets, on their side of town.

He looked for her other places too. He looked uptown, outside factories at quitting time, in the food stalls. He wished a hundred times he had a sketch or a photograph of her. He could have shown it to the people he stopped to ask if they knew anything about a Ruby Alfreda Johnson.

Confederate Day came. Max went to the parade like everyone

else. He never took a day off, which made the holiday a treat. It was a beautiful day, bright, shining, temperate. The packed streets along the parade route were a spectacle. Young women dressed in their finest wore flowers and ribbons in their hair or pinned them to elaborate hats. Young men preened for them on street corners near carts selling beer and boiled peanuts. Buskers played accordions and violins. The Stars and Bars flew from lampposts. Draped over the lintels of factories and stores, patriotic bunting rippled in a gentle breeze. Military men, including the aged remnant of Civil War survivors, marched with drum corps and white uniformed school children down thoroughfares to the tune of big brass bands playing Sousa and Stephen Collins Foster. Every third or fourth song they played was "Dixie." Each time, grown men doffed their hats and sang along with gusto. Max did too.

It was an exhilarating, exhausting day. After listening to the first few speeches, Max got bored and skipped the rest. He hopped a trolley and returned to his room thinking only about catching a couple hours of sleep. He fell on his unmade bed without taking off his shoes and snored within minutes.

Some hours later, a great pounding at his door woke him. The voice of Harold Ross rang out.

"Sassaport! Max! Open up! I need you!"

Night had fallen. Max lit a gas lamp, got to the door, and let Ross in. The latter wasted no time.

"There's been a murder," he said. "I've been with the police and there's loose ends. Lots of loose ends. We need to work together and chase them down then write 'em up, clear, concise. This one's got to be on the up and up."

"You mean no Baby Elizabeth."

"Absolutely not. This will be front page everywhere. The *Constitution* broke the news in an extra. So we won't be first. But we'll be the one that got more of it and got it right."

Ross looked around the small, dark room crowded with objects Max hoped to sell.

"This place is a dump, Sassaport. You know that, right?"

Max ignored the insult.

"Who got killed?" he asked, thinking it must be a bigwig to inspire Harold Ross to hard journalism.

The other man picked up a small brass bowl with a dented lip.

"Factory girl. Beautiful one, too. Black-haired, blue-eyed, porcelain skin, thirteen years old. An Irish kid."

He put the bowl back and ran his fingertips over a set of leather-bound books in a warped box fastened by a broad embroidered belt.

"How was she murdered?"

"So far, it's thought strangulation with probable sexual violation. They found her yesterday afternoon in the basement of the National Pencil Factory. She worked there and, the story goes, went over to pick up a her pay on her way to the parade. Never came out. Get your hat on. I'm dropping you where they've taken the body. I want you to stay there until the examiner makes an announcement. I've got interviews."

"Are there suspects?"

"That's the interesting part, my friend. A few. One of 'em is the night watchman, he's already been arrested mostly because he discovered the body. Mark my words, they'll release him soon. Another is the janitor, an unsavory character by all initial reports, but my sources tell me the one the cops want to fry is the factory manager, a New York Jew, name of Leo Frank."

"Oy," Max muttered, sounding very much like Zeyde. He took his hat from a hook on the wall and collected from a salvaged desk the tools of his trade, his notebook and pencils, which he stuck in his pockets.

Ross hadn't bothered to mention that the first two suspects were black. Factory watchmen and janitors were always black. Max knew that. He'd seen a lot and grown a lot in the months he'd been in Atlanta. He understood immediately why the authorities might want to fry a Jewish Yankee factory manager rather than a local black man. He read the papers.

Mrs. Hearst's pet project was doing well. The *Georgian* railed daily about the harm and injury inflicted upon child factory workers. Their heartrending stories of accidental maimings and endemic disease broke hearts all over the city, especially in its moneyed parts. Thanks in large part to the *Georgian,* protest against the hiring of minors had lately increased. But families were dependent on the cheap goods and plentiful jobs mechanized industry provided them, which made the issue complex. Most were a generation away from farm stock. Children had always worked the family rows from dawn to dusk. Schooling was for the fallow season. Folk couldn't claim the use of young workers per se troubled them.

Instead, rather than face contradictions on the fair and square, whenever tragedy struck they blamed those damned Yankee Jews. It was them who owned and operated the factories; those "foreigners" who'd given birth to modern Atlanta, the jewel of the New South. They revolutionized everyone's lives in the span of a few decades for both better and worse. It didn't endear them that some bosses made millions for themselves and the bankers while tenement children made petty scratch. The yellowest of journalists, including that yahoo Watson over to the *Jeffersonian,* dubbed factory owners and managers "bloodsucking Hebrew overlords." Insinuation of all kinds of perversity festered in *Jeffersonian* stories of poor tykes crushed or stabbed by machines, the ruination of young lungs and hearts. Whenever one appeared in a broadside, handbills appeared all over the city featuring cartoons of big-nosed Jews carrying bags of gold.

Ross had parked his Model T Roadster Pickup close by. It was a gorgeous car, red with black trim and brass fittings, white walled tires. He flipped a couple pennies to the street kid he'd hired to watch it and stood on the running board. He swung one long leg then the other over the door, slid his torso down the leather back of the front seat and settled in. Max entered from the opposite side in the conventional manner, opening the door and climbing up to the passenger seat. He'd got used to riding trolleys in Atlanta, but a ride in an automobile was a rare experience. He knew it showed in his wide eyes and quickened breath. He hoped he didn't look too much the rube to his boss. Ross put on a pair of goggles against road debris and handed a spare pair to Max.

"Here, kid." He flipped another penny to his watcher. "Crank her up."

The kid bent over the crank shaft and obliged. The car shook and sputtered a tad but took off with enough speed that Max put a hand on his head rather than lose his hat. Most Atlantans rested from the day's festivities. Only scoundrels, beggars, barflies, and newsmen were afoot and not many of those. Both auto and horse traffic was light.

That meant they could speed. How fast they went was a mystery to Max. He only knew they moved faster than he'd ever moved before. He was excited enough to be unaware of anything else and missed the route his boss took to the Bloomfield Funeral Home. When required, a municipal morgue was set up at the back of the mortuary's main floor. Ross eased into a parking space in front between two police cars.

"Gang's all here," he muttered.

Ross knew every cop, undertaker, cub, stringer, and reporter crowding the vestibule of Bloomfield's. He cracked jokes and asked for family members by name, glad-handing like a pol. Someone let slip in his ear where in that rambling building Mary Phagan's body lay and he snuck off to find it, leaving Max behind after whispering in his ear, "Any reporter tries to follow me, get rid of 'em. I don't care how." Max froze where he stood, breathing heavily, wracking his brain trying to figure out how to control the movements of a roomful of large, bold men.

In the end, it didn't matter. The saloon down the street sent a boy to Bloomfield's to let the press know they were open. They left en masse for the joint, telling the boy to stay and fetch them when the examiner was ready to make a statement. The cops and undertakers joined them. Max alone remained in place. Half an hour later, while he gazed out a window, idle and bored, Ross appeared at his elbow, startling him.

"C'mon, Max," he hissed *sotto voce* as if they were in a crowd. "Change of plans. We're on the move."

They rushed to the car. Max cranked them up and jumped onto the running board on the fly.

"Did you get something?" he asked Ross when he'd caught his breath.

Ross reached in his breast pocket and pulled out a crumpled piece of paper on which were scrawled words Max could not decipher as the paper was streaked in soot.

"I got the mother lode."

He cackled like the wild card his mama raised, stuffed the papers back in his pocket.

"L'il Mary wrote two notes before she succumbed," he said. "That, my boy, was one of them."

Max whistled. How'd Ross get his hands on that? Under the very noses of the police? The man was a marvel. A legend. Ross spoke again.

"Look. I have to get to the office to write this up. I need you to take over an interview for me, OK? It's with one of my informants. Actually, a friend. Someone I trust."

OK? It was more than OK. It felt like a breakthrough. Max had never been charged with an important hard news interview before.

"Absolutely, Mr. Harold!" he said. His boss cackled again.

They pulled up to a three-story rooming house undistinguishable from the row houses that snaked through the industrial neighborhoods, including the colored town near Decatur. Its paint was blistered. There were missing shingles on the roof although the tar paper underneath looked whole. Two of the windows were boarded up and the panes of three more were cracked. It was just past the dawn. Lights flickered inside. The residents, factory employees all, were surely up and readying for their ten-hour workday.

"I'm talkin' about a colored gal I know works at National Pencil," Ross said. "I want you to go in there, tell her I send my regards and regrets (always treat your informants with respect, kid, remember that).Then ask her everything she knows about Newt Lee, that'd be the watchman, and Jim Conley, the janitor. Leo Frank too. I'll be back at the shop, filing this." He tapped his breast pocket. "Get back to me soon's you can."

He asked Max to crank him up yet again. While he did so, the cub reminded him he hadn't told him the interview subject's name.

"It's Ruby," Ross said. "Ruby Alfreda Johnson."

Max's mouth fell open. His head twitched and his eyes went damp. Any other day, Ross would have wondered what his odd expression meant. But he was hell-bent to beat the rest of the boys on the murder of Mary Phagan, so he didn't. If his years as a newshound had taught him anything, it taught him what stories were going to be big, maybe national. This was one of them. It could make his career. If he managed things right, he could rise to the stratosphere and take his rightful place alongside Menken and Sinclair. He could go to New York and start up a magazine. All he needed from Max was that he do his job.

"She might have left already," he continued. "She likes to get into work before the others. When I meet her at the factory, I usually meet her outside the southeast entrance the coloreds use," he said. "Ask someone going in to fetch her." He drove off.

Max felt lightheaded but he worked to compose himself. He steadied his breath, marched up to the front door of Ruby's rooming house, and knocked. As Ross suspected, she'd gone to work. Turning about, Max walked the short distance to National Pencil in a fog. It lifted gradually, step by step. By the time he reached the factory, his back was straight, his chin up, his chest forward, full of air, his step sure. He was determined to conduct himself in an honorable and manly fashion when he at last gazed upon the face of Ruby Alfreda Johnson.

8.

The National Pencil Company was housed in a four-story granite and brick building with heroic arches. It ran the entire block of South Forsyth Street. There were multiple entrances for multiple purposes—one for the bosses, one for buyers, a loading dock, an unloading one, two entries for the white laborers, one for the black. Max waited outside the entrance marked "Colored." He stopped a young boy and asked him to send out Ruby Alfreda Johnson to meet a messenger from Harold Ross. The boy seemed to know her. Max waited in the shadows. Anticipation made his heart race. It crushed his lungs. Luckily, he didn't have to wait long.

His first look at Ruby shocked him. It shouldn't have. He'd imagined her grown-up a thousand times, but she was no longer the untamed, rambling girl who gamboled through the woods with him. She looked every inch an adult now. She appeared contained in an unfamiliar way. Her walk, her facial expression, the way she filled her clothes, everything about her bespoke maturity.

Her hair was piled up on top of her head and covered with a kerchief without regard for vanity's sake to protect it from the perilous teeth of machines. She wore a cheap, shapeless dress. Despite all that, she was as Mayhayley Lancaster had predicted, a beauty. For Max, she was a vision of perfection. She stole his breath. He stayed within shadow until he could order himself while she glanced around looking for the messenger of Harold Ross.

She found him. The perfect eyes widened. The perfect mouth made an "O" of surprise. A perfect hand flew to her perfect throat.

"Max!" she said, knowing him at once despite their five years apart, his neatly trimmed beard, his height and broad shoulders. "Max!"

He forgot all caution. He stepped out of the shadows, grinning with his arms raised, eager to embrace her. She held up a hand to stop him.

"Not here, Max," she said softly.

She tilted her head and rolled her eyes to cue him that they were hardly alone. A steady stream of black workers came and went through the factory's colored entrance while white ones passed en route to their own. More than a few glanced at the pair with a wary curiosity. Max was no fool. He knew the need for discretion. He stood three feet apart from her and dropped his arms to his sides, hands clenched to keep them low and still.

One of the parks where Max sold his second-hand goods on Saturdays was close by. It had a clearing surrounded by a thick cluster of flowering bushes where they might be unobserved.

"Can you leave here for just a bit?" he asked.

She looked from side to side, searching.

"I'm supposed to meet someone."

He stood a little straighter.

"That would be me."

Her brow wrinkled then smoothed again.

"You come from Harry?" she asked.

"Yes."

It struck him she didn't say Mr. Ross or Harold Ross or even just Harold. She said Harry. Max never heard anyone call Ross Harry before. It irritated him that Ruby did. His brow knit. He scowled.

"So can you leave for a li'l bit or not?"

She saw he was annoyed, which confused her. But she nodded. There wasn't much going on at the factory with the police all over it. Cops and reporters disrupted every workroom. Her job was largely custodial although when there was a deadline looming and not enough workers, she got better paying work. That would not happen today. He gestured for her to follow him. He took her deep into the park to the clearing that would hide them from view. As soon as they were under cover, they stepped into each other's arms and hugged. Joy shot through them both. They released each other slowly. Ruby asked how he wound up at the *Journal*. He told her.

"You always were so smart, Max," she said, touching his arm.

"And you so brave," he said, touching hers.

Neither let go. They stood in half-embrace, each marveling at the other's presence. Max started to blab a mile a minute, telling her what he knew about her family, gossiping about the kids they worked or went to school with. The more he talked, the more the old affections eased through the years that had passed. He could see again the child she once was in her eyes and mouth. She laughed or sighed without effort where he hoped she would. A factory whistle sounded. They were out of time. She had to get back to work.

"I finish at eight," she said. "Meet me at Dark Sally's at eight thirty. It's off Decatur."

Max knew the place. It troubled him that she knew it too. Dark Sally's was a shady joint with a honeycomb of private dining rooms upstairs and off the bar. All manner of race mingling occurred in those rooms. It was a place where whites and blacks did clandestine business together, hatched plots, had love affairs, and quarreled. It was where prostitutes met johns and thieves fenced their goods. When he first got to the city, Max went there hunting for human interest stories but patrons were tight-lipped around strangers at Dark Sally's. Ask too many questions, and you could get hurt. He only went there now on assignment.

As they walked back to the factory, Ruby remembered Harold Ross.

"What did Harry tell you to tell me?" she asked, although she could guess. Harry was one hundred percent newshound and the biggest news since the Hanna Mines blew had landed at her place of employ. The murder victim was someone she'd had unhappy dealings with and Harry knew that too. It only surprised her that he hadn't come himself but sent his cub. Who, most astonishingly, was Maxwell Isadore Sassaport.

Max slapped his forehead.

"Dang, Ruby! You always did drive the sense out of my head. Ross sent me here to ask you about the murder. Particularly what you know about Leo Frank, Jim Conley, and Newt Lee."

Ruby's mouth twisted.

"And Mary Phagan? Did he ask you to question me about her?"

"No, but he was in a hurry. I'm sure he meant to. Did you know her, Ruby?"

Ruby smacked her tongue against her teeth. When they were children, she did so in a delicate way, barely making a sound. Max teased her about it, calling her The Silent Scold as if she were the villain in the traveling show or leapt off the flicker screen. He smiled to hear her do it again.

"She hated me," Ruby said.

Her words sobered him.

"Why?"

They'd arrived at National Pencil.

"Harry knows why."

She slipped through her entry portal, calling back:

"See you at Sally's."

A dapper man in a dark blue suit with lavender piping walked by and overheard her. He grinned and tapped Max on the back with the tip of his ivory-knobbed cane in tribute as he passed. It was Eli Bohert from *Vanity Fair.*

Vanity Fair. If even Eli Bohert had been roused from his feather bed at this hour, the murder of Mary Phagan was as big as Harold Ross hoped. By now, the crime was known to every hungry reporter in the county. A pack of them gathered on the factory's second floor outside Leo Frank's office where they waited for the police to escort them to the murder site, a dark, filthy basement. They scribbled descriptions of the manager's office, its lobby with the big black safe and elevator to pass the time. They argued and stole each other's best quotes from supervisors and shift bosses. Max joined them a few steps behind Bohert.

The elevator creaked. The room went quiet. Everyone stared at its ascending cage, waiting. It arrived carrying a burly uniformed policeman with a billy club in his belt. He stood aside and said: "Five at a time, lads." They pushed and shoved, but the copper bellowed for order while slapping his palm with the club. The pack settled into an orderly queue.

The first group and every group after went down into the basement of National Pencil sharp-eyed with notebooks at the ready. They ascended looking grim with a handkerchief over their mouths.

Max descended with the final group. More police waited for them on the basement floor, a dark and dismal place covered in soot, scrapings of lead, cedar shavings and whatever refuse workers tossed there. A detective in a baggy suit held a lantern aloft. He looked like a member of the press, disheveled, in scuffed shoes, his fedora stained with grease at the crown, except that he had a sizable silver star on his lapel. He barked them along the route where someone had relieved themselves maybe ten hours earlier, judging by the color and stink of it. They filed past the coal furnace, to a spot near the boiler where the white chalk outline of a thirteen-year-old girl's body had been scraped through a crust of dirt. Though the corpse was gone, the stench of death and filth lingered. It overpowered. Hard men coughed. Covered their mouths. The detective gave them what the cops wanted the press to know.

"Young Mary Phagan was found here, beat to a bloody pulp, knifed, and strangled. Poor lass. She came to the factory to collect her pay before taking in the great parade. If you could look at her now. Her own mother wouldn't recognize her. When she was found, her garters were undone and her underpants was ripped by the crotch. Blood ran down her legs and up her belly. She was on her side with her arms folded across her chest, but her face was turned and pushed into the trash heap. Now why, you might ask, did she lay so? It's my opinion"—he rose on the tips of his toes then descended for emphasis—"the murderer felt pity for her once the dirty deed was done, and at the same time, he felt horror at what he had accomplished, which is why he crossed her arms like an angel but turned her dead gaze away. He put a scrap of her drawers over her neck, too, to cover the cord he wrung it with, but he left the cord itself intact, coiled like a snake beneath her . . ."

Max scribbled what the detective said word for word as best he could. It was too good. The copy editor wouldn't have to do much to bring it up to the style and standard of the *Journal*, which always honored the plain speech of the man in the street. He reflected for a moment that his first reaction to the gruesome account was to consider not the victim but the ease of his copy editor. City life has made me hard, he thought. I've become a newsman.

When he was finished, the detective gave his head a long, slow shake as if to say, "the things I've seen; the depravity of man has no limit."

Max and the others peppered him with questions. Who found her? Are there any suspects? Have the parents been notified? Has Leo Frank, the factory manager?

His curled lip at the mention of Frank spoke volumes, but he'd said his piece. He'd no intention of elaborating. At the end of their tour, half the reporters went over to the Frank home and half to Mary Phagan's. The *Georgian*'s man had been in the first group to visit the basement. He was long gone. Max knew that meant he'd already visited both. Likely Ross had, too, before Max ever got in the elevator. He drew a diagram of the factory's insides, including the eraser room where Mary Phagan worked. He drew the murder site. Then he went to the *Journal* office to report in. He had the whole day to wait before he met Ruby.

Ross was at his desk, pounding furiously at the keys of an Underwood. A burning cigarette dangled from a corner of his mouth. His jacket was off, his tie loosened, his shirtsleeves rolled up. Between bursts of type, he pulled on his mane of hair until it stuck out in a dozen directions. Max stood in front of him waiting for the right moment to interrupt.

"Whattaya got for me?" Ross asked without looking up.

Max put his notes and sketches of the factory's innards, including the murder scene, down on the desk. Ross glanced at them and nodded approval.

"That's a bundle. I'll keep your notes. We can run the sketches with the victim portraits. Get with Bakersfield. He'll make your hen-scratches look like Da Vinci. What'd my gal say?"

He meant Ruby. His gal. *His* gal.

"She couldn't talk. We're meeting at Dark Sally's after her shift."

Max half-expected Ross to say that's OK, he'd take over from here and meet Ruby himself. If he did, Max planned to spill his beans and insist he be the one to meet her. He'd tell his boss about his deep friendship with "Harry's gal," one that began many years before his own, whenever, whatever that was. Ross didn't give him the opportunity.

"That's good too," he said, tearing paper out of the typewriter, putting it together with five other sheets. He stuck out his lower lip, ran though Max's notes, and put them with the typed pages. He stood. "Look, tell her I'm under the gun here. I'll catch up with her later."

Papers in hand, he strode the twelve steps to the door of the office labeled "Editor in Chief" and entered without knocking. Loud voices came from within. Max couldn't tell if they were angry or excited.

He did what he was told to do. Spent a couple hours with George Bakersfield who drew illustrations for the rag, helping him get the scale and images of the factory right. George did two renderings of the basement, one with Mary Phagan's corpse and one with the chalk outline. He also did a large one of the National Pencil building. He made cutouts of the second floor and basement in which he inserted the new and improved Max drawings and a largely imaginative one of the manager's office interior. He put everything on a draftsman's table next to a portrait of a young girl, sweetly smiling, ribbons in her hair, dressed in her Sunday-best petticoats and pinafore. It was the victim before horror struck. Altogether the illustrations were genius. The illiterate could follow the story from the images alone. And they broke the heart.

Ross remained in the editor in chief's lair. Things had quieted until a runner brought them just released special editions of the

Georgian and *Constitution*. Their headlines read: *A Mother's Heart Rended* and *Grandfather Says Mary the Most Innocent Child of the Century*. Photos of Mary's mother and grandfather accompanied them. The roaring started up again. This time, the entire newsroom could hear every word. They were falling behind the competition. The editor wanted to run with rumors to catch up. Ross wanted to stick to the facts. They could afford to wait a little. It wouldn't hurt the *Journal*, he argued. They had the death note. The text was explosive. They'd make a big splash no matter when they dropped the story.

Things quieted again. Max hung around for a while in case he was needed, then left for home. He wanted fresh clothes, and enough time to prepare his mind and heart for Dark Sally's.

Ruby didn't bother to go home and change before meeting Max. Never one to waste time or money, she walked over to Dark Sally's, stopping first at Leroy's cart. She bought two preserved peaches for supper and ate them on the way. By eight fifteen, she sat at the great oak bar with a portrait of Dark Sally hanging over it. In a queer way, Ruby thought sitting under the gaze of Dark Sally was some kind of prophecy only she didn't know what that prophecy was or when it would be revealed to her.

Dark Sally had been a street singer before the turn of the century, one who sang old field songs, spirituals, minstrel tunes, and her own compositions on the steps of public buildings, accompanying herself on banjo or violin. If the mood struck her, she danced. She was sassy, quick with a joke, and carried a knife in her boot. Hardly anyone was dirt poor in Atlanta in those days. Factories were going up almost overnight thanks to Yankees with faith in the opportunity envisioned in Henry Grady's *Constitution:* the New South, a mythical place where Southerners and Northerners loved each other, at least enough to make money together, where blacks worked for decent wages grateful of the chance and knew their place, and hardly anyone drank spirits. As their industries grew so did the population. There was more than enough work around if you wanted it.

Dark Sally didn't. She'd never spent more than a day in a factory workroom or in the back of a city shop. A motherless child, she'd grown up on her lonesome, doing what she wanted as long as the world let her. When it didn't, she found another way. Her father threw his hands up over her by the time she was ten. Luckily, Sally had a musical talent she could exploit. She made a living off the largesse of people lucky enough to be born in that time, that is, people with an extra nickel in their pockets. Sometimes, when the weather was bad and no one stopped to listen to a song or a joke, she was forced to sleep under whatever doorway or bridge she could find. But it didn't happen often.

She wasn't a bad-looking gal, tall and full-figured with deep bronze skin and lively black eyes. Many men courted her. She took up with this one or that one when the spirit moved her but she saved her heart for the day a judge fell in love with her. He'd heard her sing when she worked the steps of the courthouse. He was, of course, white, widowed to boot, and thirty years older than Sally. He loved her voice and made a study of her. He flattered her, tipped her, and over time, cozied up. Eventually, he declared himself. Sally liked him more than enough and knew a stroke of luck when she found one. She took him on gladly. They met several times a week in an abandoned storefront off Decatur, the selfsame building Dark Sally purchased after the judge died. He left her a pile of money through a straw he trusted to honor his dying wish. That man skimmed a healthy bit off the top for his services, but there was plenty enough left over. Sally took herself off the street for good and into a warm building of laughter, song, and commerce. By the time she died, she was making donations to the colored wing of Henry Grady's hospital.

What all that had to do with Ruby was a mystery, but Ruby felt deeply there was something spiritual that tied her to Sally and maybe it was about the way men loved her. Harry loved her, she knew that, the way the judge loved Sally. There was no reason for him to help her the way he did unless he loved her. Dear Max, well, he'd been born loving her and if he could give her a fortune, he would. There'd been others she'd fended off. They came out of nowhere, out of everywhere expressing an intensity of feeling she didn't understand. She wondered sometimes if she exuded a magic chemical, a scent that only men could catch, that drew them to her. By all reports, men had pursued Dark Sally like that, which made her a cousin of the soul. When she looked at Sally's portrait over the bar, she couldn't find much of herself in it beyond a similar shape and fullness of the lips. But it was enough to make her believe. Soul cousins they were.

Across from the bar was a player piano. It played ragtime and Delta blues along with Tin Pan Alley tunes imported from up North by factory men. The place wasn't full up yet, but it was jumping. Women danced together. Men did too. The song changed and the genders got mixed, with women in the arms of men and men leading the way. People ordered beers and rye whiskey but no matter how many times Jack, the bartender, offered a drink to Ruby, she didn't take a drop. It was getting on to quarter of nine. She worried that Max might not come, a thought that wounded her more deeply than she was prepared for. Seeing him again had electrified her in a way she'd never anticipated. All through her workday, she conjured up his handsome, grown-up face, his broad shoulders.

As the hours passed, she recalled a thousand times how tightly he'd hugged her in the park, and her blood, long asleep, awoke. Max felt like her damaged heart's last hope. If he didn't come, it would kill her. Then, suddenly, he was there sitting next to her, regarding her close up, leaning on the next barstool more than sitting on it. His jaw flexed. His eyes were a little wild. He took her by the wrist as if he was about to take her with him on the run. Instead, he sat still as a brick and stared into her eyes. His grip relaxed. They were both overwhelmed. She dropped her gaze while his roamed all over her. They both flushed. A palpable warmth rose between them.

"I still can't believe it," he said. "Mayhayley was right."

She put her hand over his.

"I know."

He grit his teeth, chewed the inside of his cheeks, and came out with it.

"What's between you and Harold Ross?" he asked.

There was more than a hint of distress in his tone. Ruby didn't want trouble. She searched for words.

"Harry's been a good friend to me," she said. "I work for him, too, you know. I clean for him weekends."

Someone changed the piano roll. "My Gal She's a High-Born Lady" played. A white gent in a dark green frockcoat with a magnolia boutonniere stood by the far end of the bar and sang it out good and loud.

My gal she's a high-born lady
she's black but not too shady
Feathered like a peacock, just as gay,
she's not colored, she was born that way . . .

Ruby and Max endured a mournful silence together. The song couldn't help but underscore that the entire world sought to sully their feelings for each other, the same world that had conspired against them since they were children. Ruby squinted to hold emotion back. Max spoke first.

"I imagine you needed one," he said, meaning the friend Harold Ross had been to her. "Maybe best we don't tell him about this . . ." His hand waved between her waist and his. She nodded.

. . . I'm proud of my black Venus,
No coon will come between us.

Max winced. He wanted to slug the man singing the song.

"We need to get out of here," he said.

What she said next astonished him.

"Could we get a private room?"

He would have sold his daddy's gold stopwatch to achieve it. As it happened, it was payday and his pockets were as full as they ever got, a stroke of luck he considered the very Hand of God. He located the manager and asked him the going rates. The lowest was not too dear. The proprietor knew his clientele, what brought them back, and priced the rooms, from plain to luxury, at rates the poor slob could afford and the rich man think a helluva bargain. Max made arrangements and a waiter in shirtsleeves and a long white apron escorted them to a room with a brass number five nailed to the lintel. The room had no door but a thick hooked rug hung over its entrance for privacy's sake. The waiter asked if they wanted to order anything. Ruby said no, but Max ordered whiskey. He thought he might need it.

The room was just large enough for a wide couch, a small round table, and two chairs. There was an iron-framed mirror on one wall, a painting of a cottage by the marsh on the other. There were no windows. They sat on the couch, side by side, and held hands.

"Let's not talk for a minute," Ruby said. "Let's just set here and remember what it was like to set and hold hands when we were babies. Before all this damn life happened."

Max complied. They sat quietly, listening to each other breathe. Their breath synchronized. Soon, a warm band of sentiment enveloped them both, binding them together like a rope or a chain. Neither wanted to break the mood. They kept silent until the waiter pushed back the rug after the briefest knock on the door frame, depositing Max's drink on the table and extracting payment before taking his leave.

"Maybe we should get the business part of this out of the way," Ruby said, her voice oddly thick. "Then we can just be us."

Max nodded. They roused themselves and moved the two steps to the table. Max took a sip of whiskey, and brought out his notebook and pencil from his pants' pocket.

"First, Newt Lee, the watchman that found the body while making his rounds. What's he like?"

She considered before she spoke.

"Newt's alright. He's not the smartest fellah, but he never causes anyone worry. He does his job, makes his rounds regular. It's hard to imagine he was arrested. Harry wants to know about Jim Conley, too, no? Around the factory there's some suspect him. He's a very different story from old Newt. He's drunk half the time. He's leered at me more than once, especially when I was younger. I avoid him when I can. He's got a whore comes in to visit him, and they do whatever they want right there in the factory, any halfway secluded place he can find. I don't know why the bosses don't fire him. He's supposed to keep the main floors clean. I do more of that than he does."

"And Leo Frank?"

She considered again.

"Mr. Frank's, you know, a boss. A tad strange maybe. Seems tied up in knots all the time. He looks at you through those glasses like a bug at a blade of grass. Got a soft voice, like a girl's. His wife comes in from time to time and she's the scary one. Always with a sharp edge and hoity-toity airs. Makes him look almost sweet, actually."

He asked her more questions about each of the men, trying to get a handle on them. Finally, he asked, "Who do you think killed her?"

Ruby was silent. She'd not been long in Atlanta when she learned of the riots of 1906, sparked by newspaper articles about two black men accused of raping white women. *The Clansman* played at the theater that week, which didn't help. It was a match held to newspaper tinder. On a warm night in late September, armed white men descended on Five Points and later, Decatur Street. They rampaged through the blackman's district like wild hogs. Near forty black men died before it was over. Two whites.

Reports of the riots had gone around the world, but at the time Ruby was still hiding in deer blinds with Max and in their day, parents tried to protect little ones from ugly news so she'd never heard much of it. All she remembered hearing about Atlanta from Bull and Mama was "folk don't like our kind in Atlanta," but as time went by, she heard more from others about how much money a black could earn there. When she learned about the riots shortly after she settled in Atlanta, it came as a shock. It unsettled her. She feared a new riot every time some poor brother got tossed in jail charged with a violent or salacious crime. Her neighbors at the rooming house assured her the city regretted 1906. It wouldn't happen again.

Ruby didn't believe them. She had no idea who killed Mary Phagan but she couldn't bring herself to blame black men. If one was found guilty, new riots might destroy her whole world overnight. So far, the only other suspect in the murder was a Jew. She knew the white people she shared the city with. Many were as fond of Jews as they were blacks. How could she tell Max she hoped the guilty party was a man who might put his people in the crosshairs? She couldn't.

"I don't know," she said. "It's not for me to say."

He asked her a few more questions about Frank's habits around the office, what time did he come in and was he likely to be there on a Saturday. He asked if the night watchman always inspected the basement at the same hour. Or was it unusual he should discover the victim there at that time?

She had few answers for him. At the factory, she put her head down and got the work done. She didn't get in anybody else's business or pay attention to what they did. She'd already told him as much as she knew. There wouldn't be much to report back to Harold Ross.

"What about Mary Phagan? Why does she hate you? I mean, why did she hate you."

Ruby slipped the kerchief off her head, ruffled her hair with two hands, and blew a stream of air through pursed lips to buy time. The idea of telling Max everything about her life in Atlanta was like a sharpened spike in her side. Both the Dark Sally part and the Mary Phagan part would lead to other uncomfortable questions. The answers might repel him. She wanted to spare them both. She went back to the couch, sat, and patted the cushion next to her.

"That's a very long story. Do I have to tell you now? We've only just got together after so long. Why don't we just sit quietly again. I really liked that."

"Sure," he said.

He smiled. Ruby touched his cheek. They put their arms around each other. Ruby laid her head on Max's chest. He stroked her back. He kissed her forehead. She pressed against him. He kissed her mouth and they shared a soft, lingering kiss.

The pleasure it gave surprised them both. A sense of wonder infused them. They kissed again, hard and long.

Max felt in a dream world. When Ruby left town, he was young, he'd pined for her chastely. Once, when he was fifteen, he'd called her name while with another girl, but they'd been into her daddy's bourbon, so he excused himself. Sitting next to Ruby, kissing her, he was overwhelmed by a tidal wave of emotion. He felt like a man drowning in desire. His mind was gone. He had only instinct left.

"Ruby," he muttered, "Ruby," and lifted her skirts. She lifted her hips. They rocked together. They moaned. They cried out. The rest was as natural as water flowing downhill.

Afterward, they were lost in a sentimental haze. He kissed her eyes and cheeks and lips, enveloping her in loving admiration. Ruby basked in his affection, preened for it, stretching herself across the couch and wiggling her toes.

"So this is where we've been headed all these years," she said, softly, pulling lightly on his beard.

He brushed a stray lock of hair out of her eyes.

"Our parents were as right as Mayhayley," he said.

They sighed and nestled against each other's flesh.

They'd exhausted themselves. Before too long, they fell asleep. When Max woke several hours later, she was gone. There was a note on the table written on a torn-out page of his notebook. In the same hand that wrote messages left years ago in a coffee can by the deer blind, it read "I don't want to leave this room ever, Max. I want to live here in your arms. But I've got work. Come to me later."

He'd never had a love note before. He put it against his face to inhale whatever trace of her it preserved then placed it in his left-hand shirt pocket over his heart. It felt warm there. He wondered when she wanted him to come to her and where. After work, he figured, unless she meant during her lunch. He'd try lunch and quitting time both. He left Sally's and headed to his room.

Ruby hurried to the factory in the chill of dawn. First light cast ominous shadows on the street, in the alleyways. They looked like magical creatures emerging from behind a veil of darkness. She felt one might seize her by the collar and carry her off to an underworld where dissemblers were punished eternally so she walked as far apart from them as she could get, along the curb's edge, underneath the street lamps. She walked briskly, lightly, her feet barely glancing the ground. Her mind raced.

Why had she held back with Max about her dealings with Mary Phagan? Oceans of time had passed but he was still Max! Loyal, loving Max who did everything she asked of him. Max who would hide her from bullies, who would visit witches, who would steal for her, who would follow her to Atlanta. He was her oldest, most cherished friend and now—it was so new, it amazed her, she shivered at the thought—her lover.

After Lewis Taylor, the only man who'd come close to moving her was Harry. She was fond of him and grateful but not grateful enough to let down her guard all the way. Then Max appeared out of nowhere and made her feel like a virgin again, a passionate, loving one. Only she'd noticed his face had changed when he looked around at Dark Sally's patrons, when the dandy sang that awful song. What would he think if he knew she'd once worked there? Would he believe that all she'd ever done there was carry trays and wipe down counters? Most men wouldn't. Or what if the boys at the *Journal* told him Harry's doxy came by and he pressed for her identity? They'd spill. It wasn't true she was Harry's doxy, but she'd be the first to admit their relations looked suspicious. What if he believed them? Most men would.

Max loved her but he wasn't a saint. At the very least, doubts would be planted in his heart. She'd seen it happen to other girls, both back home and in the city, that the boys they loved turned on them because they'd listened to gossip. It ate them up. He'd wind up hating Harry, too. Better Max be kept in the dark than rivals materialize out of alleyway shadows at the first ray of light and devour his tender, happy feelings.

She fell into reverie then, reliving each caress, each kiss, each thrust of the night. Her legs went weak. She leaned against a lamppost to steady them while her spirit soared. What did the past matter? She had Max again! It was a miracle! She'd felt safe in his arms. All her pain, all her regrets had vanished at the first kiss. But where could they go from here? They still lived in the world they lived in yesterday. She couldn't so much as walk down the street on his arm. She loved Max. They would have to be content with Dark Sally's in future. It would be enough for both of them if she took special care.

She thought of Harry next and fear ran through her like a knife. Max would report to Harry soon. What if he asked Harry why Mary Phagan hated her? Harry might let something slip. He might even brag about his role in it. That would be worse than if the press room maligned her. The whole matter shamed her. She had to get to Harry first. Beg him not to spoil everything.

Dawn was over and the morning had begun. She turned on her heel to face the sun and headed in the direction of the *Journal*'s offices. Harry would be there. When he was on a big story, he slept there. An urgency gathered inside her. She had to get to Harry before Max did. Dear, darling, beautiful Max. Her eyes welled. She filled her lungs with air and ran.

9.

Harold Ross was buried in paper and ink. Standing in the press-room by the long table he'd commandeered as his crisis desk, he could put out his hands and touch eleven piles of notes and half as many piles of typed sheets scribbled over with remarks, exclamation points, question marks, and arrows. His hair was at its worst, spiking out, twisting in, knotted at the back. He chain-smoked in an abortive effort to calm his frenzied thoughts. At least he had enough sense to keep his ashtray on the windowsill behind him or there'd be burn holes through the whole mess.

When Ruby entered the press room, he didn't see her at first. He didn't see anything but the tabletop and the story it was trying to tell. His mind's mission was to reach a great synthesis that would put it all in order in the most convincing manner. If he stuck to the facts, he might even solve the crime. He blocked everything else out.

A handful of reporters typed listlessly at their desks, more interested in what Harold Ross was up to than their own tasks. The typing ceased. They twisted their necks to look Ruby over. They knew who she was. She came around every once in a while. She was Ross's special friend. Some said his gal. In fact, there was an office pool with pressmen making bets from one to fifteen dollars over what the two were up to. But they couldn't devise a way to find out the truth that didn't fall short of the law. Not that they were above the odd breaking and entering or petty larceny in the pursuit of news but they feared Harold more than the cops. Harold was smart. He'd find out. He'd exact justice.

Whatever she was to him, a woman like Ruby was hard to forget. The sight of her stirred the lust of more than one of them. None had the courage to enter into such a liaison in that day, in that place. Lucky bastard, they thought. Crazy too.

The silence in the room intensified. They knew where Ruby worked and figured she must be on an errand about the murder. They waited for something to happen. A stray newsboy returned from his route, his unsold papers under his arm. He spotted her and lifted his cap. Someone slapped the back of the boy's head, either in reprimand for showing a colored girl respect or for generally being a dunce. More time passed. Ruby stood behind Ross, breathing heavily. Her breath was uncommonly loud being the singular sound in the room. Ross continued to ignore her arrival until, frustrated, somebody said, "Harold, you have a visitor."

Ross swatted at air with one hand, warning the speaker off. His eyes didn't leave the table. Ruby reached out and touched his back. "Harry," she said, and suddenly, he turned around and looked at her, at first blankly as if she were out of focus and then blinking with surprise. He said the first thing that came into his head to explain her appearance.

"Gal, have you got something for me? I sent my cub." He looked over her shoulder then glanced about the room. "Where the hell is he?"

"He's what I'm here about," she said.

"Max?"

There was confusion, disbelief in his voice. He didn't say

"What did that punk do?" but it was the question on the room's collective mind. Ruby wanted to escape. The scrutiny of the others made it hard to keep her gaze steady.

"Can't we talk alone somewhere?"

Ross looked down at his table then back up at Ruby. He didn't want to stop working, but her eyes melted him, as they always did.

"OK," he said softly then loudly to the rest, "Any of you animals touch my papers, I'll murder your mothers."

He inclined his head toward the chief's office. The chief never came in until ten in the morning, even when the news was hotter than August. Ruby followed him there. After they entered, Harold drew the blinds. He took Ruby's hands in his.

"What's this all about? If that boy insulted you, I'll have his hide."

Her skin was warm, clammy. She looked down.

"No, Harry, it's not like that."

He sensed by her tone that a revelation was coming, so he kept silent and squeezed her hands as encouragement. Tell me, baby doll, his squeeze said. She complied.

She told him about her and Max, their loving childhood, their trip to Mayhayley's, her work at the plantation next door, how she met Lewis Taylor, a man of whom Ross already knew more than he wanted to. At the mention of Taylor's name, his back straightened. His cheeks flexed. But he kept quiet to let her continue. Ruby told him how Max had helped her flee her home after Taylor abused her. The rest of her story, the Atlanta part, he knew already.

Two years before, Ross met Ruby while she was in extremis. He was a spanking new senior reporter trawling the city looking for news in the wee hours when he heard a girl cry out over and over. Then it stopped. He followed the sound to an alley between a bar and a flophouse hotel. A white man had Ruby cornered against a brick wall with his knife at her throat. "Release her!" Ross shouted. He set himself on the balls of his feet and raised his fists like Gentleman Jim, the boxer. The man was a low-life drunk. He swayed on his feet, imperiling Ruby's jugular. "Release her!" Ross shouted again, adding a growl of rage at the end. The man gawked open-mouthed at the gent challenging him. He blinked. Confrontation could have no good ending for him. He withdrew his knife and ran.

Ruby assessed Ross and adjusted her clothing. Her eyes never left him. They narrowed, studying her situation to determine if she'd gone from frying pan to fire. Nothing about her spoke of panic, only survival. Here's an extraordinary creature, he thought. Awful good-lookin' too. He extended a hand. She didn't take it but shrank back against the wall. Arms spread, she moved sideways along it, inching away from him.

Ross was not about to let her go. He tipped his hat. They might have been in the grand ballroom of the Peachtree Hotel instead of a grimy alley off Decatur.

"How do y'do?" he said. "I'm Harold Ross. Are you alright?"

Ruby nodded slowly.

"Was that someone you knew? Or a stranger who grabbed you from the street?"

Her mouth opened but she did not speak. He tried to soothe her.

"I don't mean to interrogate you. I'm a newsman. It's how we think. You be quiet if you need to be quiet," he said. "Do you want me to take you somewhere?"

Her eyes got huge. They seared into him. He could not look away. He thought himself a hard-nosed journalist, pitiless, able to stare down every story through an impersonal lens. He'd worked at newspapers from the time he was twelve in Colorado, Utah, California, Panama, and New Orleans. Yet this strange, beautiful black girl made his brow break into a sweat. She spoke.

"Yes," she said.

That was unexpected. He asked her where, she pointed to Dark Sally's across the street and down half a block. He gave her his arm. It was late enough. No one would see. She felt weak, she needed to calm her breath, so she took it. He didn't know why, but it felt like a grand favor bestowed by a queen rather than a bold gesture by a poor black girl just minutes before abused by one of his own.

In those days, Ruby worked weekends at Dark Sally's. She'd been laid off at National Pencil more than once when wood or lead or sheet-brass was in short supply and their delivery slow. A second job kept a roof over her head. At Dark Sally's, she served drinks to half-naked lovers, card sharks, socialites, men in business, anarchists, and strongmen. She ran their errands if they paid her. For enough money, she turned many a blind eye. It came with the territory at Dark Sally's. Since she came to Atlanta, she'd learned how to defend herself and kept a knife in her boot like Sally did. But the night she met Harold Ross, a man had taken her by surprise. She'd hauled empty bottles out the back of the club as she often did, tossing them into the trash bin one by one, enjoying the tinkling sounds of breaking glass. Her assailant grabbed her from behind then dragged her to the spot where Ross discovered them.

Everybody knew her inside Sally's. As soon as they entered, people started giving her orders, patrons and barkeep alike. "Hey, Rubes, fetch me a gin!" "Porter, gal! and quick!" "Get this tray to room sixteen, pronto. They've been waiting long enough to turn to stone." She went directly to the bar, picked up the tray for room sixteen, and climbed the stairs. Harold thought she'd forgotten him. He went to the bottom of the stairs to watch her ascend. At the top step, she turned, smiled at him, and mouthed "Thank you." It pricked the hair on the back of his neck.

He was sunk after that.

He courted her as diligently as he might any white woman he knew. He became a fixture at Dark Sally's, bringing her small gifts she could accept without feeling compromised, things like fancy ladies soap, a tortoiseshell comb, and a silver ring to wear around her thumb. Whenever he could, he walked her home at the end of her workday, telling her stories, making her laugh. Although the streets were deserted in the hours before dawn, caution was necessary. They grew adept at separating quickly if late-night carousers happened by, reuniting as soon as the way was clear. He helped her quit Sally's by matching her pay of six bits a week, making up domestic chores for her, again, so she wouldn't feel compromised. She washed his clothes on weekends, prepared food, kept his rooms polished and swept. Sometimes, he used her as a courier, because he trusted her to run articles to his sources for review and correction. But despite what the boys at the paper thought, she was not his doxy, never was. He would have been delighted if she were. It wasn't for lack of trying. He'd tried. From the beginning, he played up to her to gain her favor. He felt she liked him, more than enough. But the one time he made an unmistakable advance was a sad, awkward failure.

She came to him one Saturday morning while he was still abed. When the doorbell rang, he put on his velvet slippers, his fez, and a robe with quilted satin lapels to answer it. When he saw who was calling, he apologized for being in disarray and she laughed at him because although she'd surprised him by coming for work early, he was, as always, elegant.

"Why, Harry, look at you!" she said, gently chiding him. One can't take care of a man and his home without feeling close, she'd discovered. She considered her feelings for Ross familial in a way. "I've never seen you when you weren't playing the swell."

She said it with affection so he came up close to her and tried to embrace her. Her reaction was immediate. Her face went sour. She put a hand out and stopped him.

"I won't come here anymore if you act like that," she said quite seriously. He could tell she meant it.

He put up his own hands then and, patting air, backed off. He felt humiliated. He apologized but not profusely.

Ruby saw that she'd hurt him. Harry had been good to her and she'd known for a long time he was attracted to her, she couldn't deny that. She felt she owed him an explanation. With difficulty, she told him about Lewis Taylor and what he'd done to her, that intimacy came hard for her because of it.

"I don't like it when men touch me," she said.

He understood. Apologized some more.

Two years later, he hadn't approached her again but he thought about it. Sometimes, when he thought of about it intensely and his thoughts grew dense and dark, he figured maybe he was just biding his time, waiting for her to weaken.

Then came the Mary Phagan incident, which bound the two of them more powerfully than if they'd shared the fiercest carnal pleasures.

The incident involved the cover-up of a crime. Thoughts of his role in the matter always made Ross cringe. He'd do it again to help Ruby, he'd do it in a heartbeat, but that didn't change the fact that he was a reporter dedicated to the pursuit of truth and the unveiling of civic corruption. Yet, for Ruby he lied, he bribed to bury a thing that would have landed her in prison.

It happened at the factory. Mary Phagan loved a boy there who gave her no notice. He worked on another floor where machines drilled holes in wood cylinders and inserted lengths of lead. She saw him every day when he delivered boxes of unfinished pencils to the knurling room. Mary operated a lathe there, scoring the metal tips at the pencil's end and inserting erasers into them. She wrote his name on her station then erased it a dozen times a day. At last, she worked up her courage and wrote him a note. "Why won't you look at me, Johnny? I could love you." It was so bold, she wondered whether she should sign her name. If her note were anonymous, he would have to hunt to find her. The romance of Johnny looking for her like a prince with glass slipper in hand was awfully appealing. She imagined herself lifting her gaze to his, eyelashes fluttering, the way Mary Pickford's might in the flickers. She would say "Yes, Johnny. I am she," at which point he would fold her gently in his arms and they would love happily ever after. On the other hand, it occurred some other girl might snatch him away from her while he searched. She tossed and turned on it and then signed her name.

Mary needed someone to deliver the note. She hadn't the courage to do it herself. She trusted none of the girls in the knurling room. They'd pretend to deliver it, then giggle and show it around the floor. She cast about for someone else. She'd heard what everyone said about Ruby, that she'd worked at Dark Sally's and was now a grown white man's weekend hussy. Clearly, she was one of those colored gals who'd do anything for a penny. She decided to enlist her.

Ruby was sweeping up. Mary called her over to her station. Ruby was older than she by several years, but Mary spoke to her as if she were a child.

"Gal, come 'ere," she said. "I need an errand from you and will pay you a nickel. Won't that be nice to have?"

Ruby was tempted to say she didn't need a nickel so bad. The other girls in the room twisted away from their work and stretched out their necks to observe them. Their white stares shut Ruby up.

Mary Phagan took the folded note from one pocket and a nickel from the other. She put them together and extended her hand.

"Now, this says 'To Johnny,'" she said, pointing to the letters on the front as she assumed Ruby could not read. "You give it to that good-lookin' white boy, Johnny, in the drill room."

A nickel was still a nickel.

"Alright," Ruby said.

Trouble was Ruby gave it to the wrong boy. There was another Johnny in the drill room, taller than the one Mary wanted and blond. His face was like a pretzel. He had a twisted nose and a frog's mouth but Ruby had no idea what Mary found good-looking and the floor manager pointed him out straightaway, as if he were the only Johnny there. After reading the note, the wrong Johnny immediately asked the boss for a piss break and went to the knurling room to find Mary Phagan. When he saw her, pretty as a cornflower, twice as fresh and developed beyond her years, his body rejoiced. He marched right up to her and, in a fit of reckless happiness, kissed her hard in front of everyone.

When he finished, he backed off and grinned ear to ear, his arms outspread as if to welcome a bride. She screamed, punched and kicked him, then turned about to flee the room in anger and in shame. Wrong Johnny yelled after her, "You said you could love me!" making it crystal clear the love note had been misdelivered. Ruby pushed her broom near the exit door. In her flight, Mary ran smack into her chest. Realizing into whom she had crashed, she commenced to kick, punch, and scream at Ruby too. "Stupid nigger bitch!" she yelled, "not that Johnny!" Ruby pushed her to the floor in self-defense.

From inside Leo Frank's office, N. V. Darley, the plant personnel director, heard the ruckus and left his meeting with the superintendent to see Mary Phagan collapsed in a heap and Ruby Alfreda running around a corner. In her rage and humiliation, Mary Phagan said, "That nigger gal wants to kill me! She tried to shove me down the stairs!" Ruby got away and hid at her second job, the home of Harold Ross. Tipped off by one of the girls, the police went there the next day. "Police! Open, up!" they yelled.

Harry signaled for her to hide but for Ruby, the jig was up. She answered the door holding ice in a towel against purple wounds on her cheeks. She was bruised from forehead to wrists. There were two deep bloody scratches on her neck as well. Mary Phagan had a mildly skinned knee. If anyone assaulted anyone, it was obvious that Mary did the dirty work not the "nigger gal."

The truth didn't make a whit of difference. The police felt obligated to arrest Ruby anyway. Pretty young white girls beaten by black ones were a spicy draw for the newspapers. They'd win a commission of five dollars each if they alerted the *Jeffersonian*, the *Constitution*, and the *Georgian* to her arrest. Spicy draws were circulation boosters. It was the kind of race baiting story the *Jeffersonian* specialized in. It would give Hearst's paper a chance to beat the drum for its pet cause, the perils of child labor in factories. Without question, all the outlets would make hay of it. Even the *Journal* would.

Luckily, Ross bought them off before they could cart Ruby away. He kept a pile of cash in a cigar box at home. It wasn't all his. Some was supplied to him by the *Journal*. His chief understood that on occasion, a senior reporter had to pay to get a story or to kill it. He gave the arresting officers forty dollars each to let Ruby off the hook. They freed her. He went to National Pencil and gave Darley forty dollars to keep quiet too.

Darley intimidated Mary Phagan into silence for free. She

hated Ruby from then on. When Ruby's lunch bag was stepped on or when she fell on an oil slick surface, she knew who to blame. Mary Phagan or one of her friends. Six weeks had passed since the battery of Ruby Alfreda Johnson at the hands of Mary Phagan. That wasn't very long. She didn't know how it could happen, but she feared she might become part of the murder investigation. She prayed forty dollars a head was enough to keep lips sealed, but with a brutalized girl laying lifeless in the factory basement, all bets were off.

"You can't tell Max, Harry," Ruby said. "Not how we met nor what happened with Mary. If you do, I'll kill myself."

Ross ignored her hyperbole. He was too insulted. First, she'd rejected him but favored his cub. Max, of all people! Second, she thought he himself—of all people!—might break her trust.

"Why would I betray you? If anyone finds out about the bribery, it'd be curtains for me too. I'd have to leave town at the very least. It'd be worse trouble for those I bribed. You don't have to worry about them. I'm warning you though. You keep meeting Sassaport at Dark Sally's and the truth will out that you once worked there sooner or later. Probably sooner."

She shuddered. Her eyes filled.

"I couldn't stand that," she said. "But I don't think it'll happen. Workers come and go from Sally's all the time. There's no one there now from my day. Well, the night manager. Only him."

"It's still a risk. Tell Sassaport. He's a grown man and also my cub. I happen to know he's seen worse in that capacity than what goes on at Dark Sally's. If he loves you, he'll understand, he won't think a thing about it. What he won't understand when he finds out later on is that you never told him."

She dried her eyes with the palms of her hands then wrinkled her brow to regain control.

"It's just that right now he thinks I'm some kind of angel."

Ross's voice got soft and dark.

"Well, I do too. And I know everything you're afraid to tell him. Don't I?"

She looked down and nodded her head.

"Yes, but no one's ever looked into my eyes the way Max does."

It wasn't completely true. Willie Gordon had looked at her that way. Only he'd been a child. The man standing before her had too. But he was Harry, her employer and friend. Harry didn't count.

It wasn't the way Ross saw things. He'd idolized her and treated her pretty damn good. Would it kill her to acknowledge him? He was hurt some but swallowed his pride, reminding himself that he was a hard man from whom all slights bounce. He didn't want to alienate her. Hopefully, when she got over this Max thing, she'd come to him and finally understand why Ross and Ross alone deserved her love. For now, he'd play along. He told her not to undersell the kid.

"Be honest with him," he advised. "If you're not, it'll be hard on both of you."

She sighed deeply and looked up at him again.

"Alright. I'll try. But not straightaway. I want more happy memories first. I'll need them if he leaves me."

Harold Ross gave up.

"Have it your own way."

He promised her he would get the boys at the paper to shut their traps about her. He'd threaten to get them fired. Total clam up, he assured. No one would say peep to Max. Then he suggested she leave. Sassaport could be coming through the door any minute. He was never late. She gave him a quick hug and buss on the cheek. It was a gesture she rarely gave him. Once her back was turned, he put his hand up to cover the place where she'd kissed him and hated Maxwell Sassaport a little.

10.

That same afternoon, the *Journal* published a photograph of Mary Phagan's death note. The text was nearly illegible so they printed what it said in clear typeset letters alongside. The *Journal* then questioned whether a white child who kept a diary and wrote in it often, one who penned letters to her cousins with far more properly executed grammar than expected from a factory girl, would have risen from her death throes to write:

> *mam that negro hire down here did this. I went to make water and he push me down that hold a long tall negro that hoo it wase long sleam tall negro I wright while play with me*

Thanks to the genius of Harold Ross in securing information from inside sources, they also printed the text of the second note, the one they did not have in their possession.

> *he said he wood love me land down play like the night witch did it but that long tall black negro did boy his self.*

The words themselves condemned every black man living within twenty miles outside Atlanta. There wasn't a soul in the county who didn't know black patois when he heard it.

"There are monsters preying upon our girls!" the caption to the notes read. The article beneath them began "They are monsters who would put words in their mouths after murdering them!"

The city erupted. The authorities were bombarded by demands for an arrest. Factories all over the city, not just National Pencil, were picketed and vandalized. White men assembled under the Stars and Bars to denounce the common practice of hiring black men and boys to work the same factory floor as young white girls. Women who'd never labored outside the home for a day in their lives marched down Peachtree protesting promiscuity in the workplace and society at large. Their posters pictured caricatures of Negro fancy men with huge lips and tight pants hovering, mad-eyed, over sweet blond children. In the parks, black preachers on soapboxes exhorted all in earshot to remember the love of Jesus who desired only the peace of brotherly love. They attracted few listeners. On the sidewalks, blacks and whites practiced an exaggeration of their usual separateness, keeping apart over greater distances than normal. Each feared violence from the other.

On the third day after Mary Phagan's corpse was discovered in the basement of National Pencil, Leo Frank was arrested and charged with rape/murder. The detectives on the case liked Frank best for the crime from the beginning. He had those bug eyes, that girly voice. He stuttered when he answered questions. Mary's friends said he often came into the knurling room and tried to flirt. They were scared of him. He looked at them too long, long enough to make them squirm. He was a Jew Yankee. A murderer for sure.

The police had more suspicion than evidence until they questioned Jim Conley, the black factory janitor who became their chief witness against Frank. Conley was the sole employee working that Confederate Day until the night watchman came on. His testimony was sure to convict their man. It expanded from day to day. At first, Conley told them that Frank promised to pay him if he guarded his office door when the girl arrived. He did but never saw his money. Next, he said Frank brought him to the knurling room where the poor girl lay dead and forced him to move the corpse from there to the basement. A day later, he swore that Frank dictated to him the content of the death notes, which Conley had scribbled out of fear. He was drunk every moment of his interviews. The police wanted to believe him so badly they did.

When he walked to work the morning after Frank's arrest, Max saw uniformed officers strutting back and forth on the sidewalk in front of The Temple, twirling billy clubs like batons at a parade. He crossed the street, identified himself to them as a member of the press, and asked what was going on. He was told there'd been threats against the synagogue by those who considered Frank guilty. Everywhere he went that day—on the street, at the lunch counter, in the pressroom—Max heard mutterings about the Jews, the Jews, the Jews. He blocked his ears to it. When he was a child, he'd asked his grandfather why Jews were hated in the old country. Zeyde lifted his shoulders, pointed his mouth down and said, "When did the world love Jews?" He warned him it wasn't just the old country. Pogroms could come to America too. Max didn't believe him. Pogroms in Georgia? Bullies and bigmouths maybe. But people who'd quarter your body and rape your mother? He'd had a hard time imagining it. Now vile images came easily. "Always keep your eyes open but mind your own business," Zeyde advised. He tried.

Spring turns to summer on a dime in Atlanta. By the first of May, citizens sought refuge from the heat. They lived outdoors on porches and fire escapes as much as they could. Swarms of gnats hovered heavy over the ground, rising through the thick, humid air at the first scent of human sweat. Citronella candles sold out on shop shelves and lit up more homes than gas jets. Wherever there was a stretch of grass, fire ants and snakes woke from their winter slumber to plague the unwary. By May, the most pious Atlantans doubted God had ever given man dominion over the earth. Certainly, he had little command over biting, slithery things.

Harsh weather and civic strife are volatile companions. Everyone was vehement about the Frank case. The black community was against him completely. The white was split but more blamed Frank than not. The Jewish community lined up stalwart behind him. Tempers flared in homes, at businesses, and in the street.

Dark Sally's was not immune. The manager hired additional bouncers to keep the peace. Max and Ruby weren't aware of them. They'd been unable to tryst there for lack of funds. Cheap as they were, the low end rooms at Dark Sally's were out of reach on a regular basis. But after Max had an exceptional weekend selling junk and Ruby skipped a few meals, they had enough between them to secure a room. They made a plan for a Tuesday night. Both walked on air the entire day in anticipation. They were pleasant to everyone they met and hummed popular songs about love while they worked. Ruby met the thoughtless little insults from the knurling room girls with smiles while Max met the complaints of a bad-tempered Harold Ross with apologies for wrongs he'd not committed.

Outbursts from Ross were new. He was a man who prided himself on his emotional restraint. "A journalist needs to keep his thoughts and feelings to himself," he told Max on more than one occasion. "I don't care what the provocation. Get yourself a poker face. A poker heart too." The idea that he was jealous of the lovers never occurred to Max. He figured Ross suffered under the pressure to deliver the fresh Mary Phagan items the Chief needed daily to feed the public's maw. Every paper in four counties along with wire services across the country interviewed every friend, relative, and coworker Mary Phagan ever had. They encouraged Frank's neighbors to reveal tidbits about his wife and in-laws. Some days, there were forty special editions about the murder hawked all over the city. Competing with all that, who wouldn't erupt from time to time?

That night, Max arrived at Dark Sally's first. The couple's savings were in his wallet. He spoke with the night manager who offered him a key to room twelve. It had a feather bed, he told him, and a washstand. He paid extra for it.

He sat at the bar fidgeting. His heart beat so hard he thought it might bust out of his chest. His feet tapped the bottom rung of his bar stool, his fingers the top of the bar. When Ruby walked in, his chest swelled with feeling. His shoulders went back, his neck got longer. He slid off the barstool and walked toward her, meeting her halfway.

They were finally together. It brought out the kid in them. Too excited to stand still, they bounced on their toes, talked at the same time, laughed, and tried to talk again with no success. They gave up to fall silent, oblivious to the world, all the while standing alone, eight inches apart, in the middle of Dark Sally's dance floor. They beamed like the joyous, beautiful children they once were, taking deep breaths to wrest control out of the delirium of being together at last. Their chests rose and fell in unison.

It was quite a show. Patrons of Dark Sally's front room devoured it each in their own way. Half felt sharp stabs of sentiment recalling first loves. The other half smoldered with resentment that life had not granted them much love and never would. An old whore with ink black hair sighed. The man with her put his arm around her and squeezed in a tender way.

As if to balance things, a drunk left his station at the bar and stepped up close behind Ruby while making monkey faces. The couple didn't notice. The drunk didn't favor being ignored. He made grunting sounds and scratched at his underarms. That Max heard. His blood rose high. He pulled Ruby aside, stood nose to nose with the jerk, hauled back, and punched him in the jaw. Max wasn't the strongest puncher and he had no technique. It was the first punch he'd ever thrown in all his life, but he took the drunk by surprise. He crumbled.

Dark Sally's night manager rushed over, bent down, and spoke to the groaning man writhing on the floor.

"Commissioner, sir," he said, "are you alright? Shall I get a doctor?"

While he bent over the man, a burly bouncer positioned himself behind Max. The manager gestured with one arm to the lovers. His meaning was clear: scram.

He meant leave the premises, but Max had a key to a room he'd paid dearly for in his pocket, one with a real door, a featherbed, and a washstand. While everyone crowded around the manager, waiting for the Commissioner to come to, Max held fast to Ruby's hand and ran up the stairs. He found room twelve, opened it, and locked them in. The love they made was quick, hard, and euphoric. They talked for a while and made love again, this time slowly, easily, as if they'd made love together for a thousand years.

In the morning, Ruby left first. Max got ready for work at his ease, touching a still warm spot on the bed as lingeringly as if it had been her flesh. A dazed warmth pervaded him when there was a loud, persistent knock on the door. It was the night manager. Max came alert.

"Kid," he said, "you made a mistake last night. The man you socked is County Commissioner of Public Safety. He's gunnin' for you. Lucky for you, he don't know your name, mostly 'cause I don't neither. The lid stayed on last night, but sooner or later the Commish is goin' to sober up. Point is you can't come in here again. I say this for your own good. Now, you tell Ruby she ain't comin' in here again neither."

He turned to go then turned back.

"Between you and me, kid, have caution there," he said. "A woman like that makes trouble wherever she goes."

Max noted that he knew Ruby by name. He spoke in a journalist's voice of command, sharp, curt, rude.

"What do you know about her?"

The night manager blinked but gave nothing up.

"Look. You do what you want," he said. "Ain't no business of mine. But the Lord made something out of that gal that can irk the soul."

Max cursed then packed up his knapsack. He was anxious to quit the room. He didn't press the man further. He passed him, wordless, on his way to the stairs.

"It ain't her fault," the night manager said softly to his back.

When Max told her they were banned from Dark Sally's, Ruby remarked at least they'd had one glorious night. She'd never forget it. He agreed. They looked for another place to be.

At first, they met under the cover of darkness at the park near National Pencil where Max sold his finds on weekends. Police patrols had increased there since Mary Phagan was murdered, especially at night. Twice, they'd nearly been discovered. Their options narrowed. They were on fire for each other. Both put their minds to finding a new trysting spot. It was Ruby who found one.

Pushing her mop at the factory, Ruby first wondered if maybe they could meet at Harry's place. He wouldn't have to know. It was a terrible thought. Each time it came to her, it shamed her. She'd shudder and push it away. But it kept coming back until she found another option.

Ruby knew there were places in the factory, broom closets and supply rooms, where workers who needed privacy sometimes met, Jim Conley and his women from outside among them. She followed their lead and found her own, a good-sized storage closet at National Pencil that had fallen into disuse. It had a large shute in the wall that opened up into a derelict trash bin in the alley. Ruby was inspired. She met Max in the alleyway in the dark of night and instructed him to take a shovel and bang on the outside arm of the shute until it pointed up so it could catch a breeze. They'd have fresh air coming into the closet. They wouldn't suffocate. Next, she cleaned the floors and shelves with lye. It was her job to clean. No one took notice.

Once the closet was ready, Ruby hid in the factory after hours. When everyone but the night watchman left, she ushered Max in through one of the worker gates. He brought food and drink and a blanket. They spread it all on the cement floor and took pleasure in each other. They tried to meet every day. Max didn't bring the blanket on the hottest days because the cement felt cooler. Those nights, one or the other came up with bruises. They considered them badges of love.

Despite such limitations, they settled into a fractured life made bearable by the hours they shared together, unencumbered by the world. They talked about getting to Illinois or Ohio where blacks and whites could marry each other. When the time came, they'd have to travel separately. They wouldn't be safe from here to there together. They'd have to pay for separate rooms at separate boardinghouses if the weather turned too rough to sleep outdoors. They'd have to eat in different restaurants, if they could afford restaurants at all. If they managed to take a train, they'd have to sit in separate cars. They needed a lot of money for that. The costs added up.

Whenever there was a breakthrough in the Mary Phagan investigation and the press caught wind of it, the lovers could not meet. The factory swarmed with journalists who'd failed to find anything new at the police station or the courthouse. They picked over the bones of the investigation on-site, re-questioning factory girls and managers both, hoping to find a chunk of meat to feed their readers. They would have discovered the lovers in the first hour.

Breakthroughs in the case meant that Max had to work anyway. In early May, the inquest was held. Prosecutors provided a vivid portrait of Frank as a man of violent, perverse nature. But when he was questioned, he presented himself convincingly as a man of tame temperament, a quiet, reasonable man, an honest man. The two faces of Frank gave the public much to chew on although their conclusions were predictable. Community opinion boiled down to gentile against and Jews for. Firebrands preached against Jews in the streets. Caricatures of black men hovering over white children faded away and hooked-nosed Jews replaced them. Max passed by The Temple. After the inquest, its guard was doubled. When he mentioned to Harold Ross the increased security at the synagogue, Ross gave it to him as an assignment.

"You're a Jew, aren't you?" he asked.

People usually didn't guess Max was Jewish. He didn't look like the Jew in their heads. His surname was foreign enough to Georgian ears to indicate a dozen different origins. Max nodded, wondering how Ross knew. Ross nodded back.

"Good. If anything happens at The Temple, I want you to make sure I'm the first to know."

By the end of May, a grand jury was convened. The jury was read an affidavit from Nina Formby, operator of a shady rooming house, who claimed that Frank had called her numerous times the day of the murder trying to arrange a room for himself and a young girl. The same day, the *Georgian* reported two men, a carnival worker and an insurance salesman, volunteered to testify that a drunken Conley had confessed to killing Mary Phagan, first to one then to the other, the day of the murder. The prosecution dismissed their stories. Conley's lawyer, William Smith, made a statement to the *Journal* that the tall tales of Conley's confessions were false, he'd never admitted to the crime but "unseen forces" had pushed the carney and the salesman to influence the jury in the most craven manner. Harold Ross read Tom Watson's article on the slander out loud in the pressroom. Max spoke up.

"Sir," he said, "those 'unseen forces', you do know what it means?"

Ross nodded his head, took in smoke from his cigarette, blew it out.

"Yes. Your people. The Jews," he said. "Look kid, it's not from me, it's what the man said, I'm quoting him. The *Constitution*, the *Georgian* will do the same."

Max winced at reference to Tom Watson. His newspaper was not only anti-black. It was anti-Semitic as they come and popular. Ross sounded too casual about Watson's slurs and Smith's innuendos. Max squared his shoulders. He did something he'd never done before: called Ross by his given name.

"It's not right, Harold," he said.

Ross screwed up his mouth and stared at him until an idea came.

"Do an interview with the rabbi over at The Temple," he said. "We'll run that too."

Max trollied then walked to the office of Rabbi Marx at the back end of The Temple just beyond the sanctuary. When he went off Spring Street and onto Peachtree, two young toughs in a horse-drawn cart yelled "Yid!" and tried to run him down. Max jumped into a row of bushes lining the sidewalk. The toughs rolled on down the street, laughing and whooping it up. Max grit his teeth and brushed himself off, recalling Zeyde's pogroms. Dear God, he thought. Not in Atlanta. Not here. Isolated incident, those boys. Isolated. So far.

The rabbi was in. He answered his door, looking suitably refined, dressed in a seersucker suit, starched collar, and tie.

By way of introduction, Max reminded him of the young man from the sticks he'd found sitting by himself in the sanctuary some months before. "Of course I remember you. Young men don't often show up in my pews in the middle of a weekday." Max thought he would add, "Why haven't you prayed with us?" But there was none of that. Max told him he was now a reporter for the *Journal*. Might he ask the rabbi a few questions?

"No one's asked me for an interview yet, can you believe it?" Marx said. "Come in."

The rabbi guided him to two great chairs in a book-lined foyer. They took their seats. Marx offered a defense of Frank based on his sterling character and service to the community, donor to The Temple, president of their chapter of B'nai Brith. Max told him about William Smith's rejection of Conley's two confessions. The "unseen forces" dismayed the rabbi considerably.

"Off the record, son," he said, "I didn't know people here hated us that much. Some, maybe. But now . . ."

He gave Max the date of a meeting of the Jews of Atlanta he'd put together. He hoped to mobilize efforts in Frank's favor. He gave him a list of Frank's gentile supporters. There weren't many. When they were finishing up, Max asked him,

"Do you think the mood of the city will escalate to a pogrom, sir? If Mr. Frank is found guilty?"

Rabbi Marx put a hand on his shoulder, squeezed.

"Maybe," he said.

He made a short sound that was half laugh, half groan, a rueful, ancient sound.

"It might be worse if he's found innocent."

Max wrote up the interview and showed the result to Ross. Ross drew red lines through a pile of it. "No need to light a match next to a bonfire, kid," he said as he crossed off any reference to pogroms. He kept enough, though, including the date of the mobilization meeting, and the familiar names of powerful, wealthy Jews who would attend. He gave Max a byline. It got the cub attention. Men in the pressroom congratulated him. It didn't change anything. Young toughs still roamed the streets looking for Jews. The ugly placards proliferated. Frank was indicted.

After the indictment, the attention of the press shifted to the most important players of the impending trial: the lawyers. Puff pieces were written about prosecutor Hugh Dorsey until the readers fancied him as much a hero as those by-gone cavaliers of the Confederacy. Dorsey's opinions on the case commanded lengthy columns in *Vanity Fair*, the *Georgian*, the *Jeffersonian*, and the *Constitution*.

Over at the *Journal*, Harold Ross worked those stories, too, but he was the first to report in depth on Frank's defense counsels, Rueben Arnold and Luther Rosser. In private, Harold called them Old Salt 'n' Pepper for their differences. Tall, blond, and handsome, Rueben Arnold was an earnest, trustworthy fellow everyone respected. He had a steel trap mind and perfect recall. The stories he built during cross-examinations were hard, clear, always perfectly logical. His practice did well. Luther Rosser was a more blunt instrument who battered his opponents into submission. He blustered his way through trials and negotiations, civil and criminal, quoting scripture, making his voice a trumpet of righteousness. He was rarely seen in a tie or cravat, it was said because his throat was his weapon and the sight of it red and bulging bowled over jurors and officers of the court alike. His practice did very well. The two of them together made a formidable team but in the minds of the public, a suspicious one. Atlanta found it inconceivable that anyone would defend a beast like Frank. How could they sit in the same room and not strangle him? What were the shysters up to? The *Journal* gave them answers, separating fact from rumor, reminding its readers of the right of the accused to a fair and impartial trial, and pointing out hypothetical flaws in the reported evidence.

The other papers wasted no time catching up. Reporters gathered outside the attorneys' homes and offices every day to yell out questions. Rosser believed in throwing them a bone from time to time and was more forthcoming than Arnold. His sharp wit was more entertaining than his co-counsel's too. Ross called him a newshound's holiday because "he's quick with the quotable quip." Most of the senior pressmen staked out Rosser's place while the cubs kept watch on Arnold's.

The trial was slated to begin on the twenty-eighth of July. Two weeks before, Max lounged with the others at the front gate of Arnold's building. All morning, he'd had the feeling something was going to happen. His fellow cubs agreed. A raw charge was in the air.

Midday, a cab pulled up. A woman emerged. She was an immediate curiosity. The cubs flocked to her. Max had a view of her from the back. Tall, angular, with a stovepipe hat and a boa around her neck, a puffy white shirt tucked into a long black skirt that recalled the last century. No Atlantan wore skirts that long anymore. Especially in the summer heat. He joined the others swarming around her. "Are you a witness in the case, m'am?" they asked. "What's your name?" "Where are you from?"

She didn't answer. Max still couldn't see her face. He jockeyed around his mates to get a better look when her glass eye caught the light and in the next second, blinded him. He couldn't see any of her for a moment but it didn't matter. He knew who it was. Mayhayley Lancaster.

A cloud covered the sun. Mayhayley and Max observed each other eye to eye. She, of course, was unmistakable. He wondered if she knew him. Despite the years since he sat with Bull Johnson in her cabin, she did and nodded. The cubs between them shouted more questions. She turned into Arnold's entryway. Max shouted loud enough to drown out the others: "Miss Mayhayley! Are you here as a prophetess?" She squared her shoulders without turning around and laughed from deep in her belly. "I am here as a lawyer!" she said. She walked mockingly, haughtily to Arnold's door where she was promptly welcomed in.

The others crushed around him. "Who was that?" "How do you spell her name?" "How do you know her?" "What did you mean prophetess?" He threw them a few crumbs so they'd let him go. As soon as they did, he went straight to the *Journal* and wrote a headline on his own authority.

The Seer of Heard County Arrives to Defend Frank

Underneath it, he wrote down everything he knew about Mayhayley Lancaster, teacher turned landowner, midwife, churchgoer, and sought after seer. Her reputation had blossomed since he and Ruby were kids. Her home of a Sunday afternoon often hosted a row of cabriolets and automobiles within which clients waited for their turn at her wisdom. He described the stacks of books in her cabin, wrote about the glass eye and the dollar and a dime. He remembered that before he left home, his mother told him she'd heard Miss Lancaster was studying law.

Hot damn, he thought. Crazy woman done it. Become a lawyer. When Ross arrived at the pressroom straight from an interview with the judge in Frank's case, Max showed him his work excitedly. It was the first time he could provide the inside dope on a spectacular scoop.

"Well, this is interesting," Ross said.

"I've known her since I was a kid, Harold," Max told him, having got used to using his given name. "My girlfriend and I availed ourselves of her services once, and I can assure you she is the real McCoy."

"Your girlfriend?" Ross said, acid on his tongue.

"Yeah," Max said. He knew by now that Ruby worked for Ross weekends and he wanted to add "your maid" but he couldn't let Ross know that much. It wasn't safe to let anyone know about him and Ruby. Even her friend, Harry. Maybe especially him.

Ross rewrote his headline and article.

One-Eyed Witch to Assist Frank Defense

Max thought it wrong to whittle down who Mayhayley was to one-eyed witch, but he had no control over that. At least Ross didn't change too much of the text. Ross shared the byline with him this time. When the edition came out, he bought an extra copy for Ruby.

The headline caused a small frenzy. Reporters swarmed Arnold's home and office daily hoping for another encounter with Mayhayley Lancaster. There were many efforts to find out where she was staying in Atlanta, but all came up short. It baffled the press that such a distinctive woman so eccentrically dressed would be hard to find.

The next time she was sighted was neither at Arnold nor Rosser's establishments but at National Pencil where Max was on his way to the factory to join the other newsmen gathered there, waiting for something to happen. Much to his surprise, he saw Mayhayley appear from out of nowhere in the street. He tailed her to the back entrance of the factory then followed her through the visitor's gate to the second floor. As always, a gaggle of newsmen lolled about in the hallway between Frank's office and Mary Phagan's workroom. On seeing Mayhayley, they snapped to. A boring news day suddenly became bright and sharp. They piled around her.

If Mayhayley had a flaw, it was that she liked attention and adorned herself to get it. The day she appeared at Arnold's, she'd dressed to create an air of feminine mystique while at the factory she attempted to cultivate a tone of professionalism. She wore a man's cap and motoring jacket with goggles hanging by a strap around her neck. Her shirt, tie, pants, and boots were decidedly conservative. Her sole flamboyance was a black velvet eyepatch on a red ribbon. Clearly, it pleased her to pose for a photograph and answer questions. Her chin went up, enjoyment graced her lips. She winked. She told the press that she stayed at a cousin's house and that her sister, Sallie, was with her. She confirmed she was working for the defense. She'd come to the factory to investigate. She didn't tell them exactly what aspect of the case she investigated but she asked for silence while she did so.

Scribbling away on their pads, the gentlemen of the press traipsed behind her as quietly as they could. They watched while she stood in front of the elevator and put her hands on the door. She closed then opened her good eye, oblivious to the flash of light bulbs. After a few moments, her hands slipped away. She walked across the landing to Frank's office and swept a palm over the desk. She placed two hands against the safe outside the door.

Mayhayley was not very interested in Mary Phagan's lathe, although a few strands of golden brown hair were found on it.

The prosecution thought the hair evidence of a struggle at her station before she was murdered. Mayhayley regarded it quickly, even dismissively, and ascended the stairs to the next floor where she ran her hands over more furniture and machines. She descended to the packing room. The last shipment had gone out for the day. No one was there but Ruby, who washed a corner of wood floor on her hands and knees. Mayhayley saw her and nodded recognition as she'd done earlier with Max. She spoke to the men following her.

"That's it, I'm done. All y'all can leave now. Only you, young man," she said, pointing at Max, "you stay right t'here."

The others clamored that an exclusive for the *Journal*'s cub was unfair. Mayhayley asserted a legal right to be unmolested and threatened to put a witch's curse on them if such rights were not respected. She herded them out, shut the door. They hovered on the other side, ears to the wood.

Mayhayley, Ruby, and Max huddled at the far end of the room to frustrate the eavesdroppers. Mayhayley grinned.

"So. You are together again at last. Just as I said."

They grasped hands and said yes.

"And here I am too."

They said yes again. Her features grew serious.

"Then listen to me. You are both in danger. More'n you know. There are dire events ahead. You should leave here. Max, your mother will need you soon. Don't forget her."

She said no more and left. When she opened the door, the men clustered against it gave way, parting like the Red Sea. They swarmed Max, demanding a morsel of whatever it was Lancaster told him. Ruby flattened herself against the far wall. Max held them off and led them back to the hallway before they could notice her. The lovers managed to share a surreptitious glance that said: "Be careful, I love you, we'll talk tonight."

Max pondered what Mayhayley meant by his mother needing him. They wrote to each other every week. There wasn't anything unusual in her last letter. He wondered if she was keeping secrets from him. Then he pondered what the Seer of Heard County said about him and Ruby. They were in danger.

When they met later that day, Max told Ruby about the toughs near Rabbi Marx's office.

"I haven't had that kind of trouble since we were kids," he said.

"It never stopped for me," Ruby said. "Bullies ain't nothin' unusual to me and mine. But I will say it's worse in the city than the country."

Their spirits sank together. They shared a long embrace. Mayhayley's words rang in Max's head. Under more danger than they knew and dire things coming. He grasped Ruby more tightly. She moaned.

They agreed. Half the city considered both their peoples a shade to a signpost less than human. Leaving sooner rather than later sounded a good idea. If only they had money. Then maybe they could flee.

11.

The day of jury selection for Frank's trial, Harold Ross was occupied following up on a confidential lead. If he chased his lead hard enough, he'd have an exclusive. He couldn't be in two places at once so he assigned Max to cover jury selection. Max wanted to know what made his interview so imperative he'd give up a major story to his junior.

"Now if I told you, it wouldn't be confidential, would it?" Ross's eyes were unusually bright. "Besides, I trust you. You'll do a good job."

He whistled a popular tune. The interview must be really big, Max thought. Harold never whistled a popular tune.

"When I get back, you'll know," Ross said. "We'll tack your article onto mine. Take a photographer. He'll help us fill up a couple pages. The chief will be pleased. I'll talk him into giving us an extra."

"This is what we've been hoping for, Ruby," Max said that night. "Your pal Harry is giving me a lot more to do. Maybe I'll get another byline. I think soon I can ask the chief for a promotion and a raise."

Ruby ignored the "your pal" and advised him.

"Go easy. I know Ross better than you. He loves the limelight and doesn't like sharing it."

He considered and rejected her opinion. He could get support for a raise out of Harold. He knew he could.

"Sure, he's got a swelled head," Max said. "But he's always been fair with me."

He'd always been more than fair with Ruby too. She felt shamed for criticizing him and amended her advice.

"Just don't expect too much is all I'm saying. Don't inflate your ambitions and no one will stick a pin in 'em." She kissed him again, tenderly. "You always were a dreamer. You've never seen the world the way it is."

The body she held in her arms stiffened. He leaned away from her.

"Some reporter I must be in your eyes," he said.

She rushed to apologize.

"Max, I didn't mean it that way. I just meant you've got a big imagination." She gently pulled him back and kissed him lightly. Her voice went soft. "I always loved that about you." She kissed him harder.

He forgave her.

The morning of July 28, Max entered Atlanta's City Hall through the side entrance used by the press. It was the first time he'd been inside a courtroom. He rented a seersucker suit for the occasion from Harold's tailor and looked as elegant as his boss. His photographer was an older man known to all as Barney Tea. White-bearded with a waxed mustache that curled perpetually up, Barney Tea was famous in the city. He was the pearl of broadsheet shutterbugs. He had a fondness for bourbon, hence the "tea," but he carried it well.

Max walked down the narrow corridor to the City Hall vestibule with the photographer trailing behind. A mob of reporters milled about, smoking cigarettes and cigars, waiting for the courtroom doors to open. The company of Barney Tea raised his status in their eyes. A reporter from the *Constitution* twiddled a toothpick around his mouth and said, "I know you. You're Ross's man." Half a dozen heads turned toward him, including that of a visiting dignitary, a crime reporter from the *New York Times*. Max nodded and pulled his fedora down over his brow to look fierce. Inquisitive eyes lingered on him. The courtroom doors opened.

Havoc broke out. Pressmen pushed one another aside to get the best seats at the long table blocked off for them. Even the out-of-town reporters behaved like crackers. The press table filled up immediately with representatives of Georgian outlets—they'd all tipped the bailiff—and the fight began for the chairs in rows near it. The man from the *Boston Traveler* elbowed Max, nearly catching him in the eye. His hat was knocked to the floor. His feet were stomped on twice. The first time, it took him by surprise and he jumped back, granting the stomper access to the last remaining seat in the first row of chairs behind the press table. The second time, he steeled himself to hold his place no matter how hard he was stomped. Max achieved a seat in the second closest row. The reporter from the *New York Times* was on one side of him and the *Chicago Tribune*'s man was on the other. The press was seated. Barney Tea stood in the aisle ready to scout the entire room for the best shots.

The main doors to the building were opened next and before long, a stream of private citizens flooded the place. There were more of them than there were seats. Those without one sat or stood in the back, in the aisles, or on the steps up to the witness box and judge's bench. A court officer routed those too close. Gawkers locked outside took turns sitting on each other's shoulders to see what they could through the windows that were open due to the heat of the day.

The bailiff ordered the room to rise. Men still wearing hats doffed them. Judge Leonard S. Roan arrived in a flourish of black robes flapping like raven's wings at his sides. The judge was a stern man. He had a deep, solemn voice to match. Even outside of court, people did whatever he told them to. Inside the court, no one so much as coughed.

Roan climbed to a seat at his high bench, poured himself a glass of water, and told the lot of them he was about to ask the defendant, his lawyers, and the prosecutors to enter. He wanted absolute quiet while they did so.

Arnold and Rosser entered and went directly to their respective table. Dorsey and his men were right behind them. Necks craned. Some spectators rose from their seats for a better view. There were quiet murmurs as the lawyers passed. They intensified when Mayhayley Lancaster came in to join the defense table. They got louder still when armed court officers led Leo Frank's wife and mother into roped-off seats directly behind Arnold and Rosser. A man joined them but Max only saw him from the back and wondered who he was. Judge Roan banged his gavel. The assembled quieted before he had to shout.

A side door opened and the sheriff led the accused to the defense table. He was everything Max expected from Ruby's description and newspaper photographs: thin, neat, and bug-eyed beneath wire-rim spectacles. He hadn't heard the soft, girlish voice yet, but what he did with his arms, the way he sat and crossed his legs, presaged it.

The room crackled with tension. It struggled to obey the judge's order. Those observing from the windows had no such restraint. They raised their fists and swore at Frank. A multitude of cameras flashed in the defendant's face, Barney Tea's among them. Frank flinched and shrunk into himself.

He shifted his weight from one foot to the other and repeatedly moistened his lips with the tip of his tongue.

Max described the scene around him in his notebook, "A dozen shaking fists and the air thick with obscenities. No one's got close to the defendant yet. But the scent of riot is in the air." He jotted his opinions to the side. "Frank isn't helping himself," he wrote. "He looks guilty." The unidentified man with Frank's wife and mother turned to face the room and Max saw he was Rabbi Marx. He signaled Barney Tea to photograph him.

The judge banged his gavel against his desk. The bailiff called for order. Court officers fought their way through the crowd outside and pulled the most volatile observers away from the windows. Eventually, things quieted.

By most measures, the jury selection proceeded at breakneck speed. One by one, prospective jurors were paraded into the courtroom, interviewed, and either accepted or struck from the list by prosecution and defense. The defense turned to Mayhayley Lancaster each time a candidate took the stand. She'd shake her head or nod like a Roman emperor giving thumbs up or down. After making a show of asking the candidate questions, the defense followed her recommendations to the letter except when two black jurors were called. Mayhayley wanted them. The lawyers went against her advice.

Obstacles raised by Jim Crow ensured that blacks couldn't vote, but they paid farm tax and being on those rolls got a man jury duty. Arnold and Rosser saw that both black men before them were illiterate. They'd be sure to believe Newt Lee and Jim Conley over Frank. Dorsey could easily bamboozle them if he wished, which is why the defense struck them both.

Clearly, Mayhayley was not pleased. She slapped the desktop and glared at the lawyers who tried hard to appear unmoved. Her good eye burned a hole in Rosser's back while he questioned the next prospect. He mopped his brow with his handkerchief, but Max couldn't tell if he did so because he felt the heat of her glare or because despite the open windows, the room was hot as eternal hellfire.

Not half an hour into the proceedings, the whole room pulled out paper fans and fanned like mad trying to create some relief. Their fans read "Meecham's Seed and Feed" and "Dougherty's Funeral Home" on the back. Rosser removed his tie and loosened his shirt collar, making his famous red throat visible to all. The prosecution struck candidates for bias or those who expressed they were against the death penalty. In the end, the jury was white, middle-aged, male, Baptist, Episcopal, or Methodist, and middle class.

They looked a proper gentleman's gang. Max took down their names and occupations in his notebook. By the time the selection was over at one thirty in the afternoon, he was exhausted. His writing hand cramped. His brain buzzed. Judge Roan called a recess until three. Soon as his chamber doors shut behind his flapping black robes, the courtroom was released.

Max hustled at top speed to the City Hall pressroom set up in the basement. Commandeering a typewriter and chair, he sat down and typed furiously for an hour, surrounded by newsmen from all over the country doing the same thing. No one spoke, the click-clack of typewriters was the only sound in the room. For Max, it was like music. When he was done, he ran lickety split back up the stairs. He was in the courtroom by two fifty-five.

The jurors were sworn in. The defense and prosecution presented witness lists. The initial witness for the prosecution, Mary Phagan's tearful mother, established the activities of the victim before her death—an oatmeal breakfast, a trolley ride to the factory with the stated objective of obtaining her pay. George Epps, a boy who claimed to have met Mary on the trolley and converse with her before she disembarked at South Forsyth Street, testified she was afraid of Frank and asked him to protect her from his lechery. The night watchman and initial suspect of the police, Newt Lee, appeared, giving graphic testimony to finding the poor girl's corpse.

It was a strong beginning for Dorsey. Only an idiot would badger the dead girl's mother, and Rosser got nowhere with George Epps and Newt Lee. All efforts to poke holes in their statements failed. It got late in the day. Judge Roan dismissed everyone until the following morning, when Lee's testimony would resume. The trial had begun in earnest.

At the end of that first day, Max returned to the pressroom and worked far into the night. Barney Tea developed his shots and left them at Max's elbow. A janitor emptied wastebaskets and left. At two in the morning, he was alone, reassembling his notes, re-crafting his story. He knew it was a great stroke of luck that he was responsible for a report not just on juror selection but on the trial proper's beginnings. This could be his entrée into a promotion and thereafter, an idyllic life with Ruby in Chicago. It had to be superlative.

He'd been so busy, Ruby hadn't spoken with him in two days. She was restless, lonely. Long after midnight, she left her rooming house. She needed a walk. It was in the quiet before the sun rose, at an hour when even criminals sleep. She had her knife in her boot. She could wander where she pleased.

Before long, she found herself outside the *Journal* building, looking up at the sole light behind a pressroom window. Somehow, she knew it was Max and that he was by himself, knew it in her bones, her blood. She looked over her shoulders, one then the other. No one was near. She picked up a handful of pebbles and threw them at the window. They clattered lightly.

Max didn't respond. Max likely didn't hear anything. She tried again, throwing little rocks, ones some bigger than pebbles. The sound they made was hardly much louder. She gathered larger rocks, threw them. One after the other, they bounced off the building's brick. She threw harder until smack! one hit the window next to the lit up one. It made a noise loud as gunshot. The glass cracked. Alarmed, Max threw his window up to see what was going on outside.

Ruby. His beloved.

She looked more beautiful than ever. He glanced up and down the street. He saw the world had melted away for them, they were as alone in the middle of Atlanta as Adam and Eve in Paradise. He gave her a wide, welcoming smile and gestured for her to go to the service entrance then he ran down the stairs and let her in. They embraced, gloriously alone in the marble vestibule of Atlanta's finest newspaper. He took her upstairs.

"You shouldn't have come," he said. "The streets aren't safe anymore."

She gave him a pointed look.

"They never were."

Like naughty children, they stole into the chief's office to make passionate use of the couch. Afterward, they talked about Max's day in court.

He showed her the article he'd written. She read it, praised him then asked the questions she'd earlier avoided answering herself.

"What do you think? Did Frank do it? Or did Newt Lee? Or Jim Conley?"

He didn't want to pin the crime on black suspects. He assumed she'd bristle at that. She'd have to. He didn't want to hurt her. At the same time, he believed one of them must be guilty.

“It’s too early to tell,” he said, like a juror sent from heaven.

She nodded and kissed his cheek. He felt her body relax. She wasn’t prepared for confrontation either.

“I wanted to talk to Mayhayley afterwards,” he said, “but she left in a huff. People crowded her outside. She pushed her way through like a quarterback.” Max imitated the way Mayhayley’s shoulders moved, right then left. “Reporters couldn’t get near.”

Ruby credited his initial report on the one-eyed witch assisting the defense.

“You created a monster,” she said.

They talked about Chicago then, their golden city of dreams. When they got there, he’d try for a job at the *Chicago Tribune.* Matter of fact, he told her, he sat next to a *Trib* reporter at the trial; he got his card, he planned to lobby him. Max calculated the salary he’d make once his promotion came in.

“It’ll take a year,” he said, “but if we save our money, we can do it in style. A year from now.”

They made use of the couch again. Max straightened up, left his story on Harold’s desk, and walked Ruby home, watching over her from six paces behind as the streets were just coming alive. After stopping at his own place to wash and change, he returned to the *Journal* an hour after the dawn. Ross was there, reading his article.

“This is great, kid, great,” he said on noticing him. He sat back in his chair and lit a cigarette. “Look at this.”

He handed him his own piece, the exclusive. It was dynamite.

There were two parts. The first was an interview with madam Etta Mills, a competitor of Nina Formby who swore to police that Leo Frank telephoned her bawdy house numerous times on the day of the murder, trying to secure a room for himself and a young girl. She stated as he was a regular customer, she’d done her best to accommodate him, but he never showed up. Madam Mills contradicted all that, telling Ross that Nina Formby was an inveterate drunk, incapable of remembering the truth let alone telling it. She claimed Formby never heard of Frank before the murder hit the dailies. She couldn't have negotiated with him for a room.

"Why, she so drunk every day, she don't know a boot from a slipper. Her gals run roughshod all over her" he quoted Mills as saying. "I can't imagine what they steal or whose pockets they pick once they done with 'em. None o' that happens at my house. I run it honest."

She further extolled the character and behavior of her own girls, citing the cleanliness of her establishment as proof. (Ross wasn't sure if he should include a flagrant self-advertisement for a house of ill repute. The *Journal* was a family newspaper. He cut it out.)

Ross told Max that after interviewing Mills, he did his due diligence and went by Nina Formby's joint. He'd penned a description of its interior presuming most of his readers had never been in a like establishment.

"We bang the golden knocker shaped like a horned goats head. We gain entry through the red door. A slattern in a sheer nightgown worn open over a bustier, cautions we must clean our muddy boots against the threadbare mat. She guides us through a corridor lined in gilt mirrors in discordant order of size and shape. The floorboards creak."

The slattern in a nightgown brought him to a small office. A middle-aged whore with red circles painted on her cheeks sat at a desk in a cheap suit. She looked up from her paperwork. The door greeter introduced her.

"This the night manager, Miss Ethel."

Harold asked for Mrs. Formby.

"Mrs. Formby's asleep," said Ethel, which, given the woman's reputation, Ross took to mean Formby was passed out drunk.

Luckily, her night manager was impressed by the journalist, him in his well-cut trousers, shiny boots, and magnolia boutonniere. His wild, unkempt hair added a certain panache. Gentlemen didn't often come to Nina Formby's. Her clientele was a tad rough. The reporter saw all that and went to work.

Ruby's Harry could schmooze with the best of them. He got in a persuasive position, sitting on the corner of Ethel's rickety receptionist desk with grace and ease. He offered her a cigarette, which she took, whereupon he came up close to her with a flaming match cupped in his hands. His dark eyes looked deep into hers. There was longing in them, longing for a good story, a printable quote, maybe, but Ethel interpreted it as longing for companionship of the kind she and her coworkers could provide. Imagine that! she thought, taking a deep drag of the cigarette. A gent like him!

Poor woman was bedazzled. She fell for his tricks easily, answering his every question without pretense. Within seconds, she confided that Leo Frank was not and never had been a customer there. Her employer made it up to prevent a police raid then thought better of it. Given the fierce moral indignation of the public about the murder and the publicity that would surround her testimony, she decided none of it would be good for business and might even harm it. All she needed was a crowd of Holy Rollers picketing her house. Just that afternoon, Miss Nina swore up and down to Ethel she would never testify for the likes of Hugh Dorsey and his goddamn crew of arm-twisters. Never.

It was bombshell news, the kind of charged information journalists dream of.

"Apart from the publicity, why?" asked Ross, masking his excitement.

"Well, when Mr. Dorsey produced her affidavit, he made Miss Nina sound like the worst kind of slut."

Ethel and the *Journal*'s star reporter shared a snigger, considering sluts were Nina Formby's stock-in-trade.

After a flurry of editing and typing back at the pressroom, Harold Ross left for court. He would not miss any more vital developments if he could help it. Before he left, he directed Max to catch a couple hours sleep once the chief OK'd their copy.

"I need you shipshape this afternoon," he said.

He instructed Max to be stationed outside on the front steps of City Hall during the court lunch hour. Ross would cover the trial from inside, but they needed interviews with members of the community about its proceedings. He expected a buzzing hive of Atlantans standing on the steps every day, waiting to catch a glimpse, a word of the trial conducted inside. It was Max's job to gauge their mood as well as garner quotable opinions from the man-in-the street.

It was also up to Max to present their work to the chief.

The chief was impressed. The headline alone, *The Whore Lied*, delighted him. He wouldn't be able to print copies fast enough. He added a subtitle printed a few points smaller, *Frank Never a Customer.* He reviewed Barney Tea's courtroom photos, pushed out his lower lip and read Max's columns on jury selection.

"Good job," he said, "Keep it up, Sassaport. I've got my eye on you."

It wasn't a raise and it wasn't a promotion but Max considered the chief's praise a giant step forward.

Back at his room, Max tried to rest but he lay in his bed from eight to ten wide awake, staring at the ceiling, tossing and turning, too wound up to sleep. At last, he gave in, got dressed, and walked over to National Pencil hoping to catch Ruby on an early lunch break. He didn't find her but he touched the archway through which she passed daily as reverently as if it were a mezuzah. His mind hummed with visions of their perfect life together in Chicago while he rode the trolley to Atlanta City Hall.

He was several blocks away when the trolley screeched to a halt. The crush of humanity crowding all avenues to City Hall was impossible to plow through. The conductor clanged his bell to warn the horde of men clogging the streets to get away from his cab. It was about to advance. It revved up then screeched again. None gave way.

Max marveled at their sheer number. Trial of the century, the Yankee papers called it as if nothing more dire might occur in the eighty-six years to come before the current century closed. The citizens of Atlanta agreed. No one wanted to miss it. The trolley remained immobile for five minutes before the conductor gave up and opened the doors.

Max disembarked and walked, thinking he could wind his way through the crowd faster than the trolley ever could but found himself unable to break out of it. Men of all colors, stations, and backgrounds pressed together to become a single beast, a clumsy weaving millipede stinking of sweat and beer. He was jerked along, forced to move as the crowd moved and then he stopped. Everyone did. There was no going forward or backward without trampling one's fellows. They recognized there was danger in being part of a crowd where passions ran high. They were not yet a mindless mob. Each man held fast to his ground, waiting for news.

Intelligence from inside City Hall leaked out to the horde from time to time. It was transmitted by men standing near the open windows where they overheard everything going on or by the men on the steps who received bulletins from the guards.

Inside the courtroom, men spoke quietly into each other's ears to avoid the notice of the judge. But there was no such caution by the time information reached Max who stood a distance away outside. News was delivered near him by shouts over shoulders. Much of the information passed along mutated with each iteration. It wasn't the clearest way to determine how the trial progressed.

There was consensus on one point. It seemed indisputable that Newt Lee continued to withstand the fog of doubt Frank's attorneys attempted to throw over his two-hour testimony. It should have been easy to cast guilt on the man who found the body. But Newt Lee cut through their traps and insinuations fearlessly, impressing everyone. The whites in the crowd remarked on how smart, how certain that darkey Newt Lee was. Sure enough, he'd hang the Yankee Jew. "One in a million, that niggah," someone said and those around him chuckled. The first detective called held his ground as well. It wasn't that Arnold and Rosser weren't doing their jobs but that Dorsey had done his exceptionally well. His witnesses were expertly prepared, if not rehearsed, resolute under pressure.

"Did you see the witch outside?" Ross asked Max after court closed for the day.

He handed over his notes.

"No," Max said. "Wasn't she inside?"

"No."

They both thought that curious. Max volunteered to follow up on it.

"It must be about the black jurors. Why do you think she wanted them?"

"Beats me," Ross said. "The ways of adepts are alien to me. I'm just a humble reporter."

His cub smiled. Self-effacement was always a joke with Harold Ross.

"Right now, go home, Max. You look exhausted. I need you on your toes outside tomorrow. I expected the trial to have spectators, but turn's out half the city was there today. Try to arrive before the dawn and maybe you'll achieve a place on the steps or by the windows."

Ross wasn't wrong. Max was tuckered out. He left the *Journal* to shuffle his way back to his room, his head low, his thoughts fixated on what would happen to the Jews of Atlanta when Frank was convicted, a thing that seemed more likely today than yesterday. Unlike Ruby, he'd known about 1906 pretty much when it happened, when Atlanta erupted in two days of murderous violence against blacks. His father read aloud about it at the dinner table on the day their week-old newspaper came. Max remembered pictures of burning homes and storefronts, stories of children screaming, women attacked, their men bloody and mutilated. He hadn't thought much about it at the time apart from a brief sadness followed by the distractions of playing with Ruby and working Daddy's store. He was a kid. What happened in the city felt far away. Now it gave him much to worry about.

Focused on dismal histories, he didn't hear Ruby call out to him from an alleyway close to his rooming house at first. When he did, he quickly checked his surrounds for those who might see them, and ducked into the alley, to its darkest part, where she waited. He fell into her arms. For reasons he did not completely understand, he wanted very much to cry out, an impulse he resisted with what was left of his energies.

His head rested on her shoulder. She stroked his back as a mother might a child. She whispered in his ear.

"What do you think now, Max? Will he be found guilty?"

Max nodded against her neck.

"It's startin' to look like it," he said.

He felt her chest fill with air then slowly deflate. Max could not help but think her primary emotion was relief.

12.

Over the next few days, Max split his time between the outside the courthouse and a search for Mayhayley Lancaster. He had little luck finding the latter. He had nothing to go on. He grew depressed, thinking himself a failure. The idea that he'd have nothing to give Harold Ross was more than a disappointment; it was a setback. Then Ruby remembered the surname of Mayhayley's cousin, the one she told reporters she stayed with while in the city.

She'd tried to call the name up for days. She recollected early on that when she was seven or eight, her mama hired out her sister, Celia, for service at a wedding supper. The bride was one Vera Lancaster, blood relation to the seer. They were cousins of some kind. What stymied Ruby was the name of the groom. Vera would have her husband's name. That's the one Max needed. But Ruby didn't have it.

It came to her in her sleep. She woke one day and it just flew into her head. She sought out her lover immediately. When she found him, she near burst with happiness that she could do something useful for him.

"I recollected Vera married a man from Memphis," she said. "Mama and Daddy would joke about him. He was a farrier, name of Joe Colt. They found it so funny there was a farrier named colt."

They were in the street. There were other people some distance to the east and south. Taking a chance, Max grabbed her and kissed her, fast as lightening.

"Thank you, Ruby," he said. "You've saved me."

He had a name, a profession. It shouldn't be too hard, he thought, to track down Jim Colt. But he couldn't use the City Hall records—there was no one working in the building during the trial. He couldn't use the library. They were closed for the trial's duration too. Disappointed, he tried the *Journal*'s archives. They yielded unexpected fruit. That February, a farrier rescued a stable of police horses from a fire at a city barn. His name was Joe Colt. His address was included as he'd burnt his hands and the police set up a charity to solicit funds for his medical care.

The Colt's lived in an apartment in Bellwood, the hillbilly section of town. The front door of the building had round holes where doorknobs should be. Max put his hand through one and pulled back to enter. Inside, residents hoping to catch a cross breeze stood in the hallways outside their open doors or sat together on the stairs where it was cooler. Most of the talk was about the heat and the trial.

Addressing them all at once, he asked where the Colts lived. He was a stranger and as such, suspect. Chatter ceased. Men and women whispered to one another. No one answered him.

"I'm not a bill collector or the police," he announced, hoping to defuse suspicions.

He did not. Hillbillies are stubborn. They take no one but their own at his word. Max could be stubborn too. He knocked on door frames until at last a man tilted his head to the left while raising his eyebrows. Max moved to the left to stand square in front of the Colt's open door. He rapped loudly.

He expected a worn-out couple, gray-faced, subsisting in a flat as dreary as what he'd seen of their neighbors'. He expected Colt's hands to be stumps. But when he looked inside, he found a living room that was a celebration of color and knickknacks, little carved animals and birds. A guitar hung on a wall. The man who came to the door, Joe Colt himself, was well dressed and lightly bandaged. A few layers of gauze were wrapped around his palms and wrists. He used his hands well enough and held himself erect. His wife, standing behind him, a hand on his shoulder, was ruddy and fat.

Max introduced himself and mentioned his origins, that of a country boy born next to the town along the Chattahoochee where Vera had grown up. He asked if they knew the whereabouts of Mayhayley Lancaster.

"She gone to the woods," cousin Vera said. "Her and Sallie. She said a back-home boy might come lookin' for her."

Of course she did.

"Did she give you a message?"

"Why yes. She said I should tell him to think about her words . . ."

He let that sink in.

". . . and she said she'd see his woman again. In the by and by."

Good to know.

"Why did she leave? Did she quit Arnold and Rosser?"

Jim Colt snorted.

"Let's just say there was a row between 'em."

He shut the door. Max knocked again but they didn't respond. He rushed to the courthouse. It was the end of the day. Luther Rosser was on the City Hall steps, making a statement.

"I know you all are dyin' to ask me where our witch has been. I object to that appellation. Miss Lancaster is a practitioner of the law, a God-fearin' woman, and, as it happens, a bona fide sensitive, the like of which we have not seen since Madam Blavatsky passed on in '91. She contacted us some time ago and offered her services, as you know. Her purpose with us was to assist in juror selection. That task is done. Miss Lancaster has returned to her home."

All the papers reported on the exit of the one-eyed witch. Max's report had a line that hinted at trouble between the defense and the seer on the matter of black jurors. Ross thought it worthy detail, but the chief took it out. He considered it guesswork, not reportage. Max told Ross that if he got the chance he was going to ask Luther Rosser directly about the black jurors. The chief couldn't kill a good quote on it. It would be news then not speculation.

The trial heated up so fast, Rabbi Marx moved up the date of his community rally to support Leo Frank. He telephoned the *Journal* to let Max know. He left a message as Max was out on duty. That Saturday afternoon, when there was no court, Max went to him, hoping for a statement he could use alongside a notification of changed date and venue in the Events column of the *Journal*'s society pages.

"Why have you changed the date, Rabbi?" he asked.

"There's no time to waste." Marx said, in the tone undertakers use when speaking of the dead.

His solemnity confirmed Max's worst fears, but he bit the inside of his cheeks and put on the poker face Ross advised him to cultivate.

"The trial can't last more than another two, maybe three weeks," the rabbi continued. "I've moved the meeting to next Sunday, directly after services."

"Sunday services, Rabbi?" he asked. "Whose? I never had a synagogue to go to but I'm pretty sure our Sabbath's Saturday."

Marx's smile was wan but sincere.

"That's true. But we do things differently here."

"Why?"

"We added an extended morning prayer service on Sundays at The Temple. We've found it best to be as much like our Christian brothers as possible. Blending in with them is the American way."

"You mean it's safer."

The rabbi's hands were knit across his chest. He freed the fingers, lifted and wriggled them, then let them drop.

"There's nothing wrong with working to be safe, son. We still know who our God is," he said. "To tell you the truth, I can barely get a *minyan* Saturday mornings anymore. On the other hand, people love the Sunday service."

He rose from his chair to signify the interview was over. Max rose from his, his features emotionless.

"Are you afraid, Rabbi?" he asked.

"Fear has its place in keeping us safe," Marx said. "But, like everything, it can become excessive. I pray that most of the citizens of our city are well meaning, righteous of mind, and not the sworn enemies of the Jews. I try to behave as if this is true. Whether it is or not . . ." He shrugged much like Zeyde when there was nothing to be done.

It wasn't the most reassuring of declarations. More than ever, Max wanted to leave town with Ruby. During his trip back to the paper, he weighed how important his career at the *Journal* was to him, how hard it would be to give it up. He enjoyed his work, he thought he was pretty good at it. But he'd been pretty good at making money in Sassaport's Fabrics, Fancy Goods, and Notions, too, even though he'd longed to be free of it. There were likely many things he could do and be good at. He and Ruby needed to be safe and together, openly. That was the primary thing. If he had to, for her sake, he'd give up the newspaper. He'd work in a store, he'd work in a factory, in a field. With Ruby by his side, he'd be happy no matter what. Mayhayley was right. It was high time to quit Atlanta.

He planned to talk to Ruby about leaving straightaway when the chief called him in the office. He wanted him to report on the rabbi's rally. He promised a byline. It meant more money. The opportunity to do some good for the rabbi and make money for Chicago at the same time felt serendipitous.

The rally was called for noon. Rows of chairs were set up in The Temple's recreation basement. When Max arrived, he flashed a press pass to the Pinkertons hired for the evening's security and entered a room half full with worshippers who'd stayed on after morning services. Some still wore prayer shawls and yarmulkes. Their rabbi, standing at a dais set up for the occasion, wore neither.

People from outside the congregation arrived. Some went straight to the dais. Rabbi Marx greeted them with a solemn nod and outstretched hand. They spoke in his ear. Max attached himself to The Temple's president who filled him in on the identities of dignitaries. Among the hands the rabbi shook that day were those of the Montags, who recently added a paper mill to their National Pencil holdings, Victor Hugo Kriegshaber, officer of Atlanta Loan and Savings, as well as owner of a construction company, famous fine food purveyor Mayer Wolfsheimer, and Joey Hirsch, a prince of the rag trade and City Council member. In fact, the room was lousy with millionaire manufacturers and industrialists, bankers, and philanthropists. A handful weren't even Jewish. Some were Christian clergy. The pastor of the African Methodist Episcopal Church and the pastor of the Friendship Baptist Church were both attendant. Max was comforted by their participation. If the white men of

Atlanta rose up against the Jews, maybe the black pastors would persuade their people not to join them.

Rabbi Marx addressed the rally first. He spoke of Leo Frank's good name, of his charitable works within the congregation, for B'nai Brith and for the Hebrew Orphans Home. He extolled his family. He quoted scripture, with an emphasis on the Ten Commandments' prohibition of bearing false witness, and petitioned the assembled to pray for their brother languishing in the Fulton County Tower since his arrest more than three months ago. The Tower county jail was a place no one wanted to visit, let alone reside. Crowded, cold, and damp, a proper prison would be more hospitable. Marx spoke about the danger facing the Jewish community no matter what the verdict in the Mary Phagan case. He recalled 1906. Then he introduced the honored speaker of the evening, Mrs. Lucille Frank.

There was a hush of surprise. Those gathered shifted in their seats looking for her as she'd not made herself known. They found her at their backs, near the entry, flanked by her husband's attorneys, Arnold and Rosser. Lucille Frank was young, plump, the picture of upper-class health, dressed in a smart gray-striped skirt, a ruffled white blouse and short jacket, her hat a somber affair of black feathers and netting. She stood tall with gloved hands crossed beneath her bosom. Max remembered Ruby's account of her: "always with a sharp edge and hoity-toity airs." She didn't look so proud anymore. Everything about her was forthright, down-to earth. But she was one hundred percent knife-sharp, with an edge as lethal as the verdict planned for her husband.

She strode with purpose to the dais where the rabbi awaited her. Men and women rose as she passed. A few applauded softly. She addressed them in a strong, unwavering voice, a warrior of righteousness.

"My friends," she said. "Thank you for being here in my family's hour of need. It is a dark day for my husband. Leo is a good man. Not one among you who knows him can deny he is a man of quiet, wholesome character. You know that he is innocent."

A man in the crowd yelled out: "Yes! We do!" Men and women both applauded. Some stood to say "Amen." She put up her hands to quiet them.

"But we live in a time when there are evil forces afoot. They have decided to find a man, a Jew, as scapegoat, to punish us for our enterprise. And they have chosen Leo M. Frank. Until the end of April this year, I would have told you our Christian neighbors were incapable of what I have since seen with my own eyes since, cruelty and humiliation for the sake of it . . ."

In delicate language thick with metaphors employed to avoid disturbing the women present, she described the insults the police heaped upon Leo. The day after the murder, they stripped him naked, searching for scratches and bruises sustained in his supposed attack on Mary Phagan. They did this in a station office where four men stared at his nakedness, one a doctor with a monocle, which he lent to the others after he examined one of Leo's moles. One by one, they canvassed her husband's body. Of course they found nothing. She condemned the police persistence in investigating her husband after that. She condemned Jim Conley.

"This liar, this murderer," she said, "has put my husband's head in a noose. His version of events is ludicrous; he does it to save himself!"

She evoked the martyrs of Europe's pogroms and the Roma Curia. She led them in *kaddish*, the prayer for the dead. She continued.

"We must pray for the citizens of Atlanta to regain their senses, to come to a just resolution and free Leo M. Frank . . .

and if, God willing, he is free again, we must not forget that Tom Watson will not stop, his articles of hate will only increase. Dr. Poteat will not stop. He will preach louder in the Baptist Tabernacle, when he denounces our race. Men like these will not stop. Worse than that, thanks to the murder of Mary Phagan, the entire population of Atlanta has given our enemies their ears."

Max thought she would condemn the newspapers next. But she did not. At the conclusion of her address, she went to the small Ark of the Covenant that graced the basement. It was only used during the High Holidays when there was overflow from the main sanctuary above. She opened it and with one gloved hand on a Torah scroll inside, she made an oath.

"I swear to you what you all know in your hearts. I swear that my husband is innocent of this unspeakable crime. May the God of our Fathers protect him and us."

Men and women cheered. Ranks broke, well-wishers surrounded her and the lawyers, offering support. They praised the incarcerated and wrongfully charged. The rabbi took donations for the establishment of a new order, as yet unnamed, to combat the rise of the Klan. He hoped to attach it to B'nai B'rith. The funds would pay for armed Pinkertons to guard Jewish neighborhoods during the trial and whatever came next. It would enable his congregation to distribute handbills throughout the city that protested a rush to judgment while calling for calm and dialogue. It surprised Max to hear that membership in the old Klan had expanded. He thought the Klan pretty much died decades ago. According to the scuttlebutt going about the room, there was more harassment of Jews since Frank's arrest than any of the papers had reported. Many avoided traversing the city at night. Max took names.

He left the meeting convinced his people were in mortal

danger all over Georgia. After he filed his story, he met Ruby in their park at dusk.

"Rabbi Marx expects riots," he told her. "It could be worse than '06. I don't think we should stay here after the trial's over. I owe Harold and the chief the trial. But afterwards? Afterwards, we'd be idiots to stay here any longer."

He admitted they didn't have the grubsteak they'd set as a goal before leaving. They were still far from it. There wouldn't be railcars or hotels when it rained. Ruby considered.

"I came to Atlanta with nothing. I can leave it the same way."

Max's heart swelled, proud of her commitment and bravery. He'd pondered their eventual flight for a long time. He had a plan. It was a good one. They would leave the city separately and meet up outside it where brick and iron landscape gave way to country roads, fields, and woods. They could travel together when the route gave them cover and endeavor to stay in each other's sight when it did not.

He'd bought each of them a map. They unfurled them, spreading them against the ground. Max pointed out a meeting place he'd found, a small town just over the Illinois border called Juniper. They would endeavor to meet in Juniper if they became separated. From there, they'd head to Chicago.

"I wonder if we can get married in Juniper," she said.

He put an arm around her and kissed the top of her head.

"Wouldn't that be grand."

They pooled their money. Together they had fifteen dollars. It wasn't much but they'd be alright. They planned the best route and marked it on their maps. It grew dark. They decided to meet the following night at the same place. Recently, their closet at the factory had been put to use by the packing department. Meeting in the park was worth the risk.

In the meantime, they went back to their rooms and made lists of what they could take when the day to leave came. Ruby didn't have much. In addition to the clothes on her back, she had two more skirts and two more blouses along with a thick, heavy sweater she wore all winter. She had a good pair of shoes she cherished and a lady's felt hat. She kept an apron and two cleaning brushes at Harry's. They weren't much but they were worth money. She'd retrieve them after her last day of work at the factory.

Max could fit all the belongings he cared about into a knapsack. He put it on his shoulders to test its weight. It was heavier than it looked. He felt like Uncle Morris. He tried to write Harold Ross a letter of resignation, a formality he didn't need to perform. No one cared much when cubs quit. Cubs didn't explain, they just stopped showing up and were swiftly replaced. But Max felt he owed Harold something. He'd learned a lot from him. He liked the idea of Ruby cleaning for him more than he did Ruby cleaning for one of the other jamokes in the pressroom.

He started three heartfelt notes of resignation and balled them up. It was useless. Nothing sounded right. He ceased trying to tell the truth and gave Ross an excuse instead. The final note he hoped soon to employ read: "Family emergency calls me unavoidably away. Thanks for everything. I'll be in touch." He signed it Maxwell Isadore Sassaport.

He took his knapsack to the park. He wanted to show Ruby the items he'd decided to take and ask what she thought of his letter to Harold. He sat on their rock. He waited and waited.

Ruby never showed.

He panicked. He quit the park for her rooming house. She was gone. He ran to the factory. She wasn't there. His mind went wild. He imagined her half-dead in an alleyway. He imagined her run over by an automobile. He convinced himself maybe

Ross had secreted her away someplace, to keep her from him. He banged on Ross's door. No one answered. He considered breaking a window into Ross's living room, crawling through and searching for her. He picked up a rock from the street to do so. At the last moment, when his arm was raised rock in fist, he came to reason. The smarter thing to was to go to the press-room and confront Harold there. He'd wait all night if he had to. "What have you done with Ruby?" he'd demand. He imagined having to sock Ross in the jaw like he had the Commissioner of Public Safety at Dark Sally's. He didn't want to. But he would.

A sour mix of jealousy, anxiety, and courage propelled him to the *Journal* building. Ross was outside, about to enter. Max marched up to him and opened his mouth, ready to assail him.

He didn't have to. On seeing him, Ross grabbed him by the shoulder.

"I've been looking for you," he said. "Listen to me, Sassaport. Ruby's in danger. The police came for her. There was no saving her this time. They took her in."

Max couldn't talk. His lifted shoulders asked, "Why?"

Ross tightened his lips and spoke through his teeth.

"They've got her on some trumped-up charge. My sources tell me her name appeared on a list of defense witnesses for Frank," he said. "The prosecution wants to know why. They'll hold her in the Tower until they find out."

Insanity. The world gone mad. What could the defense in the crime of the century want with Ruby Alfreda Johnson?

"I need to see her," Max said.

Ross put a hand on his forearm.

"I know."

Max shook him off. He didn't ask Ross how or what he knew about him and Ruby. Either he'd figured it out or Ruby told him. What did it matter now.

"Honestly, Max, I know how you feel. I love Ruby too . . ."

Max blinked. Harold's affirmation pierced his mind. For Max, there was only one kind of love. Ross's words confirmed his fears that sometime or other, he must have been Ruby's lover. That hurt. Max had always supposed if there'd been a romance between them, it was over before he came to town. That didn't make the idea hurt less. He took a deep breath and stored his feelings away in a dark corner until later. It didn't matter right now. Nothing mattered except seeing Ruby at the Tower, getting her out of there. If he had to, he'd subdue her guard by brute force and carry her off. She belonged to him, not Ross. It was up to him to get her out.

"You can stand here and do nothing, Harold. But I'm going over there and . . . and . . ."

Ross lifted his eyebrows and tucked in his chin.

"And, what?" he said. "Break into the Tower in the middle of the night? It's the county jail, for Christ's sake! We wait until morning. There's nothing to be done about it tonight. In the morning, I can get us in there with a press pass. Patience is key. A cool head and patience. Ruby's a strong woman. She'll get through the night and whatever else she has to."

Max dropped the knapsack he'd lugged all over the city while searching for her. He covered his face with his hands. Visions of Ruby abused on a filthy prison floor assailed him. Ross put a hand on his shoulder and this time, he was not shaken off. He spoke as gently to Max as he had to Ruby the night he met her, back against a wall looking for a place to run.

"C'mon. Let's wait inside"

Soon as they were in the pressroom, Ross secured a blanket from an unlocked chest and spread it over three chairs pushed together.

"We need to grab a couple hours. We have to be sharp when

we're at the Tower. I'll sleep here. I've done it before. You can take the couch in the chief's office."

Max doubted he'd sleep at all. He'd be better off pacing the pressroom, staring out windows. Harold insisted he try.

He lay on the chief's couch thinking about lying there with Ruby, their moments of tenderness and ecstasy. He put his nose against the cushions but the scent of her was gone. He remembered Uncle Morris's redheaded widow and called out to Ruby with every bit of intensity old Persephone Adela ever possessed. 'Round midnight, he thought he saw her, arms outstretched, near enough to touch, but when he tried to reach his love there was only air.

Atlanta was a New South city built on the ashes of the Old. She was a firebird of rare plumage. Grand buildings sprouted from her ashes. Their marble, brick, and glass radiated freshness and novelty. Heroic sculptures graced her arches and porticos. The town was a model for all Southern cities yet struggling to recover from General Sherman, fifty years after he'd burned his way to victory. Factory money was Atlanta's rejuvenator. But it found few funds for the Fulton County Tower.

The Tower was a dark brick structure looming over Butler Street. Inside, it was a metal and cement cage. There were four floors of cells in the main jail, its prisoners separated by color and gender; the Tower itself rose three stories above it. A spiral staircase snaked its way through the Tower to a notched parapet at its summit, winding past guard posts set up at rectangular battlements the height and width of a man. The confined whispered among themselves that sometimes suspects or witnesses were taken there for convincing. The unconvinced were shoved out. Harold insisted the reports of death were myth. If anyone was ever murdered by police at the Tower, he'd know about it.

"All the cells aren't dismal," he said. "Some residents obtain favor."

He told Max that Leo Frank's cell had a couch and an armchair from home. His wife brought over fresh meals on tin trays draped in gingham. She spent part of every day with him. He was permitted other visitors too. Jim Conley's cell had a chair and table provided by Chief Detective Lanford along with warm blankets and hearty food. He was the man's pet until he could testify at the trial.

"Believe me," he said. "I know. I've interviewed them both."

His cub didn't need telling. Harold's interviews with the trial's suspects were the toast of the pressroom. While Conley gave interviews to anyone who asked, Frank had only ever given one and that to Harold Ross. It was before his arrest. After that, Frank spoke to no one from the press. It buoyed Max to think Ruby might be as important to Lanford as Conley. If so, she wouldn't suffer the worst of the Tower. But why was she even there? What value could she be to the defense? How could she know anything the prosecutor's chief detective didn't already know?

Max sat on a bench outside the warden's office when guards marched past him a line of black men shackled together, shuffling forward in leg and hand irons. The stench of pain and fear suffused the air. His hope faltered. Inside the office, Harold attempted to persuade the warden to allow him an interview with Ruby. It was taking too long. Max toyed with the camera he held. He didn't know how to use it properly. It was a prop for his disguise. Harold said a cub reporter would never be allowed inside a prisoner's cell. A photographer would. Max pressed the shutter lever up and down, up and down until the warden's door opened. Harold walked briskly out. He snapped his fingers at Max, who rose and followed him.

It turned out Ruby was not in the Tower proper. A guard took them to the third floor of the main jail. A foul smell came with them. They were taken past cages of white men sharing cells in twos and threes and ones of hard, miserable black women living cheek by jowl, eight to a cell. Ruby's cell was a dank slab of barred cement down a dim corridor far from the other prisoners. She might as well have been in solitary confinement. The cell was bare, windowless. There was only a metal bed hanging from chains on the wall, a pot, and Ruby who sat on a threadbare mattress with her head down. She looked up to see who wanted her, brightened, and stood up straight, alert and still. The guard unlocked the door. Harold palmed him a few bills and he backed away, out of sight.

The lovers embraced. They murmured into each other's necks. Kissed. Harold Ross leaned against the bars of the cell door, hands in his pockets, an unlit cigarette at his lips, watching them with his poker face. After a few moments, Ruby pulled back. She smiled then broke from Max to embrace Harry also, with a lighter touch, of course, but with the same sincerity. She went back to her lover. They stood together, holding hands. They looked solemnly at Harold. He didn't know if they were asking him to leave or were waiting for him to tell them what to do. He took charge.

"So, Ruby," he said. "What's this all about?"

She sighed deeply.

"I don't know. They say I stole something from the factory. But that's a lie. They can't even tell me what it was. They keep asking me about Jim Conley. They ask about him more than they ask about Mr. Frank."

"What do you tell them?" Max asked.

"Pretty much what I told you. I mentioned he spends a lot of time drinking in the basement. I don't know if I should have told them that. They got all quiet when I said it."

"Have you been contacted by Arnold or Rosser?"

"No."

"The warden told me that the defense wants you as a rebuttal witness against the prosecution's version of Jim Conley. Lanford and Dorsey's been cleaning him up and drying him out for weeks. William Smith rehearses his testimony every day. He'll come off a sober, honest man. They can't have you undermining that."

Harold asked her questions his cub didn't understand about mistaken identities and a dust-up at the factory a couple months before the murder. Max didn't give her a chance to respond. He squeezed her hand and spoke in her ear.

"What's he talking about?"

Her lips quivered, her eyes filled.

"Oh, Max," she said.

"Christ, I'm sorry," Ross muttered. "I didn't think."

Max hated that Ross knew things about Ruby he did not. He looked from one to the other without saying a word until Ruby took him to the bed and sat down with him. She told him everything about the altercation with Mary Phagan and how Mr. Frank's director got her arrested.

"Harry saved me," she said. She dropped her voice to a whisper. "He bribed the police."

It wasn't soft enough. The guard who took Harold's money had inched back down the corridor toward them and, flattened against the wall, wrote down every word.

"I'm grateful to you, Harold," Max said and he was but it came out in a voice colored by his envy of the bond Ross shared with Ruby, whatever the Sam Hill that was.

He turned to the prisoner and, with effort, made his tone caring, calm. He told her she should never be afraid to tell him anything, no matter what. He thought she knew she could trust him.

"There are hard things in my life I don't like revisiting," she said, as if trust between them was never a question.

They kissed again. Harold coughed and spoke.

"I think I can get you moved to a better cell."

Max had no power to affect improvements in Ruby's life in jail. He thanked God Ross did, despite the bitter taste it gave him at the back of his throat. He swallowed enough of his pride to thank him a second time.

"That'd be great, Harold," he said.

The warden had given them half an hour. It was nearly up. The lovers stroked each other's backs and whispered together. The guard reappeared and banged his club against the bars.

Harold Ross said, "C'mon, Max, we have to go."

There was a catch in his voice. Neither man wanted to leave her. They left promising to return.

"Courage!" Ross said, raising a clenched fist in the air. Max did likewise.

They went from the Tower to City Hall where reporter and cub took up their stations in and out of the courtroom. At the end of the day, they returned to the *Journal* and wrote their reports, sitting side by side. Max finished first. He handed his work to Harold who barely looked up from his Underwood. He pounded away at the keyboard as if Max wasn't there. Just as well, Max thought. He wasn't ready to talk to Ross about anything but the case and Ruby's freedom. He tried to see her again at the dinner hour. He took the camera. The *Journal*, he told the warden's man, wanted more photos. The warden's man told him she'd been sequestered until after the trial. It was the worst possible news.

Harold was right. Max couldn't storm the Fulton County Jail. He couldn't smuggle her out. Instead, he did what journalists do, he wrote her a letter. In it, he reminded her she was there as a witness, she hadn't done anything wrong. She'd be let go whenever the state was done with Leo Frank. When she got out, he'd be there to comfort her, to help her forget all miseries, past and present, and start a new life. He wrote "Love and love and love" at the end as a signature. He hired a black boy from the factory to deliver it and followed him to Butler Street to make certain it was indeed delivered along with the bribe he'd instructed the boy to give the guard, using up five of their fifteen dollars.

The highlight of the prosecution's case, the testimony of Jim Conley, began the following Monday. Max got to City Hall especially early. He tried to squeeze into the courtroom with the rest of the cubs and didn't make it. None of them did. He looked around for a prime post outside. Using his elbows and feet against the torsos and legs of others, he secured one under a ladder placed against the City Hall exterior. The crowd pressed together behind him. It stretched as far as he could see. Two men shared space on the ladder's uppermost rung and hung precariously halfway into the courtroom through an open window. They reported their observations of the proceedings to the men steadying the ladder and these men relayed it over their shoulders to those behind. Max couldn't see a thing.

However, the windowsill was just above his head. He could hear a lot. Conley's speech was guttural and crude, but he was steady, certain, and consistent, nothing like the slurring drunk Ruby knew. The men of the ladder informed the rest that the witness was well dressed, close shaven, and his hair neatly cropped. This was a surprise. Men murmured approval to one another.

Conley told a story of Frank's corruption and cruelty, of the stream of young girls and loose women visiting his office on Saturdays. Frank had him lock the door when a girl came in and unlock it for him when the visits were over. They'd developed a code together. The boss stomped the floor when he wanted the door locked and whistled for an unlock. He paid Conley a dollar each time. He swore he often saw factory girls sitting in Frank's lap.

"I seen him fondle they breasts and play with they nipples."

Frank's wife shrieked. His mother jumped up and pointed a steady finger.

"You're a dirty liar, Jim Conley!" she said. "You are destined for hell!"

At Mrs. Frank's outburst, the judge hammered his desk. He ruled the testimony too grisly for feminine ears and ordered the removal of all women from the court, including the accused's wife and mother. He chided Dorsey with not alerting the bench to the nature of his witness's content. He would have removed the women earlier.

The State's most valuable witness resumed his testimony. He testified that on the day he killed her, Frank made him drag the corpse of Mary Phagan from his office to the basement. It was a miserable, fearsome chore. He'd have wept for the poor child, but he was afraid to do it in front of her murderer.

"He murdered that sweet angel," Conley said. "He's a right devil. I don't never know what he mighta done to a Negro like me."

The crowd was thrilled. No matter what they'd heard about the reprobate janitor, Jim Conley might turn out to be goods as pure gold as Newt Lee. If so, Dorsey's case was won.

Max had a letter from Ruby the following week delivered to his rooming house by a courier from the office of Rueben Arnold.

He was both stunned and overjoyed. It was written on legal-size yellow-lined paper.

"I am now aware I have a role in court," she wrote after flowing paragraphs of loving greetings and avowals. "Mr. Rosser, Mr. Frank's attorney, who has kindly offered to have this letter delivered to you, wants me to testify as to the character of Jim Conley and what I know of his behavior in the factory. I believe this will happen sometime over the next few days, if not tomorrow."

It made sense. When the prosecution rested, the defense began. For days, a steady stream of character witnesses had praised the sober, virtuous nature of Leo Frank. Their testimonies were so repetitive, jurors, spectators, and journalists alike fell asleep from time to time. It was high time to shake things up, to turn the tables on Frank's chief accuser, to expose Conley as a low-down rapine and murderous degenerate. Ruby did not say she was tormented by the idea that she was Arnold and Rosser's primary instrument in that endeavor, but he knew she was.

"I've met Mr. Rosser but not Mr. Arnold," she wrote. "They're concerned what Dorsey's men will make of me and William Smith too. We've gone over what I'll be asked on the stand several times. Mr. Rosser says I'll be set free after my part of the trial. I pray you are both right on that."

She didn't say a word about her treatment or what kind of pressure the prosecution put to her. He couldn't tell if she'd got the new cell Harold promised. She closed in a way that strung itself around his heart.

"I miss you. I long for you. It's so lonely here."

He folded the letter and put it in his pants pocket. It lay warm and transcendent against his thigh until he got to the pressroom, where he watched Harold Ross put a folded legal-size yellow-lined paper to his lips and stuff it in the side pocket of his suit.

13.

During the remainder of Ruby's stretch in jail, Rosser visited her nightly to go over potential testimony. Dorsey did the same. Their methods were opposite. On his visits, Rosser turned on the charm.

"Miss Ruby," he said, addressing her like a white woman at their first meeting. "I am Luther Rosser, attorney for Leo M. Frank."

He paused to undo his collar, freeing his celebrated throat that it might throb gloriously. He was all courtly gestures and smiles, explaining to her that it was none of Arnold and Rosser's fault that she found herself confined. Their opponents had imprisoned her in complete violation of the law. But he was here now and would look after her as best he could. He reassured her that she would ultimately be released. Were there messages he might take to someone outside for her? Was she being fed properly? He waited patiently while she sat and wrote the letter for Max and one for Harold. Then he got to the meat.

"Tell me everything you know about that reprobate Jim Conley," he said. "I will turn my face from you if you find certain aspects too shameful to discuss."

Luther Rosser was a big man, but she stood and met him eye to eye. She told him about the drinking, the leers, the whores

Conley brought to the dressing room in the middle of the day, the one girl she knew who'd fended off an attack by him in the middle of a workday.

"If he hadn't been so drunk, he would have overpowered her. I don't know what happened to her. She never came back to work again."

The lawyer seemed pleased. He took notes on his yellow pad. She asked him:

"Why me, Mr. Rosser? Why have you chosen me for this chore? There are gals throughout the factory who could tell you the same."

"You don't know? It should be obvious, Miss Ruby. They are white. You are not. Your testimony will be all the more believable for that."

"But still, why me? There are other black girls in the factory. I'm not so special."

Rosser chuckled at her naivete.

"Oh yes, you are, my dear. We spoke with your superiors. They found you for us, served you up on a platter, you might say. You are a most . . ." He paused, searching for an innocuous term. ". . . nicely put together young woman. The jury will be enamored of you and hang on your every word. You're also well spoken, far more so than the average ni . . . ahhh, pickaninny."

On his initial visit, Dorsey threatened her.

"If you malign Jim Conley, and the jury believes you," the prosecutor said, "you will rend the city apart. Our citizens long for Jewish blood. They crowd the streets outside City Hall every day salivating for it. Frustrate them by helping to free Frank and they'll turn on your people instead. Need I remind you? Your people do not have the deep pockets and power of the Jews. The Negro community will be sitting ducks. Don't think you'll be protected. They'll hunt you down first."

It was all just as she'd feared from the beginning. She'd known all along in her heart and mind it didn't matter what Rosser or Max said. Every time Dorsey paid her a visit, she knew he'd never let her go unless she did what he wanted. Caught between the two lawyers, she got the idea to make up a story about Conley that would satisfy Dorsey while presenting everything she told Rosser in a plain, unvarnished manner.

As the time for her testimony drew near, she doubted herself. Maybe the story she planned to tell was crazy, the cracked result of stress and lack of sleep. She never slept at night anymore. During the day, she slept only sporadically. Both day and night, she was kept awake by the wails of women down the corridor from her desolate, barren cell, a condition even the bribes of Harold Ross could not improve.

Ruby was called to court on Friday, August 15. The jailhouse woke her at five in the morning. They gave her a sweet roll and coffee for breakfast instead of the usual stale bread and weak tea. Two big white women brought her to the showers for the first time in the nearly two weeks she'd been confined. The shower was hot. She found it a blessing. It burnt the filth of her cell off her skin. The women gave her fresh clothes from items the police seized when they took her. The clothes smelled musty, but they were good to put on. She felt near human in them.

Two guards walked her outside the jail and into a horse-drawn paddy wagon to take her to City Hall. She was alone in the back. The ride gave her time to think, to remember the answers she'd determined Rosser wanted from her, how she could add a twist to them that they might also be the answers Dorsey wanted. She wasn't sure she could carry it off. Her mouth would be so full of lies, the Lord Himself might descend to Earth and smite her right there, in front of everybody, but if He didn't and she got away with it, she'd have the rest of her life to atone.

They kept her under guard in a small anteroom above the courtroom on the second floor until it was her turn to take the stand. She used her time to think of Max and restore her spirit. The trial would be over soon. Her role in it would be over sooner. She and Max could start their new life. She imagined their wedding. She imagined the home they'd make. They'd have two salaries to work with. It would be a nice home, one with a kitchen and pretty things. Maybe she could get a job as a housemaid. After working for five years at the factory, domestic work was like a vacation.

A bell attached to the wall above the anteroom door brought her back. It was time for her to testify. She blinked, shook herself. Her guard took her by the arm and led her down the stairs and through a side entrance to the courtroom. At the sight of her, low murmurs rolled in a wave from the front row of spectators to the back. No one but the lawyers present, Harold Ross, who sat at the press table, and Maxwell Sassaport, who had bribed his way to a prime ladder position at an open window, using up another five dollars of the couple's savings, knew who she was.

Both Harold and Max studied Ruby looking for signs of maltreatment. She'd lost weight, but there were no bruises or marks they could see. She hadn't lost so much that she was gaunt, although she swimmed some in her clothes. In their eyes, she looked fierce and vulnerable at the same time. Their veins pulsed with the desire to protect her. In the eyes of those who did not know her, she was a remarkable specimen of Negro pulchritude, enough to be unique in their experience, a cause of wonderment. They sat up straight, stretched their necks to achieve a better view. The people outside wanted to know what was going on. They pulled on Max's pantleg, demanding an account. He back-kicked them off and nearly toppled from his perch, causing him to slap his hands down on the inside windowsill, and grip hard, while from the waist down he dangled. His toes scrabbled against the brick wall as he worked to reorient his feet to the proper rung. The window men to the right and left of him shouted down "Prettiest nigger gal I ever seen takin' the oath!" and "A black Venus if ever I saw one!" to those below and someone started singing that awful song from the lovers' first night at Dark Sally's. It proved a lucky distraction. Otherwise, the crowd might have pulled Max off and down his ladder and another scrambled up in his place.

His struggles won the attention of the court for a moment, long enough for the room to take their eyes off Ruby. The judge banged his gavel against his desk and ordered that hooligan at the window be still or he'd go outside and rip him off his ladder himself. Ruby looked over and saw him and their eyes met and both of them visibly swelled with emotion, although no one except Harold knew why. Max's feet found their rung.

Luther Rosser approached the witness. In honeyed tones meant to soothe, he asked her to state her name, age, and where she worked, which she did, her eyes darting to the side to find Max. Rosser coughed to get her attention, frowned. He pointed to his own eyes with one finger and then pointed it at hers. No more gaping around, young woman, his gesture clearly said, and the courtroom tittered. Her cheeks went hot. She dropped her gaze to her lap.

The lawyer asked her to identify the defendant which she did. He asked her questions about Leo Frank. Did he have frequent women visitors, did he drink in the office, did she ever witness someone watching his office door, did she ever see him flirting with the girls in the knurling room, to wit, Mary Phagan. She answered a simple, unadorned "no" to all of them.

"Did Mr. Frank ever seek familiarity with you, Miss Johnson?" he asked.

"Never."

"He's a fool then," Rosser muttered to the amusement of the court. Even the judge and Frank himself smiled.

"And Mr. Conley—did he have women visitors?"

"Yes, sir."

"Did he drink in the office?"

"Most always he was drunk, sir."

"Did he flirt with the girls in the knurling room?"

"No, sir."

Rosser, who was walking dramatically back to the defense table, stopped and turned back on his heel.

"No? Miss Johnson, are you sure about that?"

Ruby responded as she'd been trained.

"It takes two to flirt, sir. Jim Conley leered at girls, especially young ones. He muttered things, but his speech was too jumbled up to know what he was saying. All the girls feared him. We kept as far from him as our jobs allowed."

There were a few more questions from the defense. Rosser asked about the girl who'd been assaulted by Conley and quit her job. She recited what she knew. It wasn't much but it did its job. By the time the lawyer was done, a portrait of Jim Conley as a Negro monster drooling over the tender flesh of white maidens was painted and seared into the minds of all.

It was time for Hugh Dorsey to go to work. He gave Ruby a hangman's stare, cold, intimidating, and relentless. She gathered her thoughts and rehearsed in her mind the lies she was about to tell. But Dorsey went off script.

"Miss Johnson," he said, in his firm, clarion voice, "is it not true that you and Mary Phagan were sworn enemies?"

Her mouth dried. Her throat closed. For a moment, she could not speak.

"Not enemies, sir," she finally managed.

His eyebrows went up.

"Did you not batter her outside Mr. Frank's office leading to your arrest on the seventh of March?"

She stared at him, drop-jawed, silent. Her eyes roved the sea of white men facing her, judging her as if it were she on trial. Defend yourself! she screamed inside her head and somehow managed to speak in ravaged voice.

"No, I did not," she said.

The sea of white men rippled with snorts and smirks. Black girls always lie when caught out, their judgment said.

"Did not a certain white man who enjoys your favor intervene with the police that you might escape prosecution for this battery?"

Her throat and mouth were so dry by now, she could only croak. Her words were rough but intelligible.

"Mary Phagan battered me, sir."

Tears welled then rolled down her cheeks, one after the other.

"Certainly, girl, if that is true," Dorsey said, "you must have wanted revenge."

He paused to let his suggestion sink in. The jury regarded her with fresh eyes, eyes that condemned her as—at the very least—Leo Frank's accomplice.

"It's a terrible thing to bear false witness against another, isn't it?"

Ruby saw herself back in the Tower, maybe for life.

"Yes, sir." She added hastily, "I wouldn't do that."

Dorsey's face registered a melodramatic surprise.

"You wouldn't? Then why have you told these lies about Jim Conley?"

"They weren't lies, sir."

"No? How do you explain the vast difference between the man you describe and the man these jurors have seen and heard testify?"

At last, the question she'd anticipated, the question for which she'd a ready reply, even if it was perjury.

"He took the pledge, sir."

It wasn't easy to take a man like Dorsey by surprise but she did. He knew what challenges the cleaning up of Jim Conley had presented to Chief Detective Lanford. He knew how difficult it had been to keep him sober once he'd got him that way. Conley took so many interviews, there was always some reporter around willing to slip him a bottle for an exclusive tidbit. He'd prayed on his knees that Conley would perform on the stand in direct and total contradiction of the man he was. And he had, brilliantly, thanks to the prosecutor's men who rehearsed him, over and over and over. There was no pledge involved. Quite the contrary. As soon as his testimony was over, Conley did the natural thing. He got drunk.

"He took the pledge . . ." Dorsey said because he had to say something.

"Yes, sir. He underwent a complete rejuvenation. He was reborn. He was fast in the arms of our Lord last time I saw him . . ."

Dorsey played along.

"And this was before the murder."

"Oh yes, sir. Much before. As I recall."

Arnold and Rosser fumed. They'd been suckered by the black bitch on the stand. On redirect, they attacked her mercilessly but she did not give in. Conley took the pledge. Conley was reborn. They pulled out the knives. Arnold approached her.

"Miss Johnson. Is it not true that you were once an employee at an establishment known as Dark Sally's?"

Ruby gasped. She looked over to Max, whose face had grown more and more tortured as her testimony went on. He looked like Jesus on the cross. She didn't answer.

"I'll take that as a yes. And is not this establishment a house of prostitution?"

She blathered and blabbered incomprehensibly searching for an answer. It was and it wasn't. Her mind raced thinking of all the other kinds of business that took place at Dark Sally's but none of them were exactly legal.

"I'll take that also as a yes."

Arnold turned to Judge Roan.

"Your honor, I find myself in the unfathomable position of needing to impeach my own witness. Miss Johnson has pulled the wool over our eyes. She is a liar and a cheat. I wish to strike all testimony by her from the record."

The judge asked Dorsey what the prosecution wanted. Dorsey saw an opportunity to appear magnanimous to the jury. He acquiesced. Ruby was dismissed.

She left the courtroom with her neck bent, her head down. She expected to be taken back to the Tower immediately. No one impeded her. She walked out of City Hall in the same abject posture. The crowd outside, most of whom were as yet unaware of what exactly had transpired within, regarded her with a bland curiosity. She pushed her way through them, her proud spirit humiliated, tamped down so low that she did not hear Max calling her. "Ruby, Ruby," he called out but she pushed and pushed her way to a place where the crowd thinned, whereupon she slipped down a side street and disappeared into the dark.

Once again, Max looked everywhere for Ruby. Apparently, it was his fate—always looking for his great love, sometimes finding her, never holding on long enough. He searched at her rooming house, Ross's place, their spot in the park, Dark Sally's.

The rooming house let out her room to another girl the day after the police took her. The landlady said she'd use her broom against her if she dared show her face thereabouts.

"I run a respectable house," she said. "That trash has no place here."

Ross's rooms were still as the grave, the site of their trysts in the park forlorn. Dark Sally's bustled with customers fresh from the courthouse steps, sightseers come to try a saucy taste of infamy. He found the night manager and asked him if he'd seen Ruby. The man snorted.

"Neither hide nor hair," he said. "If you find her, remind her to stay away. This crowd will hold her down and not let go until every man here has had her. I've never seen a worse gang of miscreants. They've all asked for her. What the hell happened in court today?"

Max pretended he didn't know. He stumbled his way into the street through a haze of grief. At the National Pencil factory, he tried every door. They were all locked. He despaired. He would not find her. There was no place left to look. Anguish wrapped itself around his heart like a wreath of thorns. By the time he got to the *Journal*, it was after ten o'clock in the night.

Harold and a handful of other reporters were in, working on their stories for the Saturday edition. Some had been nowhere near the trial. They were occupied instead with chasing down stories about fall plantings recommended by the Atlanta Gardening Club or an accident involving an automobile and the horse that kicked it, but they all knew what had happened at court that day. They suspected Ross was the white man Dorsey alluded to during the trial, the one who'd bribed Ruby out of the hoosegow. They also pondered the kind of woman they suspected she was. She might have half a dozen lovers and Dorsey's white savior could be anybody. Regardless, they knew their man. His gal had been dragged through the mud. He was ready to explode at the slightest provocation. It was safest to steer clear of him. They left him alone.

Ross noticed Max and scowled.

"Where the hell have you been, Sassaport?" Ross asked, with unmistakable irritation. "I need today's man in the street quotes."

"I don't have any."

Ross raised an arm and pointed a finger at the chief's office door. The sanctum had become his living quarters during the trial. He rarely went home.

"Get your ass in there!"

The reporters exchanged blank looks. The cub was in for it.

Behind closed doors, Harold's demeanor shifted. He put a hand on Max's shoulder.

"Where is she?" he said.

"I don't know. I've been everywhere."

Harold sank down to the chief's couch then smacked his tongue softly against his teeth, just like Ruby did sometimes. If he had a nerve left, Max would have suffered from the sound of it. Instead, he sat next to Harold, put his elbows on his knees and his face in his hands. Harold clapped his back.

"Then we have to wait, sport," he said. "She'll turn up."

Max raised his head long enough to say, "I'm not so sure."

Early the next morning, a letter was delivered to the *Journal* by a boy from the pencil factory. One of the reporters took it in hand.

"It's for you, Sassaport," he said, tossing the envelope across the pressroom. Max caught the letter, recognized Ruby's hand, and ripped it open. It read:

"Come to me tonight. I'll be at Harry's. I know where he keeps a key. Atlanta has become my own hell. Everyone knows who I am and all the things the lawyers said I'd done. I walk down the street and see it in their eyes. I can't breathe. I can't come into the light. We have to leave. Don't tell Harry yet. I need to tell him myself."

She did not sign it "love" or with her name. It just ended. Max ran down to the *Journal*'s front steps and looked for the messenger. The kid was gone.

Ross came into the street and called him.

"Let's go, Sassaport. We have to get to court."

Max ignored him.

"Frank's making a statement today."

"I don't care."

"Then fuck you, you're fired."

Max didn't hear him. He didn't move. He looked to be making up his mind about something and then he lied.

"I have to keep looking for her, Harold."

"Not right now you don't."

Ross took him by the elbow and forced him into his roadster.

"I'm telling you, she'll turn up. Trust me. In the meantime, we've got a job to do.

He cranked the T up himself, ran back, and jumped in the driver's side while it sputtered and shook.

"I can't believe Frank's making a statement," he shouted over the motor's racket. "It's a chump move. I don't know why Arnold and Rosser don't stop him. Right now, he's got a good shot at reasonable doubt. If the jury decides they don't much like him, that won't matter. Know how he looks to them already? Like a four-eyed pantywaist Jew Yankee."

Max bristled.

"What did you just say, Harold?" he shouted back. "Maybe I didn't hear right."

"Christ, Max, why so insulted? You don't wear glasses and you're not a Yankee." Ross chuckled at his own wit. "Besides, I'm not saying it for myself. I'm just tellin' you what the jury thinks."

He took one hand off the wheel and waved it about while he declaimed on the subject of Frank's chances at acquittal.

"The best thing Frank has going for him is that he looks too weak to kill. That and the fact that Conley looks guilty as hell. But give the jury an excuse to dislike your boy any more than they already do and no question, they'll convict."

He drove around to the back of City Hall by the courtroom windows then pressed a few dollars into Max's hand.

"Pay for a good spot," he said and left him there.

Max did so. He stood under one of the ladders placed against the courtroom windows and tried to listen to the crowd's gossip, but his mind went constantly to Ruby and how they could get to Illinois. Their voices were muffled by his thoughts of her. He didn't retain much.

Inside the courtroom, it was uncommonly still. No one wanted to be removed for cause. Even the most cantankerous observers kept quiet. When Frank stood to advance to the witness chair, the room held its breath. He stumbled, hitting his thigh on a corner of the defense table, and walked on hunched over rubbing his hip with his hand. Mumbles and whispers pursued him.

Christ almighty! Ross thought. Could he look any more like a lurching, perverse predator? Straighten up, man!

It got worse.

As soon as Frank opened his mouth, it looked like Dorsey didn't have much to worry about. He started by describing his childhood in New York, which sounded like a childhood in China to the good people of Atlanta. He praised his wife, Lucille, a local girl of reputable family, the joy of his existence.

Nobody cared.

Afterward, he launched into a detailed description of his duties as manager of the factory. He described payroll procedures and produced sample pay chits. He offered documentation regarding the ordering of supplies and described the routines of how the machines were maintained.

"That's not all," he said in his light, airy voice. "The duties of a factory manager are exacting. Let me tell you more."

He told them how he stuffed pay envelopes with dollars and coin then filed them. How he reviewed invoices. He lifted his chin and straightened his back when he described the sorting of so many cogs in the company wheel. He had pride, even arrogance about it. Ross studied the jury to see how he affected them. He could see they were annoyed. They cared less about the details of his work than they did his wife's pedigree. Why did he waste their time?

Frank wrapped up his professional résumé by explaining how orders of assortment parcels were created.

"We box poor seller pencils with high-performing ones. You wouldn't believe the complications in inventory mixing the two creates!"

By then, half the courtroom was asleep and the other half ready to bolt, the judge on his bench and Ross at his press table, included.

"Conley's such a low bar," Ross whispered to the man from the *New York Times* who sat beside him, "and this idiot's going to stumble into it." The *Times* man nodded his head and rolled his eyes.

"So now you know who I am, what kind of man, sober and responsible," Frank said. "Presently, I shall tell you what I know about the murder of Mary Phagan."

The room perked up. The longer he talked, the more alert they became. None dared so much as cough.

"They say I was nervous, twitching, that I stuttered when I was shown Mary Phagan's corpse."

Leo Frank paused, remembering. His eyes filled. He sucked in a great gulp of air. It gurgled at the back of his throat. Some of the people watching him flinched at the sound. Others tightened their lips. He continued.

"I'd never seen anything like it, nor did I ever want to . . . that poor, beautiful child, spread out like a butterfly pinned to cardboard. Her wounds. Her tattered, dirty dress. Her neck bound with linen and cord. Who among you would not tremble at such a sight?"

He reached in his back pocket, pulled out a handkerchief, and wiped his eyes. A handful of those in the courtroom, one of them a juror, did the same. Frank rejected the many accusations about his character.

"You may believe that I am Mr. Dorsey's Dr. Jekyll and Mr. Hyde. But I tell you Mr. Lanford's detectives twisted my words, my actions into the scurrilous slanders presented to you these weeks while they swallowed the lies of Jim Conley whole. His statements are nothing but a spiderweb of deceit.

"I know nothing of the death of Mary Phagan. I did not pay Conley to drag her corpse to the basement. I had no women visit me at the factory. He tells obscene lies of what I did to these phantom wantons. They are complete fabrications. I am aghast before them."

He rose from his chair, walked to the jurors' box, this time erect and sure. He looked each of them straight in the eye.

"Gentlemen, newspaper men have called me 'the silent man in the Tower.' Yes, I have been silent these many months. I've kept my counsel until the proper time and place. That time is now. That place is here and I have told you the truth. The whole truth."

He turned his back. He was done. His wife burst into tears. The court remained silent while he left the jurors' box and went to her, wrapping her in his arms. Deputies and jurors daubed their eyes.

Ross and the *New York Times* man exchanged looks of astonishment. What a marvel hid behind those glasses! John Barrymore could not have done better. If only the jurors could go directly to deliberation afterward, he'd be assured his freedom.

But Dorsey had a rebuttal to make. He produced several new factory girls who described Frank as a wicked man of lecherous habits. How Dorsey found fresh witnesses overnight was a mystery. Maybe he'd had them all along, Ross decided, kept them up his sleeve in case he needed them. They were good little actresses. By the time closing arguments were completed, the jury questioned any sympathy Frank's statement provoked. After two hours of deliberation, the bailiff announced that the verdict was in.

Word spread fast. Court followers stood their ground at City Hall waiting for the jury to announce its verdict, their feet planted, their backs braced against the pressure of newcomers behind them. Hundreds more came running. Soon there were thousands lining the streets. Max was lost among them, pushed away from the courthouse and through the crowd. Soon, he was far from his post.

The principals returned to the courtroom. Emotions were stretched thin. Every few moments, someone blurted out, "You'll hang, Frank!" or "We'll do to your wife what you did to little Mary!" The judge banged his gavel repeatedly, demanding silence, vowing to clear everyone from the room. His court officers strode up and down the aisles slapping billy clubs against their palms.

The room quieted. Judge Roan ordered the removal of Leo and Lucille Frank for their own safety. Whatever the jury's decision, he reasoned, a mob might devour them the minute it was read. The Franks were escorted out through a side door. Men stood and raised clenched fists at both of them as they left. The judge banged his gavel again. He was ignored. More rancorous voices erupted. A half dozen men were removed. The room quieted again. The jury entered. The judge asked for the verdict. The foreman of the jury rose to his feet and delivered it.

Guilty.

The word rose up, rousing everyone inside the courtroom. In a heartbeat, it ripped through the crowd outside. Guilty. Guilty. Guilty. Men whooped. They threw hats in the air. Flasks were passed from stranger to stranger. Men sang "Dixie." They lit fires in alleyways and danced. It was a bacchanal of vengeful joy. Max heard a cluster of white men say, "Let's get some Jews and teach 'em a lesson!" They let loose a tribal yell.

When Hugh Dorsey emerged from City Hall, the mob rushed him. They carried him on their shoulders through a cheering throng that clogged the streets for blocks in every direction. The great deed was done. The Jew who slaughtered their precious virgin was as good as dead.

14.

A rattled Max stood outside the *Journal* looking up in the sky, waiting for evening to fall. It took forever. As soon as the sky was streaked with the gold and magenta of twilight, he walked then ran to Ross's place. His heart pounded so hard it deafened him to the mob celebrating Frank's conviction throughout the city. The celebrants were loud and drunk and menacing. He ducked down alleyways whenever he saw them approach. He prayed Ruby was not on the streets heading to him as he was to her.

The front door to Ross's rooms cracked open at his knock. Ruby's eyes peered through the crack. When she saw him, she grabbed his arm and pulled him in. They collapsed into each other's arms. His body pressed her against the backside of the door. They murmured each other's names. They wept together. She took him by the hand and led him to Ross's bedroom. They fell on his bed and held each other.

They made plans.

Max thought they should stay in Atlanta a few more weeks until he could amass enough money to replace what he'd spent since she was jailed.

"There's only five dollars left," he said. "That's not enough for shelter or food to Illinois. And what are we going to do when we get there?"

Ruby wanted desperately to leave Atlanta straightaway but she agreed. It filled her heart that he wanted to take care of her. It was as if he were her husband already. So, overflowing with warmth, she indulged him.

"OK," she said, "we'll wait until you think it's best. I can't go out, though. I can't face people in the street. It's very hard, Max."

He knew her better than anyone else. Childhood had prepared her for many things but not Hugh Dorsey and Rueben Arnold. She'd been proud her whole life. Her humiliation would take time to heal. He hugged her and kissed the top of her head.

"Harry will let you stay here until we leave. I'm sure of it."

She had no doubt Harry would help her out. But even Harry must have limits.

"Do you think we can both stay here?" she asked Max.

There was a heavy silence between them. Ruby lifted her shoulders then let them fall. I can't help it if he's in love with me, her gesture said.

"We're a couple now," he told her. "You don't take one without the other."

"Maybe we could ask him to lend us some money," she said.

Ross would do whatever she asked. They both knew that. If they borrowed money from him, they could leave Atlanta sooner. But Max shot down the idea.

"I'm taking care of you, Ruby," he said. "Not Harold Ross."

Max used the phone in the hall to call the *Journal* and told Ross he'd found Ruby and where. Ross hung up on him before he was finished. He rushed home. Without hesitation, he told them they could stay as long as they liked as long as Max found someplace else to store the junk he'd collected for resale. The three of them hugged together. Ruby sent Max out to buy some potatoes and onions so she could cook them all a stew out of a piece of meat from Ross's icebox. Max whistled his way to the night market. When he got back, he found Ruby and Harold sitting on a couch together, holding hands. He was so relieved to see her there, so happy, it didn't bother him.

Over the following weeks, Max found his resentment of Harold's friendship with Ruby had all but disappeared. Now that he lived with her at last, he cared less. There was no room in him for anything but her, not even jealousy. Outside of work, Ruby was his singular occupation, his sole passion. Every man in love needs another to talk to. Since he was no longer a rival, Max made Ross his confidant. He talked about Ruby every day, every night. Sometimes, Harold listened. Other times, he pretended not to hear him and changed the subject. He had wounds to lick. His chances with Ruby were gone forever, but he didn't want to dwell on it. He enshrined her in his memory, did his grieving in private, and kept emotion in check.

Meanwhile, Max wallowed in joy.

"After all her misfortunes," he told Ross one day, "I need more than ever to take her away and make her happy in a new place, a place that won't condemn us for loving each other."

Then fucking take her already, Ross thought, or shut up. I haven't got any more time for this.

There's nothing like work to build a wall around the heart. Half by choice, half by happenstance, Ross was extraordinarily busy. The trial was over but hardly in the past. The public remained consumed by Frank's conviction. The papers couldn't stop talking about it, people couldn't stop reading whatever the papers found to print. Bookies ran bets on when Frank would hang. Buskers sang songs about dispatching him to hell on street corners.

Ross reported on all of it in unvarnished detail for the

Journal. He was profitable for the paper. The world outside Atlanta remained as fixated by the Frank story as the Georgians were. His chief sold a number of his articles to papers in New York, Boston, and Chicago as well as throughout the cities of the South.

The outlets loved him. The *Times* reporter told him he was a hot read in New York. People quoted his columns on the hoodlums who harassed Jews at dinner and cocktail parties. They saw the streets where rich Jews lived, the sidewalks he described, studded with Pinkertons. They devoured reports of break-ins at Jewish businesses and the multiple beatings of Jews by abusers who openly brandished weapons, mostly knives and bats. It was genius that he wrote his columns in the first person plural, the *Times* man told him. It made him stand out on the page. It brought people in. Harold began to dream of a Pulitzer, the journalism prize promised in Joseph Pulitzer's will. The first ought to be awarded around the time of Frank's execution.

Harold's counterpoint was the *Jeffersonian.* Tom Watson, its editor, wrote hateful screeds, whipping up thugs and common citizens both against the Jews. He was the lowest kind of journalist scum. Not only did he specialize in hateful bombast, he lusted for high political office. It was because of men like him and their grip on a sizable portion of Atlanta's citizenry that Ross thought more and more about leaving the South. New York City might suit him. He had a name there.

Ross covered every aspect of Leo Frank's appeals. He reported when factory girls and boys recanted their testimony post trial. They blamed their perjuries on arm-twisting by Dorsey's men. He reported the rumors that William Smith, Conley's lawyer, had regrets for his role in exonerating a guilty man and sending an innocent one to death row. It was a lot to cover. Ross needed his cub to pick up the slack.

"Max, there's a meeting at The Temple tonight. I want you to go and find out what it's about."

Max nodded and changed the subject.

"Harold, listen to me. I've got to tell you something."

Ross sighed. It was increasingly painful to look at Max who reminded him of everything he wanted to store in the past. He'd only slept in his own bed twice since Ruby surfaced. Once, he was too tired to care where he was. The second time, he heard every breath Max and Ruby took in the next room. It was torture. He couldn't live with them much longer. But he couldn't kick them out.

He regarded his cub anyway. He tapped his ears. Max spoke.

"We're going to leave next week for Juniper, Illinois. We picked it long ago as a place to reunite if we were ever separated," he said. "We'll leave in a week. I apologize for the short notice."

When Ross collected Ruby's things from the police, he'd gone through them before giving them to her. He couldn't help himself. It was his nature to snoop and he loved her. Among hair pins, a nightgown, and a bar of soap, he found a map of the route between Atlanta and Chicago, with "Juniper, Illinois" marked by a circle. At least now he knew what it meant.

They were leaving. Hallelujah. He thought a while and then exhaled a satisfied stream of smoke from his cigarette. It was a relief. If Ruby weren't around, under his nose, cooking in his kitchen and sleeping with Max in his living room, he could focus on work and begin to forget.

"It's a good idea, Sassaport," he said.

"I'll stay in touch, let you know where you can reach us."

Ross nodded. He mouthed the word "sure" but something caught in his throat. He coughed and lit another cigarette.

* * *

A ring of Pinkertons surrounded The Temple. They wore guns on their belts and frisked everyone who entered. They found a notebook and three pencils, a couple coins on Max. When he was granted passage and descended into the basement hall, he found a room not of rows of chairs set up, but ten round tables with ten seats apiece and ten pads of paper with ten pencils on top. This was no rally he attended. It was a business meeting.

Max took a seat at a table in the back. Soon one hundred men entered and sat also. More men entered who could not secure a seat. They stood at the back. A long rectangular table hosting a panel of luminaries faced them. Rabbi Marx stood up before them all.

"Gentlemen, I thank every one of you for coming," he said. "I beg you, please, when the time comes to leave The Temple tonight, leave it in groups. Our streets are full of evil. Until we return to the pleasant days of yesterday, we must be cautious.

"My guest tonight is Mr. Sigmund Livingston, an attorney from Chicago. He comes to us with a solution to the insecurities that trouble us."

Max wrote down Livingston's name and the word "Chicago" then underscored them both. All roads lead to Chicago, he thought. Once they got to Juniper, he wanted to get them as quickly as possible to Chicago. He could get work there. Surely, a big city would be hospitable to a couple like them, black and white, young. They could marry there.

He glanced around the room. He saw the reporter from the *Chicago Tribune*, standing up near the exit. He nodded at him and gestured he would give him his seat. The fellow shook his head, preferring to stand.

Livingston addressed the assembled.

"*Meine lantslaite*," he said. "*Gut ovent.* I am here on an urgent mission."

His Yiddish had a German Jewish accent familiar to everyone in the room, including Max. It was not the same accent as Zeyde's, but in Atlanta it was the only kind he heard. Oddly enough, Livingston reminded him of his grandfather. They had the same round cheeks and whisps of hair encircling a balding head. His speech was plain, unadorned, and ardent.

"I don't have to tell you, the neighbors of Leo Frank, what problems Jews face today," he said. "Anti-Semites have sworn to exact revenge upon us and not just in Atlanta. They harry us throughout this wide and fruitful country with their insults, accusations, and attacks. We cannot hide from them. They are too many. Wherever we are, they appear and disturb our peace. There is only one thing we can do. We can fight against them. We must fight against them. No more sitting and waiting for the storm to pass!"

The Jews of Atlanta sprang to their feet. After a summer spent in fear, it was now September with only a more fearful season on the horizon. They were eager for action. They applauded until Livingston pushed against air and begged them to sit.

"I propose we fight them with our best weapon."

He tapped his forehead.

"Our minds."

Each time an anti-Semite maligned Jews in the newspaper, Livingston urged they be called into the light, prosecuted.

"We must defend ourselves in newspapers of our own and those of our allies. We must prove to all of fair mind that we are not demons but simply men, men like them, honest citizens of the United States of America. We will do it with our journalists, with public speakers, handbills, and with lawsuits so bold our enemies will have to acknowledge them."

He paused and lifted his arms outward.

"Together, Attorney Charles Wittenstein, B'nai Brith, your

rabbi and I have created a weapon that will accomplish our security: The Anti-Defamation League."

His arms fell. He continued. He described the lawsuits the League planned against hotels that posted "No Jews Allowed" in their lobbies and against the *New York Times* for its defamation against the Jews. Max took down notes for another fifteen minutes when he realized Mr. Livingston could have ended his speech long before. He'd won the room over from the first. Men at Max's table had already withdrawn their wallets. He expected them to pull out fistfuls of cash and wave them in the air or produce bank drafts and wield their pens. When Livingston finished up, saying, "We will stamp out harassment of the Jewish people and secure justice and fair treatment for all!" they did exactly that. Rabbi Marx asked them further to take up the pencils and pads and write a list of others he and Livingston could personally approach for additional donations. Every head bent to write.

It was an inspiring moment. Max took the trolley to the *Journal* and spent hours there writing and rewriting his article. He wanted it imbued with the passion and certainty of Livingston, the fire Livingston had ignited in his own chest. He described how Livingston shook everyone in hearing to their marrow. At last, he was satisfied. He turned it in.

Ross gutted it.

"When you write for me, you have to write story, not oratory, kid."

It had been months since Harold had called Max "kid." He braced himself for the savaging of his report.

"It comes off maudlin. You sound like one of Hearst's hacks."

Max clenched his fists.

"Maybe you just don't appreciate where I'm coming from culturally," he said dryly. His voice had a vaguely threatening edge.

"Jerk," Ross handed him back his submission. "Bad writing is bad writing. Save this stuff for your novel."

Max turned to end the insults. Ross called him back.

"Hey, I want a rewrite," he said. There wasn't much left of his piece. Harry had crossed out most of it with his pen. "Keep the *New York Times* stuff though. That stuff's good."

Ross wasn't entirely heartless to Max. He'd grown fond of him despite his envy over Ruby. He didn't think twice of taking bills from the slush fund supplied by the *Journal* to buy up a few of Max's salvaged items. The kids needed to build up their grubstake. He couldn't let them leave town under-financed.

"Remember," Ross said, gesturing with the dented brass candlestick he'd just purchased for $2.25, an outrageous sum. "Hold on to as much cash as you can until you land in Chicago. You'll need it there."

Max smirked.

"Don't worry. My father told me I was from a long line of hoarders."

Ross glanced over the pile of junk he'd just acquired.

"I have no doubt."

Ruby was feeling caged up at Harry's place. She couldn't go out on her own. She'd been out briefly a couple times with Max following behind her at a discrete distance for protection. The first time was hard, but it went alright. The second time, she thought a man at the butcher's was one of the jurors. The way he looked at her, brow wrinkled, convinced her.

She wouldn't go out again after that. She longed so much to get away, she opened Ross's cigar box, the one filled with money, thinking he wouldn't mind so much if she stole a little. She stood over it and looked down at greenbacks neatly piled and bound with rubber bands. She touched them. Covered them up again. They preyed upon her mind. She exposed and touched them every day when she was alone. But she never stole any. Luckily, Max came through before temptation got too great to bear. One night, he announced he'd achieved a grubsteak of fifty dollars, much of it obtained by selling his Saturday goods. It was a comfortable amount. They could spend what they needed on trains and meals. Max proposed they stop here and there along the way to find work and replenish their purse. That way, they wouldn't be broke by the time they got to Chicago. She didn't care, as long as they were together. They were ready to go.

Ross embraced them both when they left. Everyone had tears. They promised they'd stay in touch.

Every mile out of Atlanta lightened their spirits. They walked to the foothills of the Blue Ridge Mountains, making as much progress after dark as the moon and stars allowed. It was slow but it was safer at night. They would rather watch where they stepped in the dark than confront bigots and malicious men in daylight. At night, they were able to walk together and talk. During the day, when they weren't tucked away in isolation catching up on sleep, they kept separate. They had a system. If Max lost sight of her on the road, he stayed where he was until she caught up or doubled back.

It took them several weeks to get to Seiverville, Tennessee. By then, they were bone weary and ready to splurge and give the new railway a try. Ruby rode in the colored car and Max in the white. The expense was worth it. The train cut a swath through exquisite mountain scenery. When they disembarked at Knoxville, they talked about the rivers and gorges they'd traversed, the waterfalls. They talked about them so much it felt they'd seen them together sitting side by side in the same car. The grandeur of the landscape excited their imaginations and filled them with hope.

"It's such a big country," Ruby said. "We'll find a place that's ours."

There was no train that went direct to Juniper. They rode to the closest station and continued on foot until they came to a sign with an arrow that said "Juniper, Population 50." They stopped and made a camp by a clearing near a creek. Max set off alone to see what was what in Juniper, to make sure they'd be safe if they entered together. Ruby stayed behind.

Juniper had a rustic mountain Main Street. It was lonelier than the main street he'd grown up on back home. There was a general store with the sheriff's office in the back, a pony express depot, and a blacksmith. No haberdashery or notions shop. No dentist or doctor's office. Most of Juniper lived on farms out of town. There were eight citizens total who lived downtown. They left their establishments to look him over as he approached. They were church people so their gaze was benign. He walked down the middle of the street, waving his hat, introducing himself so each one could get a good look. They knew the name Sassaport. A traveling salesman by that name came through every couple years, likely one of his second or third cousins. The blacksmith offered him a place to sleep in the back of his shop. He gratefully turned it down, saying he'd found a good spot to camp out in the woods and didn't mind sleeping there. He asked for work. He didn't tell them he was a Jew or that he had a black lover waiting for him in a clearing by a creek. They didn't need to know.

There was work at the pony express depot, feeding the horses and cleaning the stalls. There was work at the general store unloading, packaging, and shelving supplies. Max took both jobs. He wanted to earn back what they'd spent so far as quickly as possible.

Over the next couple days, the other forty-two residents, farmers all, came downtown on pretexts to also get a look at him. None were black. Ruby would stick out in Juniper worse than he did. They decided she should keep to their camp. While he worked in the town, she built a shed from river grass and the fallen limbs of trees. They slept on a blanket beneath eucalyptus and willow. Every day, she thought of ways to strengthen the shed's walls. It was their first home.

Max brought her things she'd missed while living on the road. He brought bacon and socks and shoestrings, face cloths, and once, a fried chicken. Most of these were gifts from townspeople. They were a charitable lot.

The town came alive on Sundays, the day of the week when all fifty residents gathered to pray at a clapboard church half a mile from Main Street. It had a cemetery. All of Juniper prayed there from eight o'clock until noon on the Sabbath, after which they visited their dead then went home for a fancy meal. Each week, a different family hosted Max for Sunday supper because it was the Christian thing to do even if he didn't show up for services. They always sent him back to his camp with leftovers, which he turned over to Ruby.

On a Saturday afternoon the third week they were in Juniper, a traveling preacher with a glass box full of snakes installed himself in the church vestry. He meant to test the faith of the congregation and set up a tent between the church and the cemetery. That night, Max went to the tent out of curiosity as he recalled Mayhayley advising him to lie with snakes when he was a boy.

The congregation swarmed over him from the moment he arrived. They were full of smiles and welcomes. They asked him if he came to testify. Was he ready to accept Jesus as his Lord and Savior? He apologized and told them "I am not yet ready." They gave him kind but grievous looks, pitying him. One old woman in a gray bonnet that cast shadow over half her face, said, "Maybe you'll change your mind, son. Keep your heart open."

The snake preacher led them in a hymn praising the courage of those who follow the Lord. He spoke on the power of faith, that the Lord never abandoned the man who possessed it, and called for his box of snakes. Two women dressed in white carried the box to him. Inside, clearly visible, were a dozen or more serpents of varied sizes and colors with different patterns on their skins. Max recognized a cottonmouth and a rattler. He wasn't sure of the others. Ruby would know, he thought. The preacher sang a hymn in an incomprehensible language while holding a Bible in his left hand and raising it aloft. He reached up with his right, tore a page out of the book, stuffed it in his mouth, then plunged his arm into the box. Snakes twisted around him, their split tongues flicking. They slithered up to his biceps and shoulders. They wrapped around his neck. Not one of them bit.

When the snake show was over, the congregation thanked Jesus in song and dance. A number of townspeople gathered around the preacher. He had second sight too. They dropped a few coins in a milk bucket placed at his side then asked their questions. Max got in line and thought about Mayhayley. When his turn came, he dropped two cents in the bucket and asked about Chicago. When would he get there? The preacher said: "Your mother needs you" and made a little cross on his forehead with a forefinger as if he were the pope.

He told Ruby first thing on his return to camp. She said, "Maybe we should go home."

"I don't know," Max said. "The word of a snake charmer just might be thin evidence."

"The word of a one-eyed backwoods prophet was enough to keep us together."

"You have a point there, honey."

Ruby had her own reasons for wanting to go home. The chance that her mother might also need her gave her sharp, bitter pangs of sorrow. She'd missed her often. There'd been so many things she wished she could ask her about, from how a man thinks to her recipe for rabbit stew. She longed for one of her father's hugs. She thought kindly of her siblings and missed them, too, even Franklin. It would do them both good to see family before embarking on their new life, whether that family was hale or ill.

There was a telephone in the Juniper general store. Max used it to call Harold Ross for advice.

"A telegram came for you," he said before Max had a chance to talk. "Just yesterday."

Few things could surprise Max these days but that did.

"Who from?"

Ross opened the telegram.

"Geez, I'm sorry, sport."

Max's tongue went dry. Not Mama, he thought, not Mama. Ross cleared his throat and read, "Your father is ill. Your mama not so good. Come home. Uncle Morris."

Max no longer questioned what to do.

"I guess we'll be going home, then," he told Ross, raising his voice through a scratchy connection that threatened to break any second.

Ross thought about alerting Max to a few things but he kept quiet. He'd made progress getting over Ruby. He didn't need to get embroiled in their decisions together. It would pull him back in.

Three months had passed since the trial. Everyone in the state of Georgia knew the name Ruby Alfreda Johnson. She was a scandalous footnote in the saga of Leo Frank and Mary Phagan. She was part of Georgia's street songs and plays. Wherever traveling companies toured, they played her in black face. On the route home, it wouldn't be wise for her to go by her own name. He could have at least warned Max about that, but he didn't.

Max hoped that the problems back home could be easily righted.

"Once things are settled there, we'll go on to Chicago," he said. "I ought to be able to borrow money from my family. We can take the train most of the way."

"Sounds good," Ross said, biting the inside of his cheek.

Max experienced a surge of sentiment. Without Ross, neither one of them would have survived living in Atlanta. He was the centerpiece of all their good fortune.

"You'll come visit us once we're settled there," he said.

"Sure, sure," Ross said. "Long as you still want me," he added but at the end, their connection finally broke apart.

15.

Heard County, Georgia, 1914

With the help of new railroad routes and packed dirt roads built after Ruby left town, they rode more than they walked from Illinois to Georgia and their walking wasn't rough. They took different rail cars and were often interrupted by others on the open road, forcing them to pretend to be strangers, but they made it home and they made it together. It took them only two weeks. When they neared the Chattahoochee and were a short distance to Buckwood, they prepared to separate and reunite with their families. After seeing their blood again, they'd meet by the old deer blind at the dawn. If one didn't show, the other would go at the same time every day until they did.

The night before they parted ways, she lay in his arms in a dry, shallow cave looking out at the stars.

"Do you remember where the blind is?" she asked him.

He laughed and kissed her shoulder, the part of her that was closest to him.

"How could I forget? I wonder if it's still there."

"If it's not, then by the creek where my daddy found us that time."

Max hadn't thought of Bull Johnson for a long time but the closer they got to home, Ruby's father often invaded his mind. He had fantasies of asking Bull for his daughter's hand. They were ridiculous, impossible scenarios, but he enjoyed mulling over them. He imagined Bull's shocked expression and refusal. He imagined Ruby defending their love before her father, how he'd step forward to underscore everything she said. He imagined how Bull would at last relent and accept him with damp eyes. He wasn't sure how his own parents would react to the news but he felt pretty good about Bull.

They kissed goodbye. Ruby took the road to home first, leaving with a back-hand wave. Max smiled. The last time he'd seen a wave like that it was Bull's when he left the family shop the day before they went to Mayhayley's house together. He waited thirty minutes to give Ruby a good head start and then walked the same road to Sassaport's Fabrics, Fancy Goods, and Notions.

Main Street was changed. The lumber mill had expanded its capacity in the last year and new families moved to town every season. New stores opened to service them. There was a hatter who also offered gloves and a café that provided breakfast and dinner. There was another new store across the street and down a few doors from Sassaport's. Its bold red and white sign read Finbar's All and Sundry. That surprised him. As he passed, he lifted his hat to two women entering Finbar's and again to another exiting. It was past noon of a Wednesday, a time the traffic at his father's shop was often heavy. But when he entered Sassaport's, there were no customers on the floor.

A redheaded woman stood behind the counter. Her presence made the home of his childhood feel foreign, altered in some inexplicable, permanent way. She was not young, but had a pleasant face, almost pretty. Her body was taut, muscular, her dark red hair long and abundant, flowing from a blue ribbon she'd tied in a bow at the crown. She had a few gray hairs, but one had to study her to find them.

"May I help you?" she said. "Looking for something special, are you?"

Her voice had a lilt to it. It rose and fell like music. It tickled his ears and identified her immediately to Max. The woman behind his daddy's counter had to be Adela-Persephone, Uncle Morris's redheaded widow. He put down the bundle of possessions he'd carried from Atlanta to Juniper, Illinois, to Heard County.

"I'm Max."

Her eyes rounded, a hand flew to her mouth. She made a half-turn toward the storage room out back.

"Morris!" she called out. "Morris come quick! It's Max!"

His uncle appeared through the back door with a tape measure around his neck and a clipboard in his hand. "*Gott in himmel*," he said. He shut his eyes briefly in prayerful thanksgiving. The two men embraced. Uncle Morris put a hand on each of Max's shoulders to draw him back and hold him at arm's length.

"You look a proper man, *Maxele*. Grown up and fit. Thank *Gott*, thank *Gott*. This is my wife, Adela. You remember my stories about her?"

Max made a slight bow, out of respect.

"Of course." He waved his hand from one to the other of them. "But how did this happen?" he asked.

Uncle Morris grinned and his wife blushed.

"I wore her down," he said.

The three nodded their heads and smiled at one another.

"My mother, my father . . ." Max began. "What's going on?"

His uncle's mouth fell open as if he were not sure how to answer. His throat moved but he couldn't come up with the words. Adela-Persephone came up next to him, cooed in his ear. He tried again.

"Your father and mother . . ."

He stopped.

"For pity's sake, Uncle Morris! I'm suffering! My father and mother what?"

A new voice, cracked with age, issued from the back room.

"They're alive, *Baruch haShem*."

It was Zeyde. The old man wasn't immobile with grief anymore. He stood straighter than Morris did. He'd gained weight. He was notably heartier than he'd been when Max left for Atlanta.

"Zeyde," Max said, tenderly. They also embraced.

"Your father has a heart attack," he said. "We don't know how he'll recover. Your mama's been nursing him day and night, keeping him going. When he sleeps, she won't talk, doesn't do much. Just sits at Jake's bedside, lookin' down at him."

Max's heart broke. His eyes stung.

"Take me to them, please. Where are they?"

Zeyde shrugged. He pointed a forefinger upstairs. Where else could they be?

Max bounded up the stairs. Inside his parents' bedroom was a scene exactly as Zeyde described. His father lay in bed, blankets up to his chin, his face pale, his mouth ajar. His chest moved up and down irregularly and he made a sound that was half wheeze, half cough. His mother sat beside the bed in a chair, leaning forward, motionless and silent, watching him.

When she saw him, Mama called out in thin but resolute voice, "Jake, it's Max!" Daddy muttered, "Max . . ." and tried to hoist himself up by bracing his elbows against the mattress but he failed and sunk back down again. His eyes were wide with surprise. Max went to him, kissed his cheek, and squeezed his hand. He went to his mother and bent and held her close. She wept against him. Daddy tried to speak. He had not the strength.

Adela-Persephone brought them bowls of soup. Max spoon fed his father, wiping his chin with squares of cloth set by the bedside to be used for whatever need arose. Afterward, his father was strong enough to whisper in his ear. There were matters that appeared to be of vital importance to him, but Max couldn't understand more than a few words. Something about the business. Uncle Morris took him into the hallway and filled him in.

"You saw the place up the street, ya? That Finbar character's been killing us. Nobody wants to do business with us anymore, now that they have a choice. I tell you, I think he's with those anti-Semites, the Knights of Mary Phagan, and gossips about us. What am I talking about. They're all anti-Semites now."

Max didn't know what to think; what his uncle described was news to him.

"Mama didn't mention anything in her letters," Max said, forgetting that it'd been months since he left Atlanta. He'd not had a mailing address since.

Uncle Morris raised his eyes to the heavens and shook his head.

"She should she upset her baby boy?"

"Who are the Knights of Mary Phagan?" Max had never heard of the group. He surmised they were a crew of country anti-Semites. As far as he last knew, there was no such fraternity in the city.

Uncle Morris didn't answer him. He went on as if Max had not asked a question at all.

"Look. Your father needs to close the business down, but he won't do it. I told him he and Rose can come live with us, at

Adela's place. Your zeyde, too. She's got land, lumber. We can build them their own cabin. He won't hear of it. And now, this."

He made a sweeping gesture toward the bedroom that encompassed Max's father and mother both.

"Two more stubborn *yidlachs*, I've never seen."

Max understood he would have to stay on as long as it took to bring his father and the business back to health. Until that time, Mama needed him. He tossed and turned the night away then made it to the deer blind first thing.

It was cold in the morning that time of year. There was frost on the ground at the dawn. Ruby brought a blanket with her and a corked jug filled with hot chicory and coffee. They sat on the blanket side by side near the creek bed, each with a warming arm around the other. They watched the creek ripple in a mild breeze. They sipped from the jug. He told her his news.

"I can't leave them right now. I can't leave until Daddy's stronger," he said. "I don't know how long that'll take."

He held his breath waiting for her to speak. He didn't want to have to do anything without her support. After a minute or so, she gave it.

"I say don't make any decisions right away. Stay on, help your parents. Take your time. Study the situation for yourself. It might not be as bad as Morris says. It might be your uncle has his own reasons for wanting them to close up shop. Maybe he wants to get back to the foothills with his bride."

Max blew out a chest full of air in relief. She'd said all the things that had come to him in the night when he couldn't sleep.

"What about you? How'd it go?"

Ruby tilted her head, half-smiled.

Her parents had been overwhelmed to see her again after more than six years. They wept, they thanked Jesus, they covered her in kisses and hugs. They'd seen the drawings and photographs of her in the newspapers but as they could not read, they'd been dependent on others to tell them what was written about her. Hat in hand, Bull had asked white people he knew to read him the articles. White people liked Bull. In their eyes, he was one of the good Negroes, honest and hardworking. At first, they were kind and kept hurtful parts of the reported news from them. She'd been a hero, they said, helping to convict an evil man, a perverse, child-killing Jew. It happened in the factory where she worked. But after a while, someone let something slip. Bull and Francine pushed for the truth from Ruby's siblings who always knew more about Ruby than they did. In the end, there was little they did not come to know in broad strokes.

Five months had passed since the trial. Time had blunted many blows. Just to see her, to put their hands on her again brought them to grateful tears. It was a holiday, a joy to have the prodigal daughter home at last. Bull was a Christian man. He slaughtered a kid he'd wanted to sell. They had a feast. Her siblings, their spouses, and children came. Some of them, she'd never met.

"You are my girl," Bull avowed, taking her face in his hands. "And you're home now."

He hugged her. Her mother stood next to him, tears on her face. She reached out to stroke both husband and daughter on the head and back. They praised Jesus.

On the telling of it, Ruby smacked her tongue lightly against the back of her teeth. Her eyes filled. A cold gust of wind came off the river. Max guided her onto her back on the blanket and covered her with his body to keep her warm.

"Is everybody healthy?" he asked. It was his nightmare that more people dear to him got sick.

“Pretty much healthy. They’re older,” she said. “Daddy’s gone all gray. His eyes have bags under them. I’m worried about him some.”

It was hard for her to see Bull gone gray and heavy-eyed.

“It’s just age, Ruby. You’ve been gone a long time.” He nestled in her neck. “Did you tell them about me?”

She sighed.

“I couldn’t. It was hard enough for me to tell them what it was like to be in the Tower. They had so many questions! It’s too much for my family to take in all at once. When time goes by, and we feel more normal together, then I’ll be able to tell them, maybe.”

He felt the same way. He hadn’t told his family about her yet either. When time went by. Maybe.

Max got busy wresting the store’s future out of Finbar’s All and Sundry’s grasp. He walked over to the competition and surveyed Finbar’s wares and how he displayed and sold them. Newspaper work had made him good at that. The clerk was a boy he went to school with. He didn’t recognize him. Max asked him how long it took for Finbar to deliver on special orders and whether he handled postal service. He bought some stamps. On colored night, Ruby went to both Finbar’s and Sassaport’s. They compared notes, made lists. Max lobbied his mother for significant changes at Sassaport’s Fabrics, Fine Goods, and Notions. She considered them, then consulted Zeyde and Uncle Morris. She recited them to her husband, who tried to nod yes or no to her. In the end, she decided to trust Max. He was her son and she knew he was clever. She told him to take over with free rein to do what he thought best. She had more than enough on her hands nursing her husband, dragging him back to health.

First thing Max did was take the penny candy out of the front window—adults spend money, he told his mother, not kids. He put the sweets under glass at the front of the clerk's desk so the kids couldn't steal it. He bought a mannequin and put it in the front window. He dressed the mannequin in clothing appropriate to the season and surrounded it with merchandise the man of summer, fall, winter, or spring might need. People loved it. It brought them back into the store where he made sure most goods were a small fraction under Finbar prices. The rest were inflated in price so that Max could offer customers a few cents off on the spot. "Everybody loves a bargain," he told Zeyde and Morris. "I learned that selling salvage in half of Atlanta's parks." They agreed. He displayed more fabrics and notions on the floor and scaled back the fancy goods. Just after New Year's, Sassaport's returned from the brink. People were happy to go to the Jew's shop if they could save money. They weren't stupid.

Ruby worked alongside her father on the farm. During the cold months before spring's first plantings, they took care of his livestock and delivered firewood together. Once a week, she went into town with him. They went on Thursdays to catch both Finbar's and Sassaport's colored night. During the worst of that winter, when the winter freeze meant she could not meet Max at their usual spots, it was the only time all week she'd see him. They'd stand near a display of cotton goods and chat like old childhood friends that had nothing to do with each other anymore, but their hearts would near pound out of their chests. Sometimes they managed to brush hands or nudge the other with a shod foot. It wasn't much but it was better than nothing. Luckily, winter was short. Worse was a wet spring. Rainstorms kept them apart until they found a huge thicket of hawthorn by the river and chopped a haven out of its center. They could sit in its middle, drape Ruby's blanket around them, and stay dry. It was enough for now.

Jake Sassaport got stronger and by spring worked a few hours a day on the shop floor. Uncle Morris declared himself certain enough of his brother's recovery to take Adela-Persephone home. Their last night with the family, Adela sang for them, an Italian song no one knew. The words were indecipherable to them but it sounded gay. Morris was right. She sang like an angel. They begged her to sing another and then another far into the night.

Morris stepped outside for a cigarette. His nephew joined him but did not smoke. It was too expensive a habit for the family man he hoped to become.

"What happened to Adela's ghost?" Max asked.

The older man shrugged like Zeyde.

"He's still around," he said. "I catch her mumbling to him. She sneaks outside when the moon is full. I know why. But flesh calls to flesh and as long as we're alive, she is mine."

He grinned and elbowed Max.

"I'm telling you, *Maxele*, it took me half my life to learn, but the best thing a man can have is a good woman by his side. I wish you the same one day."

Although it was a frigid night, Max warmed with thoughts of the one he already had. I have a woman, thank you very much, he wanted to say, and you know her. She's Ruby Johnson.

"I do too," he remarked instead.

By the time the summer rolled around, both Max and Ruby grew impatient. They had as much time together as they could steal now that the weather permitted woodsy rendezvous. But even when they had an hour or two together two days in a row, it wasn't enough. In Atlanta they would have been grateful for those hours. But here, at home, it didn't satisfy them. Their trysts in the woods made them want a place of their own, with a proper four walls, a washstand, a bed, and something to cook on.

"Daddy can handle a lot more these days," Max promised her. "He shuffles some, but he walks the floor and sells when he feels like it. I think he's got to where he can hire someone to help him out and I can go."

Ruby assessed her circumstances as well.

"My daddy's crops look great. We've got 'em rooted and growing by leaps and bounds every day. The flowers are gone and the boles look strong and full. He's got all my sisters and brothers to help him bring in his cotton in the fall. I could leave."

For a while, they both walked on air. They planned their trip to Chicago, what they'd do when they got there. It was a heady time. They spilled over with energy and ideas.

Then Ruby's mother fell down and broke her hip.

She tripped over a crate of fresh peaches that Bull laid down in the middle of the kitchen when he was too tired to move another step holding it. Down she tumbled, landing on her side. She heard a crack when she hit the floor.

Ruby's youngest sister, Marla, was still at home and she was only ten. Someone had to look after her and Daddy and tend Mama too. Max agreed. They would have to wait.

They were in Heard County more than a year before Ruby told Max her mother got around well enough for them to seriously discuss leaving for Chicago again. Jake Sassaport wasn't one hundred percent recovered, but he was close. He had Zeyde and Mama to help out. Max could leave very soon, too, but not before he tied up loose ends. He'd just ordered a telephone for the store. The phone company wouldn't be out to install it for a couple months. He'd have to help Daddy come up with a rate to charge people come in off the street to use it. Left to himself, he'd give phone time away.

It was Max's biggest money-making idea since he took on Finbar's All and Sundry. He needed to help Daddy figure out how to maximize its potential. Between waiting for the installation and helping Daddy, it meant another four or five months before they could go to Chicago. He was afraid she'd decide she'd had it with him.

"Please don't leave me," he told Ruby. "I have to do this."

Max had been so patient while she nursed her mother, Ruby felt she owed him his store telephone and told him so. He thanked her. They made wonderful love afterward. But she began to doubt they would ever leave Heard County together.

Her time weighed upon her. After years of independence, she was stuck in her childhood. Nothing she did made inroads leading to her future with Max. She taught Marla and Mama and Daddy how to read and write and that felt good, but her doubts about the future of her love affair grew heavy. She went to see Mayhayley Lancaster to find out what was what.

She picked a day neither Max nor her parents and Marla would miss her. It was a day Max clerked for his family. Bull, Francine, and Marla went to a church fair for the day. It wasn't their church, but it was a place that praised the Lord, so they were excited to go.

Ruby set out for Mayhayley's as she had when she was a child with a water jug and a piece of cheese wrapped in cloth. She made quick progress. The route felt longer when they were children. She was used to walking distances now and of course her legs were longer. Before the morning was passed, she knocked on the front door of a familiar tar paper shack.

Mayhayley Lancaster answered. She wore a plaid shirt, a man's overalls, and an eyepatch. She gasped and enfolded the girl in her arms.

"Poor child," she said, "poor child. I thought you might come. But you have taken me completely by surprise."

She guided Ruby to a chair and sat her down, then called out for Sallie to make tea and bring some bread and bacon with it. She knew everything about Ruby's tribulations. What she hadn't divined came to her in the Sunday editions of the *Journal, Constitution,* and *Jeffersonian,* each delivered weekly to her mailbox at the post office.

"I am sorry about what that beast Rueben Arnold did to you," she said.

A year ago, Ruby would have cried at the mention of the lawyer's name but these days she could hold back. She thanked Sallie for the tea and drank it, gaining a rare strength from each sip. She wondered what was in it. The chair was as good as a featherbed to her road weary limbs. She reveled in it. After a little time, she spoke.

"Max always wanted to know why you left the trial so quick," she said.

Mayhayley reached over and squeezed her hand.

"Remember when they refused the two black jurors?"

Ruby's body came alert.

"Max thought that was it," she said, proud of him.

"Yes. I took one look at those two boys and knew them as sure as if I'd nursed them at my own teat. Two hardscrabble farmers with ex-slave daddies. Rebellious of nature. They would have voted acquittal. I knew the white men on that jury were itchin' to vote guilty. But those two would rather die than vote the same way as them." She sighed. "Arnold and Rosser thought too much of themselves."

Mayhayley and her sister wanted Ruby to stay at their home that night.

"You'll get a fine supper and a good sleep," Mayhayley said.

Both suggestions were attractive. She was surely hungry and it would be a vacation to sleep away from home and not have to wake up to a household's needs. But then if she stayed, she wouldn't be able to get to the deer blind at the dawn and Max would fret.

"No, thank you, m'am, but I'd best go home this afternoon," she said.

She reached in her pocket and pulled out a dollar and a dime and offered them in an open palm. Mayhayley closed up her fist and gently pushed it back.

She put some cold ashes from the fireplace into her mouth and placed her hand on the girl's head. After a minute, it slowly slid off. She picked up Ruby's cup and poked in the leaves with the quill of a bird feather.

"I'm glad you didn't steal your employer's money," she said. "Make sure Max doesn't steal from his people. No matter how desperate you two may become."

Ruby shook her head, dismissing her concern. It was not what she'd come about.

"But will we ever get to Chicago?" she asked.

This was it. This was the big question she'd come to ask. Mayhayley said nothing.

"Please," Ruby said. "If it's 'no,' I need to hear it."

The prophet leaned forward and patted her knee. Sallie refilled her teacup.

"You'll both get there. But first you must separate for a time. A darkness is coming."

Ruby didn't know how to feel. They'd both get there but first, they'd be apart again? Why? What darkness? Hadn't they suffered enough darkness already? Mayhayley must have her pasts and futures mixed up, both of them standing on their heads.

Mayhayley only had half answers for her.

"There's a man who will cause you to part." she said. "I don't know exactly who he is, I don't have anything on his last name but his given name starts with an 'H.' Maybe Henry or Hank or Harry."

All of a sudden, Mayhayley snapped her neck up, toward the heavens. Ruby could see her white throat webbed with purple veins, the underside of her chin.

"I told your Max about the darkness years ago."

She shook herself, reached behind her, and pulled up a shawl to wrap around her shoulders. Her forecast was done.

Ruby left the Lancaster sisters with nearly as much confusion as she'd carried on her walk to see them. How could Harold Ross—she was sure it was him the oracle named; she knew no Henrys or Hanks—do anything to separate them? He was in Atlanta, hundreds of miles away. She walked home mulling it over. The next dawn, when she and Max met, she told him what Mayhayley said and asked what he thought.

Max paled and went drop-jawed. That Mayhayley Lancaster was a pistol.

"Harold Ross was the first call I made yesterday to test the phone. He was happy to hear from me. He asked for you. He told me the governor granted Frank's latest appeal and Harold needs to stay in Atlanta to keep tabs and follow it up. But he also needs to be in Macon."

Governor Slaton had commuted Frank's sentence several days before. Protests and riots ran rampant in the capital. Frank was being moved to a prison in Milledgeville, to keep him safe from all those who wanted to storm the Tower and kill him in Atlanta. How that would play out, Harold wasn't sure. Milledgeville was one hundred miles away from Marietta, Mary Phagan's hometown. She was born there. It was where she was buried. The roads between Marietta and Milledgeville were smooth and swift. It wouldn't take much to round up a gang of Marietta men to take Frank in his sleep.

Ross asked for Max's help keeping up on the Frank's transfer. The cub who'd replaced him was useless. He could write but he had no nose for news. He couldn't find the thread of a story if it was tied around his finger. Ross needed better than that.

He wanted to send Max to Macon to interview Frank at Midgeville. He'd set it up with the warden ahead of time. The paper would pay his way. It could lead to a series.

"How about it, sport?" Ross pitched. "I'll pay you more than before. Twenty cents a word. Write it long. Fatten the old grubsteak. I'll give you a byline. When you get to Chicago, and ask the *Tribune* for a job, you'll have more *Journal* articles to show. If it takes time to convince them, you and Ruby will have enough to find a decent place to live until they do."

Customers lined up behind Max while he talked. They wanted to look at the phone, maybe even use it. His father *hondled* everyone waiting with surprising ease. Max could see it excited him. It rejuvenated him. Ross's offer tempted him. Without thinking twice, he accepted.

It didn't occur to him until Ruby mentioned it, but it was the first time he hadn't discussed an important decision with her before making it. It occurred to Ruby straightaway and that troubled her. She would have told him to take the job. It wasn't that.

"But I'm here too," she said. "I ought to be part of things."

He worked long and hard from that moment until the morning he left for Macon three days later to reassure her. She was the most important thing in his life, he said, he'd do this job and come back.

"Then we'll leave. Together."

She heard him but Mayhayley's words haunted her.

"What about the darkness?" she said.

Max brushed her concern away with a wave of his hand.

"Nothing is going to keep us from a life together, Ruby. You have to trust that."

She wanted to believe him.

16.

Macon, Georgia, and Milledgeville Prison, 1915

After all the ground he'd covered with Ruby, Max found it uncomfortable to travel alone. He missed her. It was like his right arm was missing. It made him feel withdrawn. A man drove him to Franklin where he caught the northbound train and Max, the salesman, Max, the newspaper reporter, barely spoke to him. The train was slow. It made numerous stops, many clustered around towns that came before and after the city environs of Atlanta. He engaged no one but sat in a window seat with his head pressed against the glass, looking down. It was too dusty to open the window and it was hot. In the night, he slept.

By the time he got to Macon, he needed nothing so much as a bath and a drink. He had in his pocket the name of the hotel where the *Journal* had arranged for him to stay. There were only three hotels in Macon. The paper booked him into the one somewhat out of town, the one closest to the prison in Milledgeville. It was isolated, in the middle of nowhere, like the prison itself. Only lawyers and associates of the confined stayed at the Milledgeville Arms Hotel. A hired car waited for him at the station and took him there. He had a clean room with a private bath and a bed with creaky springs.

Ross told him to hire a car at the desk when he was ready to go see Frank. But when he checked in, he asked for general transport to the prison early the next morning instead. It was a Friday. The hotel was nearly full. He wanted to share his ride with the friends and family of prisoners. He thought he might catch a fresh insight into life at Milledgeville Prison that would help him write a better story.

The wagon taking visitors to the prison had benches hammered into its flat bed on three sides. Max got up onto it and sat on the right-hand bench. A number of hotel guests joined him. There were two older women who might have been mothers of young inmates or wives to longtimers, one stern old farmer who certainly visited an incarcerated son, three young women painted and tarted up for their special visits, and two plain, tired women holding the hands of small children. A trio of young toughs boarded along with the same number of middle-aged men who looked to have serious business on their minds. Everyone squeezed together on the benches and the driver took off.

It was an hour's ride to Milledegville Prison. Max passed the time listening to the others talk. The toughs tried to sit next to the dolled-up young women, but those gals were smarter than that and wedged themselves between middle-aged men. The toughs tried their luck anyway, flirting across the laps of others from the far end of the bench. The old farmer insinuated himself between them and the mothers and their kids, which the women found very sweet. They weren't afraid of toughs. They were plenty tough themselves.

Before the half hour mark, the old farmer asked the driver what he knew about Leo Frank.

"He hasn't been here long," the man said. "but everyone knows something about him."

"Some folks say the Jew didn't do it," the farmer said. "They say it was that blackie, but the Jew did it alright. He did."

The other passengers agreed. One of them claimed to have a relative, doing time for a crime he did not commit, who was on the same cell block as Frank.

"Them Jews is known for it, you know," he who had never met a Jew himself said. "They like to diddle with the babies and then kill 'em and drink their blood."

Max couldn't help himself. He spoke up.

"That's absurd, sir," he said. "In what century do you live? This is the twentieth not the sixteenth."

No one on the wagon knew what he meant by referencing the sixteenth century yet they were silenced by his superior appearance, dressed as he was in a rented suit and with a leather satchel taken from the shelves of his father's shop for the trip. The two together made him look like a lawyer. Cowed, they shut up.

When they arrived, everyone lined up to pass through the security gate and write down the name of the prisoner they wished to see. They'd come to form quick associations on the trip to the prison walls and now that they were within them, they talked and joked like old friends to while away the time. Max had a pre-written pass arranged by Ross in his satchel. He went to the front of the line and produced it.

"Max Sassaport for the *Atlanta Journal*," he told the guard. "Here to see Mr. Leo Frank."

The chatter around him went silent. His wagon mates stared at him, dead-eyed. The guard looked him up and down, then waved him off to the side.

"The warden will be here soon. You'll talk to him first."

"Alright," Max said. He stood where he was told to, put down his satchel, and folded his hands behind his back.

His fellow travelers were routed to the common room. As they passed, they studied him as if he were an exhibit at a museum.

From around the corner, the warden hurried forward. His boots made a hard click-click-click against the linoleum floor. His hands were deep in his pockets, his watch fob bounced off his moderate gut. Overall, his demeanor was grave but agitated. He shook Max's hand and gestured he should follow him down the corridor.

"It's a mystery to me why Leo Frank is here," he volunteered. "I realize back at the Tower he was in greater danger every day. But how can I keep him any safer? The Tower has more manpower and what they've got is better skilled. Off the record, our guards are not professional lawmen. They're farm boys looking to make a better living indoors. Our prisoners are convicted of commonplace crimes. They're poor men turned thieves or drunks who got in a fight with the wrong man. Our murderers might have killed a faithless wife or a cheating business partner, but Frank is the only child-raping murderer we've got. We don't even have a death row."

They made two sharp left turns.

Max hoped the warden would leave him alone with Frank long enough to disarm him, befriend him, get him to say something newsworthy. Frank's cellblock was deserted. The other inmates were out with visitors in the supervised rooms the prison provided, or under guard in the yard. As they approached, he and the warden both click-click-clicking against the hard floor, Max could see the white, shining face, neck, and clavicle of Leo Frank, the glare of his glasses, but not much else. He was ethereal, ghostlike. His whiteness seemed to hover in the air. The warden flipped a light switch. Bare bold light made a difference.

Max never thought Frank looked healthy, not at the trial anyway. That day, he looked worse. The sheen of his skin was that of a man in extremis, although he stood up straight and did not tremble. His clothes hung off him. His face was illuminated by a broad band of sunlight that streamed through the bars from a hallway window and laid itself upon him. He looked to Max like portraits of martyrs he'd seen in books.

The warden introduced them and moved down the corridor where he leaned against a wall and smoked. Frank stuck his hand through the bars of his cell and Max grasped it.

"I know your work from the *Journal*," Frank said. "You wrote about the Jewish community during my trial. I wouldn't have agreed to talk to you if it weren't for that."

"Mr. Frank," Max began.

"Leo."

"OK, Leo," he said. "Are you glad to be out of Atlanta?"

"I don't know. I miss my wife. They're going to kill me anyway."

Frank sang a song the buskers on Atlanta's street corners had about him. They'd come sing it at the foot of the Tower. It was very popular.

"We'll kill him here, we'll kill him there," he sang in a voice reedy and sharp. "From a tree, or in a chair."

He stopped. He stood in the corner of his cell and put his hands against the walls.

"I don't know how I get out of this except dead. My wife may come next week."

He shouted to the man leaning against the wall down the corridor. Max was surprised a man his size, thin as he was, could be so loud.

"Warden! You'll permit me to see my wife next week, won't you?"

"She's here, she's in, Leo," the warden shouted back.

Frank sat on his metal bed.

"That's good," he muttered. "That's good."

His head hung from his neck like a fruit too ripe for its branch. His eyes looked big beneath his glasses. They were the same bug eyes Max remembered from the trial. Poor bastard, Max thought. Frank can't help how he looks, how he sounds. He asked him how he felt about the success of his latest appeal, that execution had been stayed.

"The governor commuting my sentence is also my death warrant," he said. "I'm not safe here."

Max didn't disagree.

Frank came up close to the bars again. In one swift movement, he slipped two letters he did not want redacted by the prison into Max's inside suit pocket. He patted them. They said goodbye.

Max didn't look at the envelopes until he was back at the hotel and in his room. One was to Lucille Frank. The other was to the pencil factory's board of directors. Why does he trust me not to read these? Max wondered. He knows I'm a reporter. Does he want me to read them? He pondered for a while but because he was raised a good boy, and because Frank was, whatever else, a Jew, he went out and mailed them without opening them first.

He telephoned Ross from a curtained booth across from the front desk of his hotel. He gave him the information he'd gathered, which for Ross was plenty to start.

"Write your story and wire it to me," he said. "Go see Frank again."

Max did. He wrote up everything they'd said and gave Ross a free hand in editing it. True to his word, Ross shared the byline with him, which only made him look good as the working associate of a nationally read reporter. It would come in handy in Chicago.

The next day, Max went to the prison but Frank was not able to see him. William Creen, a lifer sentenced to thirty years for murdering his wife and child, was behind Frank while they queued up for dinner the previous night. All of a sudden, Creen reached in front of him and wrapped an arm around Frank's shoulders, restraining him. Giving out his best rebel yell, he slashed Frank's throat with the sharpened edge of a metal dinner plate. Frank fell, hand to neck, bleeding rivers. Luckily, two doctors, in prison for insurance fraud, rushed forward and stemmed the flow. He was then stitched in the prison infirmary. Max wrote up the incident and waited to see if he lived and he did.

Leo Frank wrote Max to ask him to come interview him shortly after he was discharged from the infirmary to his cell. He could talk a little. He wrote what he couldn't say. He was strong enough for that. Once again, he claimed his innocence, citing himself as the latest sacrifice to the world's long romance with hating Jews.

Now that Max was a frequent and trusted visitor, the warden allowed him into Frank's cell that very night and locked the door behind him. He sat on the edge of Frank's bed, writing everything Frank said down. There was a clamor from the hallway. He looked up.

A large suited man in a battered straw hat had the warden by the arm and a shotgun in his free hand. He pushed the warden forward.

"Open it," he said.

The warden fiddled with his keys then unlocked the cell door. Max looked out. There were twenty or more armed men lining the corridor. Four of them entered, grabbed Leo Frank and pulled him out. In the corridor, the others surrounded him and they frog-marched him along while their prey, his bug eyes afire with fear or madness, croaked in his damaged, anguished voice:

"My wife! Lucille! My wife!"

Max was the only man in cell or corridor who cared the condemned called for Lucille. He wrote her name in capital letters in his notebook.

The big man in the battered hat leaned over him, read what he'd written, and scratched his head.

"Who the hell are you?" he asked.

Max told him he was a reporter for the *Atlanta Journal* and the big man grinned.

"You're comin' with us. We want the world to see this."

Outside the prison, a convoy of automobiles, six in number, lined the entrance with their headlights on. Men, shotguns, rifles, and wire clippers in hand, exited the prison. Most got in the vehicles. Others stood on the running boards, weapons braced against their hips. A photographer ran from car to car, taking pictures. Leo Frank stood in their midst, under close guard. He looked stunned, confused, as if for all his talk of being killed, he'd never truly prepared for the moment to arrive.

"Here, write this down," the big man said. "Twenty-five good citizens of Georgia have banded together to save the honor of our great state by overriding the corrupt decisions of the governor. We have invaded the prison, cut the telephone wires, and spirited the murderer out. Now watch what we do."

He got in the first car. Someone put a sack over Frank's head. The four men who'd taken him from his cell shoved him into the car occupied by the big man. Two of the men got inside, the others mounted the right and left running boards. Max was put in the second car. The car smelled of sweat, cigar smoke, and gun oil. The men with him didn't talk.

They took off. They sped down country roads, raising great clouds of dust, their path lit by farmers holding lanterns aloft to guide them along their way. It was a hot, starry night. Twice they stopped and women came out of the fields carrying food and coffee. Men carried them liquor and cans of gasoline. They started up again and they drank but they did not get drunk. Their blood raced with a lust alcohol could not cut through.

It took them all night to get to Marietta and proceed to the graveyard at its outskirts where Mary Phagan lay buried. The cars stopped across the street from the cemetery at the edge of a wide grove of oak, each tree with long heavy limbs. The sun rose and daylight flooded the grove. Max recognized members of the mob. Their number included local residents along with men who knew what day it was and traveled from Atlanta to be there. In the mix were clergymen, retired judges, an ex-sheriff. Max recognized a half-dozen businessmen. The *Journal* often wrote about their family's births and deaths, weddings, and most lucrative deals. This was not a crude factory tenement mob. It was a mob of Georgia's most solid citizens. There was Joseph Mackey Brown, the former governor of Georgia, Eugene Herbert Clay, former mayor of Marietta, E. P. Dobbs, the current mayor, Cobb County sheriffs, current and former, and enough lawyers to defend a multitude. They raised their fists, cursed Jews, and called out to reclaim stolen justice for Mary Phagan.

"Shoot him! Hang him!" they shouted. "Cut the dirty Jew to ribbons!"

Max was terrified. What would keep the mob from going after him? He didn't think anyone knew he was a Jew; usually people (except for Ross) didn't guess, but what if they did? If he could fight this many people and save himself and Frank, he would. But to try would be suicidal. Instead, he stood his ground with a dry mouth and wide eyes, observing everything around him, while his hand shook too much to write any of it down. From somewhere, he heard Mayhayley Lancaster's voice: *For there's a great darkness comin' at you . . . So dark and so deep, you won't know what it is until it is upon you. But you need to know and you need to be prepared or you'll get sucked into the devil's pit and never get out.* His terror increased. He could barely breathe.

Men pulled Leo Frank from the car and ripped the sack from his head. Frank's face was contorted, his mouth open but there were so many calling out "Hang the Jew!" his screams were drowned out. They dragged him next to a tree with a rope wound over a thick branch. The rope ended in a noose. They pulled on it and two large men jumped up to swing from the branch, making sure it could carry a man's weight.

They slipped the noose around Frank's neck.

Suddenly, there was quiet. The mob breathed in and out together en masse, savoring the scent, the taste of justice finally arrived. Frank removed his gold wedding ring and, his hands yet bound, held it out.

"You are going to kill me. So be it. I ask only that you take my wedding ring and give it to my wife."

His glasses were long gone, crushed under the heel of one of his murderers. His eyes looked large, still like a bug's even without the spectacles. They begged for his one last wish.

The big man in the battered hat took the ring. He bit it, slipped it in his pocket, and laughed. The mob erupted in more yells and insult, until the big man instructed the others to tie Frank's hands in front of him. They hoisted him up on a table set beneath the oak. His mouth moved, perhaps in prayer. They took off his shoes, ripped at his clothes with knives and their bare hands. At a signal from the big man in a battered hat, they kicked the table out.

Frank's neck snapped. His limbs twitched. His face pointed toward the heavens. Max couldn't see his features. It was horror enough to witness the white flesh of his Adam's apple creased by the stitched red slash made by the prisoner Creen exposed above the rope.

The mob watched quietly while the life seeped out of Leo Frank. They murmured a little when his twitching slowed then stopped. People standing near him swore they heard a final gurgle. Then it was done and everything about Leo M. Frank was still. The big man pronounced him dead.

The mob erupted in cheers. They passed bottles of whiskey. Men posed for photographs next to the lynched man. Someone ripped the sleeves off his shirt for a souvenir. A man cut pieces of rope left over from the hanging into three-inch lengths and passed them around for keepsakes.

Max realized no one was coming after him, too, at least not that night. Their blood lust had been sated. The mob wanted to savor the taste of Frank's death. His breath calmed, he said the prayer for the dead inside his head, regained his strength and, with a hand that steadied word by word, wrote everything he witnessed down.

He stayed at the lynching site until evening fell. New people kept arriving, on foot, on horseback, and in cars, giving him more to report. Ladies came with lunch baskets for their husbands. They brought their children. They picknicked beneath the man's body. Many arrived with cameras, which explained the explosion of lynching postcards sold everywhere a few days after the fact. Before the body was taken down days later, hundreds visited the grove to take a look at the demon Leo Frank.

One of them, Robert E. Lee Howell, wanted Frank's body to be taken down, cut into pieces, and burned. He wove in and out of the crowd rallying support. A few agreed, but most thought the body should be turned over to the mortuary intact. The big man denounced Howell's proposal.

"What we have done here, my friends, was a just and sacred act. But it will be misinterpreted, exploited by the newspapers, especially up North. Let us display the honor of our fair county by returning Frank to his family intact."

His opinion won the day.

They cut down the corpse of Leo Frank. Robert E. Lee Howell interfered with those attempting to place it into the mortician's wicker basket, causing it to spill to the ground. He then stomped Frank's face into the dirt until the bones cracked. Max's stomach roiled but he wrote about that too.

He didn't want to write about the filth and the horror. He wanted to flee. He wanted to be as far from the Marietta cemetery as he could get. He did it, not for Ross or the job, but for the money to ensure his future with Ruby. He felt as if Mayhayley's snakes had wrapped around his throat and hands and still he wrote everything down. After Frank's corpse was taken away, he wired everything he had to Ross and called to tell him goodbye.

"I'll be needing my pay right away. Wire it to me care of Sassaport's Fabrics, Fancy Goods, and Notions in Buckwood. I'm going home to collect Ruby and then we'll go to Chicago like we've always planned. Jews aren't safe in Georgia anymore. Ruby's people never were."

Ross felt their friendship slipping away for good, and despite wanting to be rid of him nearly two years before, he found he grieved as much for the loss of Max as for that of Ruby.

"Would you like me to wire the *Tribune* about you? A letter of introduction? A recommendation?"

Max sighed heavily into the phone.

"I don't know what kind of newsman I am anymore. Maybe I'll fall back on retail. This one nearly killed me."

"You'll get over it," Ross said.

Ruby felt ill at ease in Buckwood without him. There was no way for them to communicate. Before he left, he begged her for patience and she swore to give it to him, but it wasn't easy. Ever since he left, something felt off in the world, its whole balance changed. She'd been strong through all her recent trials, because she and Max were together. Now she worried she'd never see him again.

Newspapers came to town sporadically, sometimes a week old, but they came. Ruby got hold of a copy of the *Journal* and read Max's first column from Milledgeville. She was proud of him and fearful for him at the same time. The end of the article promised a dispatch from the prison the following week, so she knew he stayed on there. Or maybe, she hoped, since the paper she read was old news, by now he'd have fired off another column then headed home. She hoped it was so. She tried to live as if he might walk through the door any minute.

The *Journal* came early, arriving on the following Thursday. Ruby discovered it when she went to shop at Sassaport's on colored night. She made sure to talk to Max's father. Jake gave her his *Journal* to read. Max's column on the throat slashing of Leo Frank by a fellow prisoner chilled her to the bone. She needed to talk to him. She thought of asking Jake if she could pay to use the phone. She could call Harold and get a message to Max through him. Then she remembered she'd promised to be patient and didn't.

All of Buckwood knew Frank had been lynched before Max's final columns arrived. One of Finbar's suppliers hauling a load of goods from Atlanta announced it. The day he rode into town, he called for attention on the floor of Finbar's shop. "Hear ye, hear ye!" he said, his voice ringing like the bell a crier might have used a hundred years before. He gave the gruesome news in what detail he had. When he was through, customers spilled into the street to spread the news. "Huzzah! Huzzah! The murderer Jew is dead!"

Ruby was in town that day. She knew all about lynchings. They were part of her people's history, part of every black child's growing up. White children were frightened into obedience with stories of boogeymen and fanged giants. Black children were frightened into obedience with stories of men in white sheets and hoods. Mythical monsters are nothing compared to real ones. The former ate their fill of children's flesh and picked their teeth with their bones. Real monsters were never satisfied. Lynchings could spread like wildfire. She witnessed the unholy joy of Finbar's customers and feared for Max's family. She went directly to Sassaport's to see if they were alright. The door was locked and barred.

17.

Heard County, Georgia, 1915–Chicago, Illinois, 1925

The next morning just before the dawn, Ruby went to the old deer blind by the Chattahoochee, hoping against hope that Max would be there, waiting for her, and miracle of miracles, he was. She cried out. They ran into each other's arms.

"Oh, Max," she said into his neck, "I've been so worried about you."

"I'm here now," he said, holding her close.

For the first time since the lynching, he felt a kernel of peace planted inside him. He told her everything he'd seen in Milledgeville, leaving nothing out.

"My poor darling," she said. "How awful for you."

He grunted. It was worse than awful.

"I can't get it out of my mind. I have nightmares. And people are riled up now. I worry about my family."

She told him his parents were, at best, holed up.

"I know. I've seen them," he said. "I used the key above the storage barn door to get in. They heard me and hid in a closet."

He tried to convince them that now was the time to head

to Morris and Adela's place. Screw the business. They'd saved enough. Let the *goyim* have it. But as his uncle once said, two more stubborn *yidlachs* he'd never seen.

"Harold tells me half the Jews in Georgia are running to other states."

Ruby nodded.

"It's somethin' terrible here," she said. "We have to get away."

They made a plan and as all plans are, it was flawed. But enthralled by the sweetness of being together again, they thought it perfect.

The first thing they had to do was tell their parents about their great love and plans to marry in Illinois. It was a risky move. Ruby was afraid Bull would lock her up. Max was afraid his father would have another heart attack. Neither announcement went well, but it could have been worse.

Ruby spoke up on a quiet Saturday morning. It was her parents' day of rest, of prayer. Mama made a breakfast of pancakes with wild blackberries, chicory coffee, and cinnamon toast with butter. They ate together and smacked the sweetness from their teeth. Marla went out to play with a friend from down the road. Bull, Francine, and Ruby were alone, seemingly without care.

"Daddy, Mama, I have something to tell you," Ruby began.

"Then, shoot," Bull said. "As long as you're not going back to Atlanta."

He and his wife shared a hearty chuckle over the idea. Francine noticed that Ruby didn't join in.

"Oh dear Lord," she said, "you're not going back, are you? I won't let you! It's the worst place in the world for you, you have to know that!"

Ruby shook her head and chewed her lip. Taking a deep breath, she let the truth spill out in a cascade of words.

"Not Atlanta. Chicago. I'm going to Chicago." She stuck her chin up. "And there I will marry and become Mrs. Maxwell Isadore Sassaport."

Their reactions were immediate. Francine wailed. Bull jumped up and slammed the nearest wall with his fist.

"No!" her daddy said. "I won't have it! Where is that boy? I'm gonna kill him."

Her mother did not dissuade him.

"Has he spoiled you, girl?" she wailed. "I'll kill him too."

To her credit, Ruby stood her ground.

"You'll have to kill me first. Mama, Daddy. I'm a grown woman. You can't stop me. Max is the love of my life and I am his."

"Damn it," Bull swore. "I always thought out of all my children you were the smart one. How wrong I was. You can't do this! It may be all honey and roses right to now, child, but he'll leave you. He'll abandon you soon as he figures out how much trouble he's got himself in. Mark my words . . ."

He waved a shaking finger at her, looked into her beloved face, and saw that threats would get him nowhere. He pleaded next, both of them did, with tears in their eyes. It was a wretched display. She couldn't bear watching them and left the house.

"Take time to think about it, Mama, Daddy," she said on her way out the door. Her body trembled with emotion inside but she made her voice as clarion clear as an archangel's trumpet. "I want your blessing. But if I don't get it, I'm still leaving. Not today, not tomorrow, but soon."

For all her bravado, tears ran down her cheeks the whole way to the deer blind and continued to do so while she waited for Max to appear. Finally, he did. It was two hours later than they'd arranged to meet.

"I'm sorry, I'm sorry, darlin'," he said, holding her close. "It couldn't be helped. My folks have a lot going on and let's just say they weren't thrilled with my news." He wrinkled his lips in disdain. "My zeyde ripped his sleeve and said *kaddish* for me."

She pulled her head back and looked up at him quizzically.

"I'm dead to him."

His chest was damp with her tears. It was a warm day but he shivered from it.

"My daddy wants to kill you," she said.

"I'm not surprised. Mine clutched his heart. He said it would erupt if I went away with you." He laughed. His laughter had a bitter sound. "They tried to buy me. They offered me a thousand dollars if I stayed. I should take the money and leave with you anyway."

She remembered Mayhayley's warning.

"No, Max. Don't do that."

"Why not? They betray me just in the offering."

Ruby noted the difference in their reactions to parental objection. She was miserable. He was angry. Alright, she thought, this is the way it will be all our lives. I'll have to learn how to defuse him.

"It's bad juju."

"Bad juju."

"Yes. Definitely."

Properly defused, he started to laugh, this time in round, wholesome notes.

"Come here, gal," he said, taking her under the cover of a willow tree by the creekbed.

They made long and lazy love. Neither wanted to go home afterward, but they did.

For a week, Bull threatened, Francine wailed, Jake clutched his chest, Rose bribed, Zeyde prayed for the dead, but none of them could change the course of fate. At last, Ross's wire arrived with

Max's pay. Bankrolled now, tired of the fight, the lovers left for Chicago one fine morning on foot. They had enough cash for a train, but Max remained shaken by the lynching. He didn't want to be around too many people. It didn't feel safe for either of them. Until the weather changed, he insisted, they'd walk. She went along with it because she loved him.

It wasn't easy to leave. They were quite sad at first and consoled each other. Max said, "They love us. They'll change their tunes after we're established in Chicago and we write them and ask them to visit."

"Sure, honey, sure," Ruby said, but she didn't half believe him.

They went east and then north to avoid Atlanta. As they trekked the foothills, they came upon a vast peaceful clearing next to a sparkling lake and decided to camp there. They caught fish, roasted it over an open flame, slept early and well until a clamor of automobiles and the angry voices of men woke them. Max froze at the sound of it, unnerved by memories of the night Leo Frank was hanged. Frank's pale neck stretched back by the noose, the brutal hunger of the mob flashed before his eyes. The color drained from his face. His mouth fell open. He made no sound. He could not move.

Ruby got him up, pushed him beyond the tree line, scrambling to throw dirt on the embers of their dying campfire and drag their belongings into the pines. From there, she watched automobiles form a huge circle a distance away. Fifty or so men dressed in white robes with hoods exited from them. They erected a tall, plain cross, doused it with gasoline, and set it on fire. They chanted ugly things about Jews and blacks together. One of them, a large man with a barrel chest and a booming voice to match, announced to them all:

"We, the former Knights of Mary Phagan, now do declare ourselves the New Ku Klux Klan of the great state of Georgia!

Let us rise from the ashes of history, to which the damn Yankees have consigned us. Let us not forget that it is our duty to protect the fair lilies of Georgian womanhood from the ravages of Jews and blacks alike . . ."

Men cheered and volunteered the names of neighbors who needed to be taught a lesson.

After an hour or more, they broke, swearing to meet prepared for action next time.

When she was certain the last of them was gone, Ruby took Max by the arm and led him to the campsite they'd quit. She took his face in her hands and studied him. He looked better. His color was back and it seemed he might even speak.

"It's alright," she told him. "We're alone now."

"I was wrong," he said, coming back to himself. "We're not safe in the backwoods. We need to take the first train we find and get ourselves to Chicago."

They made a beeline to Chattanooga then, boarded a train in separate cars, and arrived in the promised land three days later only the promised land wasn't the paradise they'd hoped. True, they walked down the streets of Chicago together without too much trouble beyond a few harsh looks from whites and blacks both. But finding a place to stay proved difficult. After a day of searching and the humiliation of summary rejection from half-empty hotels and rooming houses, they at last found a hostel in the colored section of town that would take them. At first, Max felt uncomfortable as the only white among a sea of black faces but curiosity was the worse emotion he experienced from them. He figured he could get used to it for Ruby's sake.

She was the first one to land a job, hired as a dishwasher in a swanky restaurant near the lake. The chef, a man from France, liked her. He promised he would train her to cook fine food.

She wouldn't be scrubbing pots forever. The hours were hard, but the pay was fair. It was a good job and Ruby was happy for it.

Max had more difficulty finding work. Several days in a row, he went to the *Tribune* building and paced back and forth on the street without entering. In the end, he realized he never would. His experience chasing news was too dirty, too exhausting, too terrifying to chase more of it. He took a job with a moving company hauling pianos and desks up narrow flights of stairs all over the city. It paid less than Ruby's work and on one job, a couch was dropped on his foot, breaking it. It healed mostly, he could still work, but he limped. It kept him out of the war in Europe anyway.

One job rocked him to his core. He'd got up that morning and sat on their bed, watching Ruby sleep after a long night at the restaurant. He hoped he wasn't failing her. They'd set a money goal before marrying so they could start out their new life in a home they would invite their parents to and it wasn't building up fast enough to suit him.

I need to find something else, he thought in the trolley he took every morning to the moving company. Maybe in retail. Only there's no money in clerking. You have to own the place. He arrived to work and greeted his coworkers who sat in the back of a big truck waiting for him. Soon as he situated himself with them, he thought it again. I need to find something else. Dear God, help me find something else.

That day, they were moving an office from one locale to another. When he saw the name plate on the door and the man unscrewing it for transport, he was astounded. The name plate read: Anti-Defamation League. The man was Sigmund Livingston.

"Mr. Livingston! How do you do?" he said, removing his

cap and extending a calloused palm. "I'm Max Sassaport. I used to work for the *Atlanta Journal.* I heard you speak at The Temple in Atlanta some time ago."

Livingston's eyebrows rose with surprise. He took the hand offered him and shook it.

"I remember you," he said. "I've read your reports. Your work on poor Leo's murder was brilliant."

Max blushed.

"Thank you, sir."

The other man looked him up and down, head to toe.

"And what prompted this career change? I would think the *Journal* would be remiss to let you go."

"After the lynching," Max confessed, "I just couldn't do it anymore."

His coworkers had entered the League's office and begun carrying boxes out. They scowled at him for lollygagging. He put his cap back on.

"I better get to work, sir. It was good seeing you."

He turned to his fellows. Livingston stopped him.

"Wait. For a man with a *yiddisher kop* like yours, this . . ." He gestured to the men struggling to padlock chains around a black iron safe and lug it to a window. ". . . this is a waste. I need a writer on staff. You'd write appeal letters. Brochures. Acknowledgments and thank-yous. Speeches. How about it? Leave these men and come work with me."

Max's prayer was answered. He accepted on the spot without inquiring about the pay, which, as it turned out, was double what he made at the movers and more than he made before he quit the *Journal.* He found the work at the ADL good work, important work. Every chance he got, he included in what he wrote injustices against Ruby's people along with those against his own. Livingston was pleased.

"You're right, Sassaport," he said, on more than one occasion. "The League cannot be about the Jews alone. It must be about the rights of everyone. Bravo. Bravo."

It took another year before Ruby and Max married at last. Ruby wanted a day job when she became a wife. Why, he had no idea, no matter how many times she tried to explain, but he accepted that all women were mysterious and his wife more than most. The day came that her French chef told an Italian chef about his wonder-girl in the kitchen and the Italian stole her away, making her sous chef for his lunch crowd. It was good work with decent hours for good pay.

They married in a civil ceremony at City Hall. Their honeymoon year would have been a delight but for the Spanish influenza. Though most of its victims were very young or very old, Max got sick, but not too badly, and recovered. Ruby didn't get sick at all. The city suffered dreadfully from the epidemic, but when the bad times were at their height, it allowed the couple to buy a house on the south side of town in that part where successful blacks lived. So many people had died or gone bankrupt that year, they were able to get the house on the cheap.

They weren't the only southerners fleeing a KKK rejuvenated by Leo Frank's lynching. Along with the Jews, a rising tide of black people moved up North for a better, safer life. They flooded the housing and job markets, pushing out the Irish working class already there. Resentment built. There were race riots in Chicago in 1919, a monstrous week of arson, beatings, and murder, white against black. Three houses on Max and Ruby's street were set on fire. Max thought they were spared because the hooligans who roamed the city looking for easy victims saw him as he stood behind a well-lit window with an ax raised above his head, ready to defend his wife and home and, fearful, they moved on. Ruby said it was because they thought

Max was one of them. Max acknowledged she had a point. After the riots they talked about leaving Chicago, but City Hall promised new tenements to ease overcrowding. Police presence was increased in cross-over neighborhoods. The League worked tirelessly arranging interfaith and mixed-race conferences to promote understanding. In the end, Max and Ruby decided there was no place less hostile to go. They might as well stay on.

Once they started having children, their parents could no longer stay away. It took two boys and a girl, a hundred letters and photos sent, long, arduous phone calls, and prepaid train tickets, but eventually there was a day Ruby and Max, Bull and Francine, Jake and Rose all sat together in Ruby's restaurant while their little boys behaved themselves at table and the little girl ran around like a maniac.

Their parents were uncomfortable and stiff with one another, so they focused on the children.

"He's got your mouth, Bull," Francine said of the eldest boy, her voice sweet as warm honey.

"The baby's got Bubbe's eyes," Rose said to Jake.

She didn't really. The little girl's eyes were round where Bubbe's were oval and they were the wrong color, but Rose was in no way going to be shown up by Francine. The Johnsons and Sassaports disagreed about everything that day; the weather, the train ride, the cleanliness of Chicago streets. They felt themselves trapped in a strange purgatory, doomed to suffer one another eternally for the sake of the grandchildren. For Ruby and Max, their visit was a beginning and it was heaven.

They kept in touch with Harold Ross. A few more years went by, and Ross called them from New York where he was about to publish a new magazine, the *New Yorker.* He asked Max if the League was interested in submitting an article about their various projects and law suits.

"You'll come to the city. Stay at the Algonquin. I belong to a club there," he said. "I think you could raise some serious money at our table."

Max promised to think about it. He never went to New York though. He did file a story about the League with Ross but Harold thought it "too grim" for his publication and asked him to lighten it up. "It's too literary. Too intellectual. I'm going for urbane, witty here."

How Ross thought anything could be urbane or witty about racial injustice, Max had no idea. He withdrew his article without rancor but felt badly about disappointing his old boss who had taught him so much.

"Don't concern yourself, honey," Ruby said. "Harry's just trying to rope you back into the game. You know how he is."

Max wasn't sure he did but she knew Harold so much better than he.

"Harry's the past," she said. "These babies here." She swept her eyes over the children playing on the living room rug. "They're the future."

He put his guilt away. Whatever else he knew, he knew his wife was always right.

Historical Personages

- **Mayhayley Lancaster**, one-eyed backwoods prophet, landowner, teacher, journalist, legal consultant to the defense in the Leo Frank case.
- **Leo Frank**, manager of the National Pencil Factory, accused and convicted in the murder of Mary Phagan
- **Lucille Frank**, wife of Leo Frank
- **Rabbi David Marx**, Reform rabbi of The Temple in Atlanta
- **Harold Ross**, reporter for the *Atlanta Journal*, later founder of the *New Yorker*
- **Eli Bohert**, reporter for *Vanity Fair*
- **Newt Lee**, National Pencil's night watchman, witness for the prosecution
- **Jim Conley**, National Pencil's janitor, chief witness for the prosecution
- **Mary Phagan**, thirteen-year-old worker at National Pencil, a murder victim
- **N. V. Darley**, National Pencil's personnel director
- **Tom Watson**, publisher of the rabidly anti-Semitic newspaper, the *Jeffersonian*, later U.S. senator representing the state of Georgia
- **Hugh Dorsey**, prosecutor of the Leo Frank case, later two-term governor of Georgia

- **Rueben Arnold**, defense attorney for Leo Frank
- **Luther Rosser**, defense attorney for Leo Frank
- **Leonard S. Roan**, judge in the Leo Frank case
- **William Smith**, attorney for Jim Conley
- **George Epps**, witness for the prosecution
- **Nina Fomby**, madam of an Atlanta hotel/whorehouse, witness for the prosecution
- **John Marshall Slaton**, governor of Georgia who commutes Frank's death sentence, precipitating his lynching
- **Sigmund Livingston**, founder of the Anti-Defamation League
- **Henry Grady**, founder of the *Atlanta Constitution,* later owned by **William Randolph Hearst**, visionary of the New South

Acknowledgments

I came to write about the tragic fate of Leo Frank and its effect on the Jewish and Black communities of Georgia in a circuitous way. I discovered a song first, the Lonesome River Band's "Mayhayley's House," which introduced me to a fascinating true-life personage, Mayhayley Lancaster. Mayhayley gained fame as a one-eyed backwoods psychic, land owner, politician, entrepenuer, and lawyer. Straightaway, I wanted to write about her but had no hook. Her life was out of my wheelhouse.

Later, I discovered she'd often bragged about working on the Leo Frank defense. Mind you, there is no official record of her participation. But as an author who has devoted her writing career to creating historical fiction about anti-Semitism and racism, I knew instantly there was something there for my imagination to sink its teeth into.

Mayhayley led me to Steve Oney's remarkable, prize-winning *And the Dead Shall Rise: The Murder of Mary Phagan and the Lynching of Leo Frank*, a nonfiction text representing the best kind of journalism. Written in total command of an enormous body of facts while telling a gripping story, it brought the case to life for me, filling it with fascinating players ripe for fictive interpretation.

Of all my resources, his was the one I relied on the most. What I learned from that book lends mine an authenticity that is the ambition of every historical novelist. I will be forever grateful to Steve Oney for writing it.

I have a lot of people to be grateful for. PatZi Gil of radio's syndicated broadcast, *Joy on Paper*, has been an outstanding supporter. PatZi has guided me through many of the scariest and most befuddling chores authors must perform in the shiny new paradigm that is publishing today. She has been far more than someone who loves my work. She has been trainer, inspiration, and friend. Thank you, PatZi.

My beta readers, author Bernie Schein, Felicity Carter, Jeanne Kowalski, Lisa Cermak, Charlotte Stengel Goldman, and Sandra Brett are invaluable to me. I hope you all know that.

None of my acknowledgments are complete without a huge thank you to my fabulous agent, Peter Riva, who has been my knight on all worthy occasions, and I must cite my publisher, Mara Anastas, and her No. 1, Emma Chapnick, especially for their patience, ingenuity, and steadfast responsiveness. Copyediting is an artful task requiring an extreme focus I do not possess and I applaud my copyeditors, Sidney Rioux and Joan L. Giurdanella, because they do. The sparkling creativity of my publicist, Crickets PR, also deserves a deep and reverent nod.

Last, I am grateful to he who is usually first, my husband, Stephen K. Glickman, who is the reason all my novels are love stories and happens to be a damn fine editor too. *Todah rabah*, my *beshert*.

About the Author

Born on the South Shore of Boston, Massachusetts, Mary Glickman studied at the Université de Lyon and Boston University. She is the author of *Home in the Morning*; *One More River*, a National Jewish Book Award Finalist in Fiction; *Marching to Zion*; *An Undisturbed Peace*; and *By the Rivers of Babylon*. Glickman lives in Wadmalaw Island, South Carolina, with her husband, Stephen.

MARY GLICKMAN

FROM OPEN ROAD MEDIA

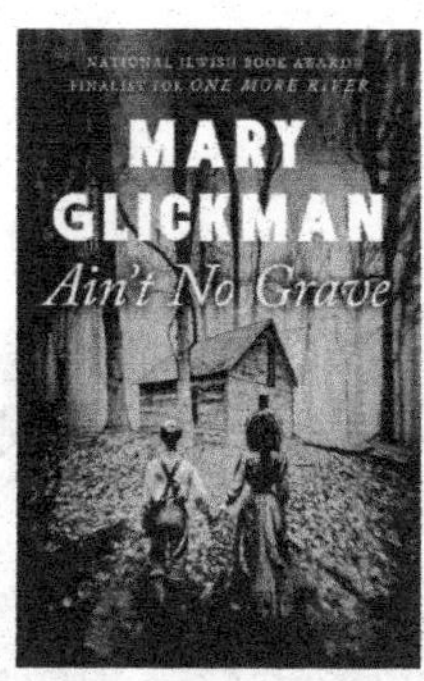

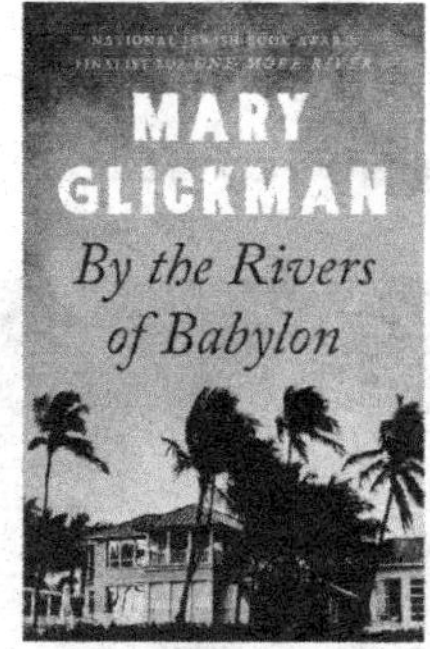

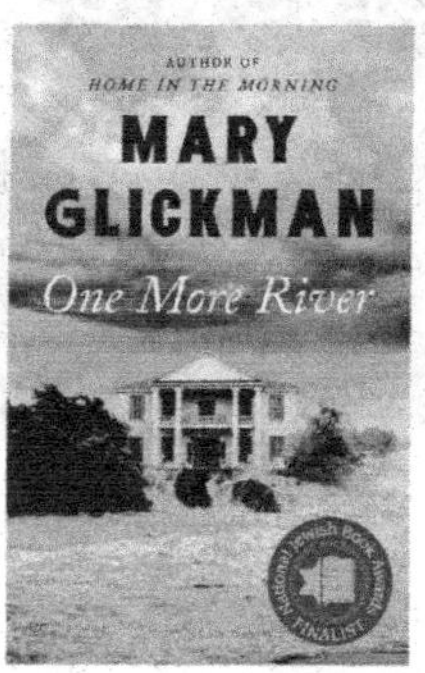

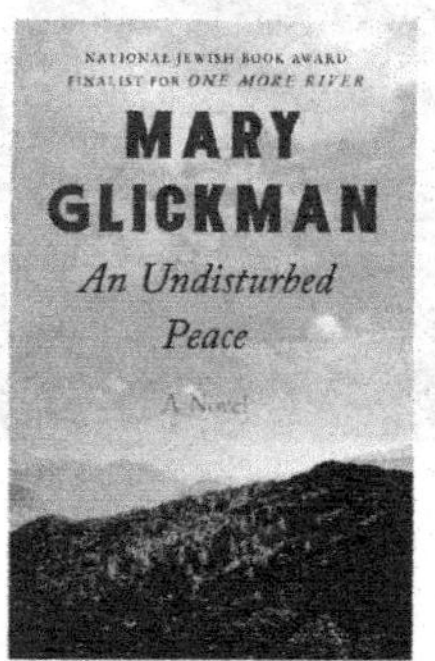